SAGA OF A NEUROSURGEON SERIES, BOOK FOUR

THE
LONG CLIMB

Young M.D., Garven Wilsonhulme,
engaged in a social poker game of winner takes all

Carl Douglass

Neurosurgeon Turned Author Writes with Gripping Realism

PO Box 221974 Anchorage, Alaska 99522-1974
books@publicationconsultants.com—www.publicationconsultants.com

ISBN 978-1-59433-357-6
eISBN 978-1-59433-358-3
Library of Congress Catalog Card Number: 2013930991

Disclaimer

This is a story, a fiction, where all but a very few names have been changed to protect the people deserving of great respect and are, in all cases, cast in a deservedly positive light. They are minor characters in the book and its story. Other characters and the part they play in the *Saga* are loosely based on real people, including the author, whose names are changed; the places they work in the book are fictitious or different from where they were actually encountered by the present author. Some of the experiences described and the characters depicted are amalgamations of persons, places, and actions, and some diluted and altered autobiographical remembrances. There are healthy dollops of whimsy running throughout even the autobiographical hints.

The world of Garven Wilsonhulme is indeed fiction, but while not exactly real, it is faithful to an era of neurosurgical training and experience that is almost entirely a thing of the past. The independence and cowboy experience of being trained in a blood and guts trauma hospital in that era is not an exaggeration. There are some of those old men (and women) out there who will smile as they read and remember. If nothing else, the experiences of those semi-pioneers are the stuff of legend, humor, and pathos that invite endlessly fascinating yarns by all those consummate raconteurs.

The world of medicine and surgery is far more sophisticated and genteel now, far more of a closely controlled corporate money and legalistically driven environment. No longer can residents work 120 hours a week by federal and state law. It is all but unthinkable for a trainee to act with cavalier unsupervised independence in the closely monitored environment of the programs of the twenty-first century. A Garven Wilsonhulme would never make it into or through the training or the vicissitudes of neurosurgical practice in today's world without a very considerable amount of refinement and bowing to the ethical, moral, legal, and scientific standards of the present day. But then, neurosurgeons are eminently tough and adaptable. Maybe even Garven could make his way in the new paradigm as he did in the era of forty and fifty years ago, when this *Saga* took place. The author would like to think he could.

Dedication

The series of books is dedicated to those giants upon whose shoulders I stood, including: Harvey Birsner, MD, my partner and friend; Shelly Chou, MD, PhD, my great mentor; Kemp Clark, MD, The Chief; Stephen David Durrant, PhD, professor of biology/evolution/comparative anatomy, a curmudgeon, humorist, inspiration, and friend; Lyle A. French, MD, PhD, the grand master at Minnesota; William Wallace Newby, PhD, professor of biology/embryology, my greatest friend and help; Lito Porto, MD, The Indian; J. Charles Rich, MD, my worthy opponent in premed and the consummate neurosurgeon and contributor to the neurosurgical community; Theodore Roberts, MD, my start; Duke Samson, MD, the great builder of neurosurgery and foremost of brain vascular surgeons; Charles Sternbergh, MD, the rock of integrity; Clark C. Watts, MD, JD, my friend and support during the lean years.

Acknowledgments

The author acknowledges with appreciation the direct contributions to the books of Harvey Birsner, MD; Keith Hooker, MD; Kim Oliver, MD; Brent Pratley, MD; Charles Stewart, MD; and all of the general surgery and neurosurgery interns, residents, and professors in California, Utah, Minnesota, Texas, Virginia, and the men and women of the navy who served with me.

"David Stark is the best there is. He's not real big on publishing papers; nobody is at this place. But Dr. Stark has the best hands and the best judgment of anybody you'll ever see. He runs a very tight ship. I mean, he is from the old SOB school of neurosurgery. Everybody hates him. He is as mean as a cornered snake, but he is fair, and he can make you into the best neuro guy there is. If you survive it."

"Boy, it really sounds like a lot of fun," Garven said.

"Forget about fun for the next four or five years, if you come here. But you will do ten times more surgery than you would ever think of doing at a place like the Mayo Brothers. That's the main trade-off. You have to make a decision early on about the kind of education you want. You can get into a nice, clean university hospital, or especially into a private hospital. You won't work all that hard, and you'll know the literature like nobody's business. You'll probably even publish a few articles. That's the way to go if you are interested in academics. 'Them as can, cuts—and them as can't goes into academics' is the way the expression goes. You won't do much surgery in one of those clean places, but you will get a little time off. You might even think of yourself as having a life."

"Those Himalayas of the mind,
Are not so easily possessed;
There's more than precipice and storm
Between you and your Everest."

—Sir Edmund Hillary, [Written as he descended from Mt. Everest after he and Tenzing Norgay became the first men to reach the summit.]

CHAPTER
One

Garven took one interview trip each weekend for the last two weeks of January and the first weekend in February. All of the visits were made on borrowed money. He had to take out a second loan and felt like he would drown from the debt. His first trip was to Minneapolis. The hospital complex was part of the university campus and was set on a low hill on the eastern bank of the Mississippi River. The buildings were neat and uniform of brown brick. They were massive and spoke of solidity.

Having gotten a taste of pediatrics, medicine, and psychiatry, Garven had had enough to do with the nonsurgical specialties. Despite the well-meaning advice of the medicine faculty and many of his uninformed classmates, he had made up his mind to do a straight surgery internship. It was unusual to make such a choice; most students in 1956 opted for the traditional rotating internship to give them a well-rounded approach to medicine. Garven Wilsonhulme had sufficient "well-roundedness." He wanted to be a neurosurgeon, and he selected the hospitals for his internship on the basis of which would give him the best neurosurgery education, and into which one he could get accepted.

The surgery program at the University of Minnesota was one of the most prestigious in the country. It was notorious for its hard work and famous for its graduates, who were beginning to fill the department head chairs all around the country. The program was almost unique for its insistence on the candidates getting a PhD in medicine as well as fulfilling the requirements for clinical medicine.

At Minnesota, neurosurgery was a department of its own, not just a division, a fact that bespoke the great strength of their program. Owen Wangensteen was the venerable head of surgery, and Lyle French was the chief of neurosurgery. They were two of the most outstanding men in American surgery at the time.

Garven was met in the entrance lobby by Norwood Simons, a general surgery intern, dressed in an outfit that made him look like a barber or a bellhop. It was a starched white tunic, buttoned at the shoulder and with a mandarin collar. He wore white pants, socks, and shoes. Garven made his first mental note: he hated the uniform; he thought it made the young doctor look more like an orderly than a physician.

"Hi, I'm Norwood. You're Garven, right?"

"That's right."

"Look, I don't have much time. I'll tell you about the program while we take a whirlwind tour. You have to be back at ten o'clock for your interview with Dr. Wangensteen anyway."

Norwood ran Garven around the confusing array of buildings, wards, operating theaters, X-ray departments, and house staff quarters, talking at machine-gun speed the entire time. Norwood was doing his surgery internship and was hoping to get into Dr. French's program, "the best in the country." He explained the call schedule (every other night), the journal clubs and mortality and morbidity conferences (once a week), and the chance to see great surgeons do great operations. Norwood waxed hyperbolic. However, about the chance to do surgery oneself as an intern—he did not have much to say on that subject.

Dr. Wangensteen was an institution himself, venerable, arrogant, brilliant, and full of bizarre ideas for research that he laid on Garven, a senior medical student, like an artillery barrage. He talked nonstop. Garven's questions were to be answered by the house staff.

There was a similarly brief meeting for Garven and the ten other internship applicants visiting that day with the surgical staff and faculty. They were strong-willed, dynamic, opinionated young men. The only older man—the only other full professor—was a domineering bearish man named Oliver Valdo. The young men launched into a heated argument over the relative value of the Billroth II versus the old vagotomy and pyloroplasty operations for gastric ulcers and more or less forgot about the applicants. Dr. Valdo stood around looking menacing—reminiscent of Dr. Cartral at UA—a man to be avoided. The house staff men whom Garven talked with told him as much.

12

Garven was lucky enough to get an interview with Lyle French, the head of neurosurgery, himself. The man was a stern Presbyterian, a fact that he told Garven almost as soon as he entered the neurosurgery office. He was absolutely ramrod stiff, all business, and the most brilliant and personally forceful man Garven had ever met. He came away from the fifteen-minute meeting with his head spinning and full of enthusiasm for the University of Minnesota Hospital's surgical training programs. He had long since dispelled any doubts about his choice of specialties for his career. The conversation with Dr. French had the affect of sealing down his resolve.

The following week, Garven flew to Dallas to see the University of Texas, Southwestern Medical School program. In outward appearance, the contrast between the University of Minnesota and the Dallas institution could not have been more complete. Minnesota was neat, green, and well groomed with handsome matching brick buildings, and nothing but white faces. UTSWMS existed only in the ramshackle building of Parkland Memorial Hospital. The place was a confusing assemblage of add-on buildings that seemed to have been placed without regard to convenience, esthetics, or comforts. The building was old and ugly, a broad-faced, tall edifice on the outside and dirty and hectic inside. There was no air conditioning—not necessary for the charity patients. Ninety-nine percent of the faces Garven saw in and around Parkland—in contrast to Minnesota—were black.

Garven was met this time by an exhausted first-year resident. The interns were all "tied up in scut work," he was told. Whereas Norwood Simons had been all togged out in gleaming white, Anderson John Dimit Purlitz was dressed in scrubs. His clothing was bespattered with blood and suspicious brown and yellow spots. It was wrinkled and probably had been in place for at least two days.

"There's not much to see, really," said Dr. Purlitz. "The 'Lands' is just another big hospital, like any big city hospital. Seen one, you've seen 'em all. Let's go see the 'Pit' and the OR. That's where it's at here."

"I'll just follow," Garven said.

What time's your appointment with Dr. Shires?"Anderson asked (Tom Shires was head of surgery).

Anderson insisted on being called by his first name.

"Eleven."

"Okay. Follow me."

He led Garven to the emergency room, more accurately, suite of rooms. It was teeming with walking wounded, crying children and mothers, running interns and nurses. The floor was old and splattered with patches of fresh blood and vomitus. A Negro man scurried around, trying to mop up the new accumulations, but there was no way he could keep up.

Anderson introduced Garven to the surgery resident in charge of the surgical ER.

After the briefest of social amenities, the resident rushed on into one of the two major trauma rooms, explaining, "Gotta GSW to the abdomen. Think he got big stink. We're heading him upstairs ASAP."

Garven and Anderson slipped in, making sure they did not get in the way. A harried-looking intern aspirated feculent material from the hole in the Negro patient's abdomen.

"Yep, big stink," he said. "Set us up for a colostomy. T and C six units of whole blood. He's bleeding BRB not just packed cells," the surgery resident in charge ordered.

The intern rushed out to follow the bidding of his resident.

"Who does the surgery?" Garven asked over the hubbub in the ER.

"Interns and residents. Period. Staff men come in to help and to teach. No self-respecting res. would ever live it down if a staff guy did his operation, except for their own private patients. Even then, the chief residents usually do those cases."

"Sounds like my kind of place," Garven said.

"It is, if you're one of the toughest dudes around. You don't get any sleep, decent pay, edible food, time off, or respect. Since I got here, I decided that 'sex' is just that number between 'five' and 'seven.' But I'll tell you, when you leave here, there won't be anybody who can out-operate you. That's why I'm here. I won't weigh more'n ninety-six pounds soaking wet, and my 'nads will probably have shriveled up to nothing, but I will be an operating fool. You see everything and do everything there is here. I hate it. Wouldn't go anyplace else!"

A tall, slim, balding, altogether patrician man in a crisp shirt and tie and a long, clean white lab coat approached the exit to the ER suites where Garven and Anderson were standing. He was accompanied by a short South American man dressed in scrubs as dirty as everyone else's in the ER and a white coat like the tall man's. They were a Mutt and Jeff team.

"Hey," Anderson said, "aren't you interested in neuro?"

"Yeah, I am."

"That's Dr. Clark and The Indian. Kemp Clark is the head of the division of neurosurgery and Lito Porto—everybody calls him 'The Indian'—is the only resident. That poor booger works all the time. He is the toughest guy I ever met. Dr. Clark has only been here a couple of years. He is slick. Great hands. He is the coolest head under fire I ever saw. If I didn't want to do general so bad, I'd get into Dr. Clark's neuro program. Nobody can touch them for the amount and kind of surgery they do. Wanna meet them?"

"You bet!" Garven said.

He had not been able to get an appointment with the head of neurosurgery, so this was his golden opportunity.

Anderson stopped the Mutt and Jeff combination and introduced Garven.

Dr. Clark said, "Sorry, I don't have time to talk right now. If you come here, we can get together and go over my program. I think you would find it exciting. Speaking of that, why not follow us? We have a case I think you would find interesting."

Garven looked at Anderson. The general surgery resident took this as his chance to disappear, and Garven tagged along with Dr. Clark and The Indian.

The two neurosurgeons stepped aside and opened the curtain front on the exam cubicle. Garven walked in and almost jumped out of his shoes. There, sitting propped up on the gurney, was a thin, wasted-looking Negro derelict with a hatchet imbedded in the right side of his forehead. He was alert and moved around as if there was not a thing the matter. He was talking to the nurses' aide when the three men walked in on them and stopped to see what the doctors had in mind.

"Well, C.M., we have to shave off your head and take you upstairs to the surgery to get that ax out of your head," The Indian said.

"Awraht, you is the doctah," said the patient.

They might have been discussing a brake repair job.

Garven felt a little shaken. He had not been expecting anything quite like that.

Dr. Clark was on his way to his private clinic.

He said to Garven, "It's like that every day here. You will get the best experience in the world at Parkland. If you decide to go into neurosurgery here, and if I accept you, you will be treated like a neurosurgeon from the first day, and will be expected to act like one. That's the contract. Give it a thought."

He heeled about and strode off.

Garven spoke to Tom Shires and came away even more impressed. The chief of surgery brimmed with ideas and enthusiasms. His big interest was in the treatment of shock, a new and demanding discipline all by itself. He worked to get Garven interested. Garven went home full of excitement and enthusiasm. His order of preference was now Parkland, number one; Minnesota, number two.

Garven Aloysius Carmichael Wilsonhulme, the urchin—the coyote—from Cipher, Arizona, was going to be a brain surgeon. How he would have loved to rub that in the face of the father who abandoned him when he was ten and gave him his atrociously pompous name.

CHAPTER
Two

On Monday morning, back in Phoenix, Garven started on the ortho-pedic surgery service. In no time, he was up to his elbows in cast plaster, ACE bandages, and slings. He worked alongside an intern, and the two of them reviewed X-rays and set simple limb fractures nonstop until noon. The occasional complex fracture, or broken hip, was sent promptly to the residents to take to the OR. It was a very efficient service, but Garven had a sense that he was working with carpenters. None of it seemed very scientific, or even doctorly. He was sure that a technician could do what he was doing. It was fun anyway. The house staff and nurses were a jovial, bawdy bunch, in contrast to the taciturnity that he had seen on medicine and the chronic exhaustion he had seen on general surgery.

They received a Hells Angel who had run his Harley Davidson into a parked car and developed a C2 fracture-subluxation. He was neurologically intact—at that level of injury, to be alive meant that you were intact, Garven learned. He was placed in traction on a sandwich board turning bed using tongs drilled in head and pelvic pins and sent to the ward. The ward nurse turned him from front to back, but neglected to do one small thing—to secure the Hells Angel on the frame. When he turned fully onto his abdomen, the bottom of the frame fell off, and the biker hung suspended from his head and his pelvis, teaching the ward help nuances of vocabulary. Garven and the clinic resident, Dr. Flanders, had to rush up and place him back on his back.

"I'm outta here, you mothers," said the biker. He then said some more things.

Chapter Two

"Keep your shirt on. We'll get your back in alignment and put on a cast; then, if you want to be dumb enough to do it, you can go."

"Make it quick. I ain't stayin' here no more'n I have to. It ain't safe!"

Garven could not argue with that legitimate observation.

Dr. Flanders cranked the traction up to seventy pounds and checked another lateral cervical spine X-ray.

"Alignment's okay. Garven, you are going to learn how to put on a Minerva jacket."

He and Garven put on the body and head plaster jacket with the biker in traction. The Hells Angel insisted on the traction tongs and pins being removed as soon as the cast was in place. Before the heavy cast was dry, he walked out of the hospital AMA and was last seen riding out of the hospital parking lot on his high rider. He was speeding, and was conspicuous in his white jacket. He had tied his Coors Beer hat to the head portion of the Minerva jacket.

The first patient of the afternoon turned out to be the next opportunity to be impressed with neurosurgery. A middle-aged Mexican laborer was brought into the clinic with a severe limp. He was almost dragging his right leg. The intern was not sure what was wrong with him. The man spoke only Spanish— more accurately, Spanglish—and no one could get a decent history from him.

"*Me duele la cinturon*," he kept saying.

"Any idea what that is?" asked Dr. Flanders, the ortho resident.

"Something about his belt hurting," the intern said. "Beats me."

The three of them examined the man, who, if nothing else was evident, appeared to be in excruciatingly severe pain. The resident carefully measured the circumferences of his legs and thighs and compared them. He tried to get him to stand up straight. The man remained in a severely bent position and stood on the tiptoe of his right foot.

"I think we have a case of severe sacroiliitis. Looks like it's caused by his right leg being so much shorter than the other one. Get him a shot and some codeine to take home and send him to prosthesis clinic to get a shoe insert for the right foot. Make it a two-inch lift, he looks way off," Dr. Flanders ordered the intern.

"Man, can you get that much pain from just having one leg shorter than the other?" asked Garven.

There was something wrong with the picture, but he did not know what.

"I guess so," Dr. Flanders said. "He seems to."

17

The intern looked perplexed. "Maybe he's got something wrong with his back. Whatta you think? Get a neuro consult?"

"Okay by me," said the ortho resident. "But get the surgeons, not the swamis."

Dr. Radcliffe, the intern, called the neurosurgery resident.

The neuro resident was Cliff Howell. In fact, he was just a general surgery resident doing his tour on neuro. He was not sure what the matter was with the poor guy, either. He did not have the sense that there was any faking; the guy was in real pain, and that there was really something the matter. He called Dr. Harralsen.

"Ruptured disc. Classical and acute," said Dr. Harralsen before he even touched the man or asked a single question. "*Donde le duele, amigo?*" he asked the Mexican.

"*Me duele la cinturon, señor doctor,*" responded the unfortunate man, obviously relieved that, finally, someone understood him, and more, that he was being believed.

"*En la espina, señor?*" asked Dr. Harralsen.

"*Si, si. Y en la pierna. Me duel mucho. Ayuda me, por favor.*"

The man was almost crying.

"He has terrible pain in his back and leg. This guy needs a myelogram right now and an operation to get rid of his ruptured disc this afternoon, agreed, Dr. Howell?"

"Yes, Sir. That's my dx," said the orthopedics intern.

Garven raised an eyebrow. "What about his short leg?" he asked Dr. Harralsen.

"Forget about it. He's just splinting. I'll have him walking normally tonight. Come by 3-B and see him about eight o'clock."

3-B was the neurosurgery ward.

"I'll do it. I guess I'll have to learn Spanish to be able to do neurosurgery. It gets tougher all the time."

Dr. Harralsen smiled. "If you work in a blood and guts program, you'll have to pick up some Spanish, or you will have a heck of a time communicating. The Negroes have their own language, too. You'll have to take a course in that as well. Come to think of it, it is tough. Are you coming on the service before graduation, Garven?"

"Next quarter, Dr. Harralsen. I'll brush up on my foreign languages."

"We'll make you a neurosurgeon yet, Garv."

CHAPTER
Three

When Garven had walked out of Arthur Fletcher's study after their acrimonious confrontation on the day of the meet-the-folks dinner, he had gone straight to the music room, where Elizabeth and her mother were sitting expectantly.

"How did it go?" blurted Elizabeth before Garven could say anything.

The look on his face suggested that it had not gone so well.

"I think we should speak privately, Elizabeth," Garven had said.

Mrs. Fletcher had more than a fair inkling of what had transpired.

"Please, Garven. I don't want to intrude, but I really must know what Mr. Fletcher had to say, if I am to be able to function. I am sure you understand. Could you tell me that much?"

"All right, Ma'am," he said.

Garven was not good at verbal sparring, and for practical purposes, he did not know how to beat around a conversational bush. He presented a succinct but accurate version of the meeting and offered the voided check as evidence. Mrs. Fletcher sat in stony, irritable silence. Elizabeth was visibly angered, gritting her teeth at first, and shedding wrathful tears as Garven finished his brief rendition.

Elizabeth pleaded with Garven not to let her father destroy their great love. She vowed never to sign a prenuptial agreement even if they had to live in poverty. Garven had mixed emotions about that declaration.

Mrs. Fletcher had the last word. "Garven, here's something you can take to the bank. The two of you will be married. There will be no foolishness about disinheritance or nastiness. I will deal with my husband. He will behave himself. Elizabeth and I will set about to arrange the biggest, best wedding ever seen in Maricopa County."

Garven liked the part about taking "something to the bank" and knew he could live with the rest. Weddings were for women, and he would perform the groom's traditional role of being an ornament, just like all the legions of grooms before him and, undoubtedly would be, after him.

Neurosurgery kept cropping up. The next time Garven encountered his chosen service was when he was spending his week on ophthalmology in May. He and an excited resident saw a very obese young woman in the eye clinic. She had vague complaints of blurred vision. On the eye exam, Garven had seen a very peculiar blurring of the borders of the optic nerve disc. The insides of the eye grounds, the retina, appeared boggy, as if they were wet. He called the resident to look at the phenomenon with him.

"Will you look at that!" exclaimed the eye resident, oblivious to the sensibilities of his patient. "That's papilledema, Garven. The reason her eye grounds look wet is because they are swollen, and the reason they look that way is because her brain is swollen. This is the first time I ever saw it. This girl has a brain tumor!"

The young woman had a look on her face as if she had been poleaxed and left for dead.

Garven thought something was odd. For having a big brain tumor that caused all that swelling, the girl seemed so normal mentally. He did a quick neurological examination, hampered by her fat, but there was nothing asymmetrical or otherwise unusual about her. The resident made an emergency call to the neuro service.

Dr. Harralsen himself came. He took his time getting there, which made the resident both nervous and angry. Since Harralsen was a professor and staff man, the resident had to let it go.

Dr. Harralsen put his hand gently on the patient's forearm.

He smiled at her and said, "Relax. I'll ask you some questions and then tell you what I think is going on. I am in hopes that it is a benign problem."

"What does 'benign' mean, doctor?" the girl asked in a small voice.

"It means 'not bad.'"

"I hope so," she said, almost in tears.

"Now then, tell me, when was your last period?"

The young woman looked at the neurosurgeon with curiosity. It was a strange question to ask about an eye problem. She wondered if she had misunderstood that the man was a brain doctor.

Nonetheless, she answered, "About two years ago."

"I thought as much, Miss Appleton. You have a well-known syndrome, and you do not have a brain tumor."

Garven was astounded that Dr. Harralsen could be so sure. While he had waited for the neurosurgeon to arrive for the consultation, he had read up on papilledema, and everything he read made the finding seem very ominous.

Dr. Harralsen continued. "You have what is called 'pseudotumor cerebri.' That's a problem of swelling of the brain without any mass in the head; no brain tumor, no blood clot, or anything like that."

A look of profound relief came over the young woman's face. The ophthalmology resident slapped his forehead as he remembered the pearl one of his professors had tried to teach him about fat, amenorrheic young women with severe papilledema. It was a classical mistake for an ophthalmological novice to make, and he was very annoyed with himself. He knew he had lost face with the medical student.

"The condition is treated with a series of spinal taps. Do you know what that is, Miss Appleton?" Dr. Harralsen asked.

"I think so."

Her face was retaking on some of the terror that it mirrored from her soul when she had thought that she was going to die from a brain tumor.

"It's not all that bad," Dr. Harralsen said. "And we have an expert right here to do it. Right, Garven?"

"See one, do one, teach one"—the old principle came back to bite him. "Yes, Sir," Garven said with full confidence that he did not feel.

She was huge. He wondered if they would even have a needle long enough. He knew he would not be able to feel any of the landmarks in her spine.

Dr. Harralsen and the ophthalmology resident left Garven; so, they could have a brief teaching session. It was a humbling experience for the resident, but a lesson he would remember. Garven set about to get an extra-long needle and to do the lumbar puncture. It took more than one stick that first day, but for the rest of the week, he got better and better until on the last day, when the pressure was nearly normal, he could get the needle into the subarachnoid space, where the CSF is contained, on the first pass.

The contribution of neurosurgery to the Ears, Nose, and Throat service was much more spectacular. The door over the clinic read: "OTORHINOLARYNGOLOGY." As such, it was a useless bit of communicational fluff for the patients because many of the clinic patients were functionally illiterate. The

21

nature of the business was made manifest on the clinic doors by the addition of schematic drawings of an ear, a nose, and a gullet.

In among the legions of runny noses, chronic congestions, sore throats and hoarse voices, infected and wax-plugged ears—the stuff that made ENT an intolerable specialty—there was a thirty-one-year-old man who had suffered with terrible headaches constantly since adolescence, and who was established to have a treatable cause. He had a severe, chronic sinusitis involving the ethmoid sinuses located in the very top of the sinus system above and behind the nose, and just below the thin base of the front part of the skull. His ethmoiditis had been stubbornly resistant to antibiotics, nasal lavages, and painful probing.

Garven happened to be the lucky student who saw him in clinic on the day the chief of staff of ENT finally threw in the towel and agreed to operate on the miserable man. Garven was allowed to be second assistant; the chief resident, who had not seen very many of these cases, was to be first assistant. The chief scheduled himself to do the operation because the man was his private patient.

The surgery started promptly at seven o'clock on Thursday morning, a privileged hour vouchsafed for chiefs of surgery. Dr. Trappel, chief of ENT, had to get back to his lab early that day. As Garven had presumed, it was difficult for him and for the other two surgeons to see. From the very start, Garven could tell that he was not going to like "booger surgery." It was like operating through a keyhole in the first place. And Garven did not care for having to suck out accumulated nasal mucous to get to the operative site in the second place. Dr. Trappel frequently ran a probe up into the top of the nose then took lateral face and skull X-rays to be sure that the probe was in the correct location in the sinus. He was also concerned about running the probe too far in and penetrating through the thin skull floor and into the brain cavity, or even into the brain.

The surgeon worked and probed, drew masses of thickened mucous membranes out of the sinus, and lavaged with antibiotic solution. He was nearly done. He used cupped, cutting curettes to scrape out the last vestiges of infected material. He probed one last time and suddenly froze in place.

"Oh no!" Dr. Trappel said. His brow knitted in hard wrinkles. His eyes looked upward in an attitude of wishful prayer. "Get another lateral while I hold the probe in place. Stat!"

The X-ray was hurriedly done. The tip of the probe was located two centimeters inside the innermost line of the floor of the skull. It had to be sticking into the frontal lobe of the brain.

Dr. Trappel looked sick.

"Call Harralsen. Right now!"

The circulating nurse scurried off.

In a few minutes, she returned and told Dr. Trappel, "He's giving a lecture. They won't disturb him."

"Forget that! Send someone over to the amphitheater and have them march right up to him. This is an emergency. I can't hold this probe forever! Get him in here before this turns into a catastrophe!"

The nurse conveyed the message with all of its ramifications to one of the supervising nurses. The supervisor left the operating suites and delivered the message herself. While they waited, Dr. Trappel broke the uneasy silence.

"The worst thing about this is that the probe has been mucking around in grossly infected snot—a scientific term denoting nasal mucous—then went through into the brain. He is a dead setup for a brain abscess. He'll have to have a craniotomy. I can hardly wait to explain that to his family and then to him when he wakes up."

Dr. Harralsen stopped his lecture almost mid-sentence and came directly to the OR.

He looked at Dr. Trappel holding the probe and at the X-ray, then said calmly, "Have to do a crani. I presume you realized that, Steve. Young Wilsonhulme can help me if that would suit you. The problem is that you'll have to hold that probe where it is until I can get down to it. Otherwise, I will have a deuce of a time trying to find where it went into the brain. I have got to debride out the potentially infected brain. It's the best chance we'll ever have to help this guy."

Dr. Trappel groaned. His day was completely trashed. He nodded resignedly.

Garven was first assistant on a craniotomy on a live human being. It was the first time he had even seen the operation that sets neurosurgery apart from all other specialties. Once inside the cranium, Dr. Harralsen had Garven hold the probe with a mosquito clamp while he debrided the damaged brain around it. Dr. Trappel was able to release his cramped fingers from his end of the probe.

"Thanks, Oliver," he said to Dr. Harralsen. "I owe you one. I guess he should be transferred to your service, eh?"

"That would be best," Harralsen said.

He continued to suck out the brain that had been mulched by the probe tip. When he finished, there was a hole about the size of a boy's marble.

"That's first grade and accordion lessons," the neurosurgeon joked as he completed the last vestige of the removal of brain.

Garven followed the patient postoperatively on the neuro service. The man was a trifle slow mentally and inappropriate for two days, then returned to complete normalcy. Garven's only problem was about himself, wondering how he was going to be able to stand to wait through an internship and a core year of general surgery before he could get into neurosurgery and start doing this stuff himself.

Wedding plans were started. So far as Garven was concerned, the marriage could take place in the office of the justice of the peace that weekend—except, in fact, he had to make his internship interview trip to Los Angeles then. But it could be anytime soon. The two women would have none of that. It was shaping up to be the biggest wedding of all time, and it would take until mid-July before the plans could possibly be completed.

Elizabeth acted strangely. At least, Garven thought it was odd. She told him over and over again how much she loved him, but she made him keep his hands off. Their few kisses were brief and chaste.

When Garven asked Elizabeth if anything was the matter, she said, "No, silly. I am saving myself…us…for our wedding night. I want it to be perfect. If I let you get me started, I just know I won't be able to control myself. You understand."

Garven guessed he did.

Mrs. Fletcher took a time out of her dedication to the wedding project to ask Garven, "Would you please have another talk with Mr. Fletcher? He feels differently now. He is not a man who can say he's sorry, but I know he wants to make amends. He is a typical silly man and is too proud to come to you. Won't you please go to him?"

"I'd about as soon be poked in the eye with a sharp stick," Garven said.

"I know. But do it for me…for Elizabeth. We have to get beyond this. It would be terrible for us all if we let this thing get to the point where we can't even talk. I'm thinking of the years down the line."

Garven acknowledged to himself that he owed Mrs. Fletcher. The wedding, and the answer to his grievous financial problems, would not take place without her good offices. He knew that he needed to mend the figurative fences between himself and Mr. Fletcher. He called the MFD offices the following day and was put through to Arthur Fletcher's secretary. It took some cajoling, but finally, he got the woman to ask her boss if he would meet with his daughter's fiancé that day. It was a good omen that the meeting was scheduled for five o'clock in the afternoon.

Garven was on time. He was kept waiting for ten minutes before the CEO of the conglomerate came out of his office and signaled to his secretary to bring Garven in.

Garven took a seat.

Without preamble or amenities, Arthur Fletcher said, "You are a tough competitor, Garven."

Garven took a small pleasure in the observation that the man was using his given name and was not using the deprecatory, "son," "boy," or "young man."

"I have to admit that I like the forthright way you presented the check to my wife and Elizabeth. You have a good head on your shoulders—that was a coup the way you got me to write the check. I could use a man like you in the company. You sure you want to be a doctor?"

"I'm sure," Garven responded.

Mr. Fletcher was making a real effort to be friendly. It was as near as he was going to get to conveying an apology; Garven was certain of that.

"The reason I asked you to meet with me," Mr. Fletcher said, skimming over the fact that it had been Garven, not himself, who had asked for the conference, "is that we got off on the wrong foot. For Elizabeth's sake, I hope you can be man enough to let bygones be bygones and to let us start afresh. Think that can be done?"

"It can on my part, Mr. Fletcher. I can understand that you have to be protective of your daughter. I will show you that my intentions are proper," Garven replied.

He kept all traces of the animosity he felt out of his face.

"That's the spirit, Garven!"

Mr. Fletcher was beaming now. He had smoothed over the rift. This would mollify his wife, and it had not cost a dime. It was just possible that the young man was on the up and up. But despite himself, he maintained his doubts. He strove not to show them outwardly.

The two men shook hands. It was too soon to be anything but wary. There was little warmth in the gesture. Garven was about to go, when his future father-in-law stopped him.

"I hope we can put the past behind us, where it belongs. I look forward to a cordial relationship between us."

Garven was not inclined to have to put up a totally false front for the rest of his life. He decided to set some ground rules with which they could both live.

He said, "I appreciate that, Mr. Fletcher. But in all candor, I think it is unlikely that we will make it all the way to 'cordial.' What do you say to something more on the order of 'civil,' or at least 'polite'?"

Mr. Fletcher looked long at Garven the way a weasel looks at a coyote. He had underestimated the sagacity of the young man. He would not be inclined to do so again.

"Well said, Garven. I think we can both live with 'polite.' Consider that you and I have made a bargain. I keep my bargains."

CHAPTER
Four

Garven's appointment in Los Angeles was postponed by a week, and he had to pay extra to change his ticket. That had obliged him to borrow again from Gordon, and he knew that he would have to get the payback from Elizabeth. That galled him, but there was nothing he could do about it at the moment.

It was raining furiously when his Braniff Airlines flight finally landed half an hour late in the Los Angeles International Airport.

The business man seated by him groused that it was predictable. "Braniff is the world's largest unscheduled airline."

Garven had almost forgotten how big the greater metropolitan area of LA was. It came home to him when he asked how much cab fare would be to Osterlund Memorial Hospital, located out in downtown LA. Too much, he decided, and rented a little budget car, a Volkswagen bug, for the two days he would be there. He bought a *Thomas Guide* and followed the maps as best he could. The traffic was fearsome, but it was not difficult to get through the freeways, up the 405 and east on the 10. It became more difficult and dicey to get off on the correct street to get to UC Osterlund Memorial on the corner of Hill Street and Eighth. He got flustered and turned off too soon, and went northwest on Figueroa instead of southwest. He had to wind around through the rundown sections of central LA in his little car, feeling like he should be in a tank. He eventually stopped and oriented himself with the map, got onto Washington, traveling more or less southeast, until he hit Hill Street. He made sure that he was going the right direction this time; it all began to look the same to him. He knew he was headed where he wanted to go because the con-

27

dition of the buildings and of the people progressively declined as he passed 16th, Pico Boulevard, 12th, and finally rounded the corner onto 8th Street.

He was in the heart of darkness. There was not a white face to be seen anywhere. And there were thousands of faces. He wondered briefly if there was some sort of holiday because there were so many people crowding into the streets. It was unnerving, and Garven felt very insecure. His insecurity mounted when he passed a couple of parking lots near the hospital and saw guards patrolling with what looked like automatic rifles slung on their shoulders. He was leery of even going near those places; so, he turned into the side driveway of the hospital proper to see if he might get lucky and find a place to park where he would not have to walk through that urban jungle. Garven's insecurity turned to near panic when he found himself ascending the loading ramp on the far side of the main entrance.

His fears were justified. As he slowly drove up, knowing he was in the wrong location, he saw an altercation taking place in front of one of the roll-up metal doors in the delivery section. As he passed no more than ten yards away, one black man held a long-bladed knife high overhead and then stabbed his opponent square in the chest.

Garven blinked in disbelief. "'*Balls,' cried the queen*," he muttered to himself.

He drove over the top of the rise and out of sight of the homicide, thinking he should just keep going right on out of the hospital grounds and back to the airport, and forget the whole thing. But he had come that far; and he determined to suck it up and to get into the hospital, where it was safe, somehow. He ended up parking in the last space in the visitor's parking lot, and considered himself lucky to have found that slot after three passes through the lot. He got out and walked as fast as he could toward the hospital.

He found himself in an accumulating throng of Negroes headed in the same direction. At least, they seemed to know where the entrance was located, which was more than he could say for himself. The people who had engendered such fear as he was driving seemed much less disturbing up close. They were poor, and many of them were dirty. They had missing teeth, and some had absent limbs. They carried their own lunches, and the women all had some handwork with them. They were obviously old hands at the long waits in the clinics and brought something to do to while away during the hours of wait. Some were friendly and smiling; some downcast and beaten. They joked and laughed, and some of them were singing as they walked along in the heat of mid-morning in Los Angeles; others sat in stony, stoical silence, monuments to suffering. There was nothing threatening about them, and Garven relaxed. As near as he could tell, his was the only white face in the crowd, and it did not seem to matter.

The hospital was contained in one gigantic, fifteen-story building, large enough to fit the Salt River Valley Medical Center inside it without noticing it was there. There were 2,000 charity beds. The building was old and looked even older than its years. It was made of cement blocks that were dirty and devoid of new paint in over a decade by Garven's reckoning. The building was strictly utilitarian and had probably been built without esthetic enhancement to assuage the complaints of the taxpayers. There were no lawns or gardens or flowers or trees. As far as Garven could see, it was a stultifying world of cement.

Garven followed the throng into the cavernous main waiting room. It was large enough that the voices and clatter of carts produced echoes. There were a few benches, all occupied. Most of the people in the waiting room were sitting on the floor, which was grimy and gray; some families were picnicking. There were harried women with gaggles of squalling small children, shambling addicts, derelicts looking lost, and carts and gurneys being pushed by dwarfs and retarded men. The walls were dilapidated. Paint peeled here and there, and there were patches of broken plaster and splotches of nondescript stains noticeable every so often. A series of holes, stitched across one wall at abdomen level, bore mute testimony to the violence that came to the hospital.

Garven had an appointment at eleven, and he was early. He advanced into the hallways leading off the main lobby and instantly knew that he would get lost if he tried to wander around. He had wondered at the propriety or the wisdom of his instructions to meet his guide in the main waiting room, but he could now see the obvious reason for the choice.

He stationed himself in the exact center of the large room and established a routine of surveying the panorama of human misery, hoping he would be able to pick out his guide when he or she came in. He stood out because he was dressed in a conservative suit, white shirt and tie, and had on well polished shoes—an ensemble that made him unique. Had he been taller, he would have been conspicuous.

A little past the hour, a stringy, thin Caucasian walked briskly into the waiting room. He was dressed in a white lab coat—at least, it had once been white—and rumpled, splotched green scrubs. He had to be the one. Garven picked his way through the sea of bodies, trying to avoid the human shoals, so he would not step on anyone. He met "Dr. Howard Richter, general surgery," as the man's lab coat embroidery announced, halfway across the room.

"Dr. Wilsonhulme, I presume," said the greeter and extended his hand.

29

Garven was glad to see that it, unlike the man's clothes, was clean. They shook hands.

"C'mon with me, unless you are of a mind to continue rubbing shoulders with the great unwashed for a while longer."

He turned and headed for the exit.

"Lead on," Garven said.

"You want the grand tour or the extended lecture? I am best at abbreviating either or both," said Dr. Richter.

"How about the shortened version? I'm supposed to meet with Dr. Lyons at noon and the head of neuro at twelve-thirty."

"I hope you're a good walker. This place is a maze. Don't even try to get oriented. I promise that I won't get you permanently lost. I can walk and talk at the same time, despite anything my mother would tell you," Dr. Richter said, and he was already moving out briskly.

True to his word, the resident swept Garven past the X-ray department, the surgery clinics, the ER suites, which were bristling with frenetic activity, the medical and surgical wards with their barracks arrangements of beds, and through the G-U ward, which smelled of stale urine. There was no furniture in any of the halls or on the wards other than patient beds. Dr. Richter explained that it had all been stolen by the patients and their families and never replaced. They sidestepped little puddles of bodily fluids of all kinds scattered about the halls and aisles, and peeked in at the huge operating room complex. It was as busy as anywhere else in the immense hospital, but there was a clearer and more relaxing air of efficiency and purpose in the suites. And it was the only place Garven had seen since he entered the building that was convincingly clean.

Dr. Richter talked almost nonstop as the two men walked quickly through the labyrinthine halls, stairways, and entrances. He had an encyclopedic knowledge of the place.

"This is the tour to let you see the uptown parts of Osterlund," he said. "We want you to come here to do your slave labor; so, I left out the dirty and dangerous parts."

He rattled off the surgical statistics, the house staff routines—such as being on call every other day for the first two years, then all of the time after that—and the way things worked.

"You have to make your own IV solutions, push the patient's gurney if you want to get him anywhere, find your own X-rays, which is usually well-nigh to impossible, help the nurses clean up, talk nice to everyone, and take crap from the staff, nurses, patients, you name it."

"How do you stand it?" was about all Garven could come up with in the way of questions.

"There is one great saving grace. You will be the best cutter and sewer that there ever was when you get out of this program. You're interested in neuro, right?"

"Right."

"David Stark is the best there is. He's not real big on publishing papers; nobody is at this place. But Dr. Stark has the best hands and the best judgment of anybody you'll ever see. He runs a very tight ship. I mean, he is from the old SOB school of neurosurgery. Everybody hates him. He is as mean as a cornered snake, but he is fair, and he can make you into the best neuro guy there is. If you survive it."

"Boy, it really sounds like a lot of fun," Garven said.

"Forget about fun for the next four or five years, if you come here. But you will do ten times more surgery than you would ever think of doing at a place like the Mayo Brothers. That's the main trade-off. You have to make a decision early on about the kind of education you want. You can get into a nice, clean university hospital, or especially into a private hospital. You won't work all that hard, and you'll know the literature like nobody's business. You'll probably even publish a few articles. That's the way to go if you are interested in academics. 'Them as can, cuts—and them as can't goes into academics' is the way the expression goes. You won't do much surgery in one of those clean places, but you will get a little time off. You might even think of yourself as having a life.

"Here, you will work your butt off from the day you arrive until the day you leave. You will learn to operate, and you will do boo-coo surgery. You won't have to worry about the 'publish or perish' bull; you will be too busy cutting. Believe me, you will see everything here—every disease, every complication, every kind of strange character, and I don't mean just the patients. Got to choose, Garven. Give it a lot of thought. This is not the place for everyone. You have to have leather balls to work here."

"Thanks, I appreciate getting it straight," said Garven.

"It's only fair," said Howard Richter. "Hey, I have to go. It's nearly time for your staff man meetings anyway. Good luck."

They shook hands and Dr. Richter walked down the hall. He had arranged their tour so that Garven would end up standing in front of the head of surgery's office door when they parted.

The most singular aspect of his meeting with the chief of surgery, Dr. Peter Lyons, was that the eminent surgeon genuinely seemed to want Garven to come to Osterlund. He spoke with the same candor that had characterized Dr.

Richter's communication during the brief guided tour. He was neither arrogant nor pompous, but he came across as anything but a friendly man. He was all authority and business. He let it be known with emphasis that he would not suffer fools, and that patients were the most important persons in that hospital. He had Garven understand that he would have to abide by that dictum throughout his stay. If he could not put patients first, he should find another place.

Dr. Lyons' secretary handed Garven a disappointment. She had a message from Dr. Stark's neurosurgery office that he could not see Garven. There was no explanation. It did not matter that he had come all the way from Phoenix and had an appointment that had been made months before and verified as recently as two days ago. Garven shrugged his shoulders.

"Where's the neurosurgery ward?" he asked the secretary.

She gave him directions, even drew a map. "You will get lost," she said when she had completed her drawing. "Just ask somebody when you get somewhere near the place."

She was right. It took him a frustrating half an hour to get to the ninth-floor ward. He was puzzled that it had been so complicated. He introduced himself to the head nurse on 9B and told her that he was thinking about coming to Osterlund for his internship and to try to get into the neuro training program. She gave him a look that indicated that she regarded him as mentally defective and shook her head in genuine sympathy.

Garven poked around until he met an intern doing his scut work on the ward.

"Got a minute?" he asked.

"Nope," the intern said. "I take it you are looking at this place for an internship, right?"

"Yeah. I'm going to go into neuro."

"As in surgery?"

"Um hmmh," answered Garven.

"Boy, you must have a thought disorder if you are thinking about doing your neuro here," the intern said.

"How come?"

"Because Stark is the meanest slave driver you ever saw. He is a prick with ears." The intern looked quickly around to see if anyone was listening. "These guys work harder than anybody else in this dump, and that's going some, believe you me."

"So, is it a good training program?"

"The best."

CHAPTER
Five

Garven sent in his final choice list to the National Intern Matching Program center just before the deadline of May first. He put down the University of Texas, Southwestern Medical School as first choice; Minnesota, second; and Osterlund, third. He was on the senior student surgical subspecialty rotation, on plastic surgery at the time. The following day, he was to start his neurosurgery rotation. He would finish up the year just before graduation on the easiest rotation in the medical school—radiology.

Garven found that he liked plastics. It was fun helping to make nice breasts, to straighten noses, and to make flop ears not stick out so badly. He had gotten real satisfaction in helping to repair cleft lips and palates. The children of the poor people were often neglected by their parents and suffered by having to face the horrified glances of people they met. They were often eight to ten before they were brought into the university center; sometimes they were neglected until they were teenagers. Many of them wore handkerchiefs across their red, open faces. A few wore hoods to hide themselves altogether. It was sad to see them. Teenagers were so painfully shy anyway that Garven could only imagine how hard it had to be to face life with a grotesque face. The problem was compounded by the ignorance of the parents and the community, especially in the Hispanic sections.

Many of the people thought that the disfigurement of their children's faces was a punishment from God for some infraction or other. Some viewed their children as being possessed by the devil, and that the face was the outward manifestation of the demon. Both of those ideas led people to keep their afflicted children hidden away; that resulted in serious emotional trauma to the children and lifelong social retardation. If Garven needed any further evidence to make a choice between religion and science, this would be sufficient. Nothing made Garven feel happier that he had chosen medicine as a career than to see the wondering exultation of a little girl whose face had been repaired and now knew that she would be able to face other people.

Garven now spent all of his spare time with the Fletchers, at least with the Fletcher women. He arranged for his mother to come to Phoenix for the obligatory meeting of families. He made her promise that she would tell the Fletchers that his father had died. She agreed most reluctantly to extend the fabrications to the extent that he had been a doctor, and for that matter, that her name was Wilsonhulme. Rachel was used to her simple but livable home. The Fletchers' mansion all but struck her dumb.

Afterward, when she and Garven had time to talk privately as she drove him back to the hospital, she said, "That is the most elegant building I was ever in. It is the biggest house I ever saw. It seems sort of sterile to me, though. Like you couldn't really walk in it, and kids would have to be quiet all the time."

"Yeah, I think you're right, Mom. The family's a little like that, too."

"Including Elizabeth?"

"When you get right down to it, I guess that's pretty accurate. She has had a funny sort of life, nothing like the regular folks we know. I think we haven't got a clue about how really rich people live," he said thoughtfully.

"But you want to be rich. That's what this is all about, isn't it, Garven?"

It was more an observation than a question, and it pierced like an awl to the heart of the matter.

Garven nodded slightly but did not answer. The answer was evident in his face.

"I'm sorry you have such a need, son," Rachel said. "Be careful about what you wish for; you are likely to get it."

They pulled into the hospital driveway and approached the main entrance.

"Will you be up for graduation?" he asked.

"Wild horses couldn't keep me away. I think Dr. Wilsonhulme is going to try to come, too. I told him on the phone that the trip would likely kill him; but he said that it would be a good way to go, seeing his son graduate from med school," she said.

"Good. I think the Fletchers will put you up. Elizabeth and Mrs. Fletcher will go to the ceremony. I don't think her father will make the effort, though."

"I take it you two don't get along all that well."

"You could say that."

"Better watch out. He's a powerful man. You don't need him for an enemy."

"I know that, Mom. I am trying the best I can. It's just that he doesn't think I'm good enough for his daughter."

"I presume nobody would be."

"That's about it. Maybe in time…"

His voice trailed off. They were at the entrance.

"Garven, I have a question. You don't have to answer, but I need to ask anyway. It's the woman in me. Do you love the girl?"

"I'm not even sure I know what that is, Mom. I'm not sure at all."

Mark Witherspoon was the general surgery resident on the neurosurgery rotation. On Garven's first day on the service, Mark was going to get to do his first case as surgeon. It was about the simplest case in all of neurosurgery—a carpal tunnel release. He wanted to do it because it was a borderland type of case; plastic surgeons, orthopods, and general surgeons, as well as the neuros, did them. It was indicated; the nerve conduction velocity of the median nerve across the wrist was markedly slowed by the neurologist's electrical test, and besides, Mark had never done one. Garven assisted him.

Garven scrubbed the wrist, hand, and forearm himself. A pneumatic cuff was already in place and the IV anesthetic, called a Beer Block, nothing to do with the beverage, had been administered and the arm was numb. Mark would not trust anyone else to do the draping even though it was simplicity itself. Mark had the textbook, Henry's *Extensile Exposure*, open on a Mayo tray beside the operating table. He had it memorized.

The carpal tunnel—anatomically, the transverse carpal ligament—sometimes gets thick and compresses the median nerve as it crosses the wrist to fan out into the hand. That gives rise to numbness and tingling in the nerve's service distribution, then leads to grip weakness, and finally to atrophy of the muscle mass at the base of the thumb. The thickening is attributed to repetitive trauma from handwork, and that is often the cause. The operation is simple, just snip through the thick ligament until it splays open and relieves the nerve. It was one of the best operations in all of surgery because of the accuracy of diagnosis, the high success rate, and the low complication rate.

Mark did an excellent job. It took him an hour, but only because he was so exquisitely cautious. The nurses were careful not to make comparisons with the skill and efficiency of the staff men. Mark put in the closing sutures, and Garven was supposed to tie them. For all his familiarity with surgery, Garven had never been first assistant. The most he had done in the operating room was to cut sutures after the first assistant had tied them. Big deal. He had found that even that idiot job could have its difficulties. About half the time, he cut off the knots and the suture had to be replaced, and Garven had to endure another short lecture. He hated short lectures.

He was in for one now. He knew how to tie knots. He had practiced in his room. Everything seemed harder in the operating room. The suture was fine and slick, unlike the string he practiced on in his room. The knots would not hold, and Garven was making every one of them loose. He fumbled and tore a hole in his glove, then he caught a piece of his glove in a knot, then he broke a suture by pulling too hard.

The lecture was very short. "You look like a panda bear in boxing gloves playing with himself. Do you have that much trouble tying your shoes?" Mark asked.

He was working hard to remain patient as Garven fumbled.

Garven was sweating—the thick, smelly sweat of stress. It was ridiculous, but finally, he was able to get the deep edges of the wound cinched together and the knots secured.

"Feel like doing the skin?" Mark asked with hopeful negativity in his voice.

Garven thought he had put Mark through enough for one day. "Nah," he said. "I don't think either one of us would be able to live long enough to get through the operation if I do it."

Mark and the nurses laughed. They were glad that the medical student was not overly sensitive. A lot of them would have insisted on blundering ahead and turning this little case into an all-day affair with lunch on the grounds.

"Good, because I want to make this skin as plastic a closure as I can," said Mark.

He put in very fine silk sutures, and it was a work of art to behold. He was pleased with himself.

Garven thought he had gotten to do quite a bit as well. It had not been a bad day for him, either. He vowed to tone up his simple skills, however. This was the last time he was ever going to look like a club-handed bumbler. He took a handful of sutures with him to his room.

The neuro service was not particularly busy during Garven's rotation. They averaged two cases a day, which was pretty slack, even for a new program. Dr. Harralsen took out a big Glioblastoma Multiforme, the most malignant and, unfortunately, the most common of the brain tumors, did three lumbar discs and a cervical one, and one cerebral vessel aneurysm. The aneurysm burst during surgery, and it was very exciting. Garven was addled by the compli-

36

cation, but the brain surgeon took it in his stride and got the bleeding and the aneurysm under control. Garven learned one of the grim realities about neurosurgery on that case; the patient never woke up.

The results from the Intern-Hospital matchups came on the last day Garven was on the neurosurgery service. He matched with his third choice, straight surgery internship at UC Osterlund Memorial Hospital Medical Center in Los Angeles.

"Congratulations," Dr. Harralsen told him. "Stark has a great program. You'll have to be tough. They don't call him 'Black-hearted Dave' for nothing."

Garven scarcely went to the radiology clinic, as was required of him, his last week of medical school. He was busy talking about wedding plans, getting ready for graduation, and packing up for his trip to Los Angeles. He had five days between graduation and the first day of the internship.

Dr. Wilsonhulme made it up to graduation. He looked pale and winded, but he made it. Rachel Carmichael, who accepted the name of Wilsonhulme for Garven with grace, was annoyingly proud of her son, like every other mother in attendance.

"My son," or "my daughter, the doctor," was heard coming from the little clusters of conversation around the large University of Arizona auditorium.

Garven graduated with high honors, magna cum laude, and was elected to AOA—Alpha Omega Alpha—the medical honor society. Garven and thirty-one others in his class walked with swelling chests in their caps and gowns with the three black bands on the voluminous sleeves to receive their genuine sheepskin diplomas.

His old friends Ray, Bubba, and Lyle, and even Edward Sespootch—looking more debauched than ever—were there to see Garven's triumph. Rachel, Dr. Wilsonhulme, Elizabeth, and her mother all shed a tear as the UA undergraduates, with one voice, cheered the recipients of the doctor of medicine degree, and the grads themselves cheered the nursing graduates. Mr. Fletcher could not make it—press of business—he had told Elizabeth. There was silence in the great hall as the dean of the faculty of medicine led the new physicians in their recitation of the twenty-five-hundred-year-old code of medical conduct, the Oath of Hippocrates:

"I swear by Apollo, the physician, and by Health, and by Æsculapius, and by all the gods and goddesses that I will

37

look upon him who shall have taught me this Art even as one of my parents. I will share my substance with him, and I will supply his necessities, if he be in need. I will regard his offspring even as my own brethren, and I will teach them this Art, if they would learn it, without fee or covenant. I will impart this Art by precept, by lecture, and by every mode of teaching, not only to my own sons but to the sons of him who has taught me, and to disciples bound by covenant and oath, according to the Law of Medicine.

"The regimen I adopt shall be for the benefit of my patients according to my ability and judgment, and not for their hurt or for any wrong. I will give no deadly drug to any, though it be asked of me, nor will I counsel such, and especially I will not aid a woman to procure abortion. Whatsoever house I enter, there will I go for the benefit of the sick, refraining from all wrongdoing or corruption, and especially from any act of seduction, of male or female, of bond or free. Whatsoever things I see or hear concerning the life of men, in my attendance on the sick or even apart therefrom, which ought not to be noised abroad, I will keep silence thereon, counting such things to be as sacred secrets."

CHAPTER
Six

Everything Garven owned was in the backseat and trunk of his old coupe. He left Phoenix with a week to spare before he had to be in Los Angeles. Elizabeth had given him enough money, so he "wouldn't have to stay in awful places." He made it something of a vacation, taking the long, scenic route up Arizona 60 and 93 through the mountains to Kingman. He passed the shaving cream signs: "THESE SIGNS ARE NOT... FOR LAUGHS ALONE... THE FACE THEY SAVE... MAY BE YOUR OWN... BURMA SHAVE," and the collection of Indian hogans on the outskirts, then on into town. He stayed overnight in a motel with a swimming pool. The weather was already insufferably hot, and the pool was a luxury he had done without for years. He vowed that he would have a pool in his own backyard one day. The following morning, he got on US 40 and drove into LA.

When he got to California, Garven found a cheap motel back from the oceanfront on Newport Beach and spent two days luxuriating. He watched the parade of beautiful girls, the territorial surfers, and the general crazies of California from his vantage point on the beach. He was glad to be back in the "Golden State."

Two days before he was to start work, Garven reconnoitered the area around Hill and Eighth, checked out the safest parking places, and checked in early to get a decent room in the interns' quarters. That was a wise move because, although there were no decent rooms by any civilized judgment, there were not even enough rooms to go around. The latecomers would be stuck with broom closets and old storage rooms.

39

The room to which Garven was assigned was still occupied by the intern finishing up his year of medicine-peds mixed internship. Garven could not get into the room, and he was out of money because of his splurge at the beach motel. He spent two fitful nights in his car, half aware of the sounds of the night in the parking lot. His instructions required him to be in the Doxey Auditorium at seven o'clock in the morning, July first, for orientation. He cleaned up in a service station and was there on time.

The room was small and hardly merited the title of auditorium. It was crowded with new interns, a few residents, and staff people. At seven-fifteen, the orientation talks started with a speech of welcome from the administrator and followed by a short spiel from a staff doctor from each of the subdivisions of the medical staff, all of whom had university positions as well as their clinical responsibilities. There was little new in what they had to say. The interns were broken up into groups, without regard to type of internship, and taken on tours of the hospital by the house staff as guides.

The huge medical center was just as dirty, crowded, and noisy as it had been the day Garven visited and had his interview. The residents had the same sallow complexions and uncaring expressions, splotched lab coats, and rumpled scrubs. The tour served to confuse Garven as much as anything. The hospital had accumulated over decades with new buildings and additions being built without regard to any coordination or master plan. The new interns walked up or down short sets of stairs to find themselves in a new hallway with an entirely new set of numbers; the seventh floor became the eighth simply by walking through a pair of heavy closed doors. Some parts of the hospital were inaccessible from others, and it was necessary to go outside and walk across the parking lot to get to the other.

There were dozens of clinical wards, the great majority for the indigent, and a few private wards located near the university professors' offices. The charity wards were all very much alike. They were large, long, rectangular spaces filled to capacity with old-fashioned metal frame hospital beds. The patient beds were lined in three rows perpendicular to each long wall, and in the center, a single row of beds was oriented in parallel with the walls. At the far end of each ward were the windows and the nurses' work area. Just off from the entryway of each of the wards was a small room that served as sleeping quarters for the resident on call—the "call room." The wards were all busy; the floors were dirty and splattered with an accumulation of blood, pus, urine, dried diarrhea, and vomitus that had been waxed over enough times to achieve permanent enshrinement, like bugs in amber. The nurses looked overtired and unhappy, and there were too few of them.

At ten o'clock, the interns reassembled in the auditorium and were given two long, white lab coats and their clinical service assignments for the year. A second sheet informed them of their payroll numbers. Garven and his contemporaries were to be paid the exorbitant sum of fifty dollars a month—a twenty-dollar raise over last year's stipend. They received the yearly admonishment that they were not to wear scrub suits, which were the hospital's property, except in the operating rooms. And, like the generations of house staff that preceded them, the intern class of 1957 promptly forgot the admonition.

Garven was assigned to cardiac surgery as his first rotation. A notepaper clipped to the schedule read, *"Be on the floor by ten."* Garven was already late for work on his first day due to circumstances beyond his control. He thought, ironically, that it was a great start and hoped that the lack of control over his life on the first day was not a harbinger for the future.

Since he was already late, Garven took another hour to move his meager belongings into the dorm room he was to share with Michael Dortmund, whom he had yet to meet. Garven was there first and took the bed on the right for no particular reason. The previous occupants had made no effort to clean or even to shove the rubbish aside. Garven made room for his things and hurried off to find the cardiovascular-thoracic surgery ward.

It was easy to tell the junior resident from the other people on the ward. The nurses were women; the patients were horizontal; and the resident was angry.

"Well, little man so spic and span, where were you?" he demanded before Garven could even introduce himself.

Garven was wearing a pair of new scrubs he had scrounged from the main linen station rather than from the usual illicit OR source. He was conspicuous in his gleaming white lab coat.

"On orientation. This is the first day, you know," responded Garven.

"At least you're here. Seen anything of your partner, name of Landers?"

"Nope," said Garven. "I wouldn't know him if I did."

"Look, I'm John Parks, the ward resident. I have to get to the OR right now. Dr. deCastro and Devlin Peters, the chief res., are waiting on me. My butt's probably already in a sling. Here's the scut list." He handed a scribbled list of "to-do's" to Garven. "And here are the three by fives."

Garven received a small stack of white cards labeled by the nurses' desk imprinter with the name, age, hospital number, and ward of all of the patients on the service. There were handwritten historical and exam notes and updated lab data on each card.

"Thanks," he said. He did not know what else to say.

"When your lazy, no good for nothing intern partner ever gets here, he can help. For now, all the scuts are up to you. It all has to be done before evening rounds. You two 'things' have your work cut out for you, so you better get on with it."

Parks was on his way out of the door.

Although he did not particularly like being called a "thing," Garven had heard that all of the interns were so designated, and he refused to let it bother him. What did bother him was the enormous list of scut work he now held in his hand:

Hernandez	*– Old chart, chest films, present Hx to deCastro and Lillornan*
Stephens	*– Cut down, change chest tube bandages, repeat labs*
Pandella	*– Clean wound, get C&S of pus, repeat chest X-R. Find old films*
Anderson	*– Clean wound, Ck C&S. Change antib. if necess.*
Dickens	*– Needs anoth. chrt summ., graph labs*
Nelson	*– Fever W/U - 2 Bld cults., also get stool, sput., urin., ck wound again*
Shrecker	*– Clean trach. Maybe new cannula*
Harvey	*– N-G tube. Check gast. pH, take out every other suture and put on butterflies*
Garandelle	*– Remove chst tubes, post rem. chest film*
Porter	*– Clean and redress wound. Get him up. Rpt labs*
Ovellen	*– Procto, all suts. out, butterflies. Irrigate chest tubes*
Jones	*– Perit. tap—get amylase, blood and fluid*
Terkel	*– Una's boot on leg ulcer, draw new set of labs, clean trach*
Hansen	*– Procto, EKG. Start new IV other arm. Foley for surg, T&C*
Tucker	*– New chst tube, new site. Post tube film. Transfuse 3 units*
Banttle	*– Close leg wound by 2nd intention, use wire*
Violan	*– Blood gases, old chrt, ck chest film from yester.*
Opprerro	*– Order complt. bwl series, mouth to an.*
Smythe	*– Head lice: shave scalp, Kwell shampoo X 2. Clean her up— gasoline and a wire brush*
Withers	*– Pelvic exam, ?PID. Get a Wasserman, Etherize maggots in leg ulcer again*

There were two additional sheets and a list of twelve new admits who would have to have H&Ps done before the close of business. The resident had included a call schedule for the interns, residents, and junior staff. The interns and junior resident were on every other day—thirty-six hours on and twelve off, if the intern could get the work done in that time frame. The chief resident was on all of the time, and the junior staff men were on every third day.

Don Landers, the other intern, ran onto the ward, breathless and apologetic, about the time Garven had done the first four items on the list.

Garven cut off Landers' litany of excuses and said, "And where were you, little man, so spic and span…?"

Don completed his, excuses saying he was sorry about twenty times.

"'Sorry' doesn't cut it, Don. We just have to get here and get the work done," Garven said when Don finished his apology.

He handed him half the scut list and his copy of the schedule.

Don's face fell with disbelief, followed by a hangdog expression. "We'll never get all of this done."

"Not and sleep," Garven observed.

"Well, I'm not about to kill myself for a surgery specialty. I'm just a rotator. I plan to go into peds. I'll do what I can, and that's it."

He was fat and effeminate, with pudgy hands and chewed nails. He had a petulant, stubborn expression. Garven hated him from the first minute.

"*Typical pedipod*," Garven said to himself.

The scut list was efficiently arranged, taking bed by bed up the seemingly interminable rows. Garven was not sure he could decipher the miserable handwriting—some of it looked like inverted Sanskrit—and had not had much experience in doing most of the procedures. He did not let that stop him. It was a great deal of sweaty work for him, and a predictably awful and unsafe day for the patients as it was every first of July, when the new crop of green interns arrived on the services of the hospital.

Garven had a terrible time finding veins in the wizened old men and in the drug addicts, with their needle-hole pocked and scarred limbs. He stuck every IV he tried at least twice. When he did the radial arterial puncture in the wrist, he made two complications out of one simple procedure. On his first stick, he put the needle into the man's median nerve somehow, and caused him to squawk bloody murder about the "electrical shocks" in his hand. He got blood on the next pass, but forgot to put pressure on the puncture site and gave the poor man a nutmeg-sized hematoma in his wrist. Garven put a Foley catheter in a woman's vagina instead of her bladder. He got blood when he did a peritoneal tap and had to remove the trocar before he could try and get peritoneal fluid. He learned to pray—this particular time that he had not stuck the aorta. Nothing came of it; so, Garven reasoned that it had been some minor bowel vessel; and he canceled his prayer, saving it for something more serious.

When he removed the chest tube on a post-op heart, he did not clap a Vaseline gauze bandage over the hole fast enough and gave the patient a pneumothorax, with air collecting in the chest, but not in the lungs, under pressure. And all of those problems occurred before lunch.

Each task was a learning experience for Garven over and above the suffering endured by the patients unlucky enough to be in the hospital—thereafter called as "the house," in keeping with the medical and nursing staff parlance—during that house staff transitional period.

He learned how the X-ray department worked, for example. None of the X-rays were done, or if they were done, they were unfindable. The charge nurse on the c-v-thoracic ward took pity on him, and showed Garven the likely places to lay hands on lost films—scattered on the ward, tucked away in residents' and interns' secret hidey-holes for safekeeping, or sequestered in staff men's offices.

He learned the standard joke of the hospital that first day as he dealt with the problem of locating X-rays. In the radiology department, he discovered the "Return Films" slot on one door in the department. When he could not find one of the new patients' chest X-rays, the radiology secretary took him to the room behind the "Return Films" slot. Garven had expected to find a neat box with half a dozen film folders in it. The reality was a room half again the size of an ordinary bathroom. It was waist level deep in film jackets.

"Go ahead and see if it's here," the secretary said indifferently as she returned to her work.

It was not in her job description to look for films in that mess.

Don Landers annoyed the ward head nurse by moving as slowly as he could and leaving Garven with three-fourths of the scut work; so, she ignored the fat intern's pleas for help. Garven learned that, in order to hope to get one chest film on a patient, he had to order them be done twice. He wrote the orders several hours apart. By the laws of chance, he was able to come up with X-rays on about two-thirds of the patients for whom he ordered films by that stratagem.

By evening rounds, Garven had gotten through the important things on the scut list, had redone some of Don Landers' work when the nurse told him that it had been done carelessly by his "partner," and had his six workups done. He

44

had forgotten to eat, and suddenly discovered that he was famished. Rounds were in half an hour and the cafeteria was closed. He grabbed two candy bars and a Twinkie out of the only remaining viable vending machine in the main hospital waiting room. They were fresh, at least. Candy in the hospital's vending machines never had time to get stale. The house staff depended on candy for energy and survival. The patients considered the packaged bars to be their main staple, the most important food group, and the machines sold out several times a day. It was a gold mine for the distributor and the hospital.

As the residents and staff men came in for evening rounds, Garven had a chance to give himself a visual assessment. Whereas he had been clean and starched when he arrived, he was now filthy—splattered with blood and colored bodily fluids, coffee stains, and the pant legs of his scrub suit had a multitude of scribbled notes in ink. His image in the mirror was haggard and harried; he needed a shave; and he had taken on the standard house staff man prison pallor. In short, he looked just like the rest of the old hands—the experienced house staff—and he was eminently satisfied with his personal presentation.

He ran down the scut list and rattled off the lab values and results of the procedures on all of his patients and, out of necessity, on most of Don Landers'. He skimmed over the complications he had caused. He gave quick and pertinent histories and physicals on the six new admits he had seen. Unlike the medical student presentations, these were short and to the point, nothing superfluous. The charge nurse had warned him of the need for brevity and efficiency. She had left Dr. Landers to dangle, and he had only gotten around to doing one admit and had gone to absurd lengths to ferret out irrelevant details on that one. It was a history and physical that would have made his old medical school professors proud. As Don went through his tortured descriptions, excuses, and history, Garven changed his mind about hating the guy. Don was so bad that Garven could only look good by comparison. He was glad that Don was on the service to serve as counterpoint.

The head of the division of cardiovascular-thoracic surgery, G.V. Lillornan, everyone called him G.V.—not Gerald or Vaughn or even Dr. Lillornan— even the house staff, was a prominent, even famous, heart surgeon. He was better known for his national committee involvement and better respected for his research, some of which was considered revolutionary, than he was for his actual care of patients. In fact, the medical cardiologists at the university, and therefore in the hospital, would not refer their patients to him for surgery. They thought his morbidity and mortality was too high, but the statistics were hard to find in that institution. Dr. Lillornan had a protective wall

45

of secretaries, nurses, and house staff to insulate himself from the slings and arrows of his questioning colleagues. He spent about ten minutes in rounds and turned full responsibility over to Dr. deCastro, as he always did.

Aldo Ramirez deCastro was a thirty-five-year-old nervous dynamo from Venezuela. He was a superlative diagnostician, surgical technician, and gentleman. He was not a genius like his boss, Dr. Lillornan, and that was, perhaps, his greatest virtue. He received all of the consults and referrals from the medicine department and attended their cardiology conferences, unlike his arrogant superior. The house staff respected him, and had real affection for the man. He was the only man on the staff, or even on the house staff, who did not enjoy heaping insult and abuse on those beneath his station. He said that he could recall all too well how he was treated during his internship and residency, and he saw no reason to perpetuate the traditional oppressive pattern. Garven wished that the residents would take what Dr. deCastro was preaching to heart, but held his peace, knowing that his lone voice would fall on deaf ears.

At the end of rounds, John Parks took Don Landers aside to read him the riot act. The nurses had told Dr. Parks all about his poor work and bad attitude. Don appeared chastened, and Garven eavesdropped shamelessly enough that he heard Don promise that he would shape up. Garven thought that he would have to reserve judgment on that. Dr. deCastro presented the X-ray results on his patient for surgery the following day.

"Ca of the esophagus eroding into the diaphragm and pleura. It's going to be a bloody one. Garven…that's right, isn't it?

"Yes, Sir."

"I think the rotation is for you to be second assistant tomorrow, if I am not mistaken. Make sure that we have plenty of blood for the case, okay?"

"How much is plenty?" Garven asked.

He hoped he did not sound dumb for asking, but he did not want to make a big mistake on his first day in the OR.

"Twenty units," Dr. deCastro said and paused to see the effect on the chief resident and the junior resident's faces.

"Whe-eeh uuu!" whistled John Parks. "You really do think it's going to be bloody!"

"I'll warn the blood bank, Aldo. With as much infiltration as this tumor looks to have done already, we might even need more," said Devlin Peters. "We'll be in the hole with the blood bank for the rest of the year."

46

"You'll just have to con some more donations out of the families, Devlin. You hold the hospital record for any one year, I understand," said Dr. deCastro. He was grinning.

"I have passed the baton to my noble successor, Dr. Parks, meaning that I don't have to do that stuff anymore. He will have to whip the 'things' into line and get them to get us back on good terms with the blood bank."

"Okay, bright and early tomorrow," said Dr. deCastro.

He gathered up his notes and left for the evening. It was nine o'clock.

"Get some rest," he called back over his shoulder.

"Yeah, right," laughed Parks. "You on your way, too, Devlin?"

"Yeah. My wife's got me going to a PTA meeting tonight. She threatened me with bodily harm if I failed her again. Hold down the fort. Don't call me unless the place is on fire or something else really big. See you guys."

He left to change into his street clothes.

The junior resident called the two interns together.

"Ordinarily, we quit after rounds, and the guy who is not on call can go home. Out of decency, we try to help out if there are still a lot of workups or scut to do. I can't do it tonight. I have a bunch of ER consults waiting for me. It's up to you guys. I'll let you work it out between the two of you. Remember, if you don't help your pard, he isn't going to stick around on the night when you need it."

John left the floor.

Garven picked up the scut list and surveyed the remaining items that had not been checked off. There was still a daunting number, and five of Don Landers' six new patients had yet to have histories and physical exams done and written up.

Don said, "Hey, leave the H&Ps. I'll do them tomorrow while you're in the OR."

"You must be kidding," Garven said. "We'll have another twelve or fifteen then. It is hard enough to do them today. Can you imagine what it would be like to be behind by five patients to start off the day? Forget it. We'll get them done tonight. I'll help, but after today, you have to do your own patients. I can't bail you out every day."

"Don't trouble yourself, *Dr.* Wilsonhulme. I don't take orders from you. I'll do them when I get good and ready. I have to go to a peds journal club tonight. I'll be late if I don't leave right now. See you in the morning."

The chubby intern began to collect his things and made as if to leave.

47

Garven's notoriously limited patience was exhausted. This was one of those times when you had to hit the mule over the head with a two by four to get his attention, he decided. He stepped up to Don and slapped him hard across his fat face with the flat of his hand then backhanded the other cheek. Don looked at Garven in consternation, then violated the core commandment of the code of manhood and started to cry. Garven watched him without a shred of sympathy.

When Don calmed down, Garven said, "Now, let's get to work."

He still looked very threatening, and Don Landers trotted right behind the smaller man and started to do the scut in earnest.

One of the LPNs who had been peeking in on the two interns ran to tell the night nursing staff, and they all had a great laugh. They were hardworking people with a well-developed sense of justice, and they loved seeing the jerk doctor get his comeuppance.

At eleven o'clock, Don went home, and the admits from the ER began to appear on the ward—five new ones by two o'clock. They were all worked up by three, the work being interrupted by two cardiac arrests, one on the ward and one in the cardiac ICU. The ICU was largely the first-year resident's responsibility, but John was swamped in the ER and could not get away. Garven had had very little experience with resuscitations and looked pretty green when he did show up as the doctor in charge. To his credit, he admitted his inexperience to the head nurses, and let them teach him something from their large stores of experience. The main lesson he learned during that long first night as a doctor was that it was critical to make the nurses his friends. A little humility on his part went a long way toward that end. He did have the rudiments pretty well in hand by the time the next arrest occurred in the ICU, around four-thirty in the morning. All three patients who arrested died that night.

The head nurse in the ICU told Garven frankly that two of them would have made it if it had been October instead of July first. She was just stating the situation as it was, no insult intended. It was a dangerous time to be a patient. Garven was feeling very low when he finally dragged himself to a quick cafeteria breakfast at six o'clock that morning. He would have to be in the OR in fifteen minutes to help John get started. His teeth were fuzzy from lack of brushing, and his armpits wafted a bad odor. He was a thoroughgoing mess.

He sat by a diminutive young woman intern. He was about to tell her his woes of the preceding night. He needed to unload on someone. But he saw that she was crying. She was a picture of exhaustion and bereavement.

"You okay?" he asked.

"No-oo," she cried. "I am a total failure. I think I'll quit!"

Her face was knotted in anguish.

"Want to talk about it?" Garven queried gently.

"Not much to say. I'm on peds, on the cancer service. I killed eight children last night," she sobbed.

Garven waited for her to collect her emotions.

"I had eleven kids with leukemia, and overnight, eight of them died. I could never be a pediatrician. I can't stand it!" she said.

Her fists were clenched.

"What was the matter with them, I mean, last night particularly?" Garven asked.

"Oh, the nurses said that the outgoing house staff people just held them together long enough that they could die last night instead of the night before. They were all terribly sick—no platelets, white counts of 500,000 or more, incredible anemia, infections, you name it! I killed them. I did everything I could all night long, but they just kept dying on me. I'm a basket case."

And she was. Her eyes were puffy and red from long crying. Her hair was sweaty and stringy. She was filthy. She was all in.

"You'll look at it differently after a little rest," he soothed. "Remember, this is the worst day of the year for patients. You did the best you could do. We are just human. Our best is all anyone can ask."

Just saying it seemed to make Garven feel better. He knew that what he had said was true.

"I guess so. But I'll tell you, I hate to think of facing parents again like I had to last night. Jeez, what an awful night. I don't get to go home for another twelve hours. I don't know how I'm going to make it."

Amen to that, thought Garven. "Hey, I have to get to the OR," he said. "Hang on, it'll get better. It has to."

She rewarded him with a trembly thumbs-up sign.

Even at six-fifteen, Garven was late in arriving in the chest room in the operating suites.

John Parks chided him. "Where've you been?"

"Got a little breakfast," Garven said.

"You seem to think this is some sort of country club; this isn't the Mayo Brothers, *the* WFMC, you know." He was referring to the World Famous Mayo Clinic. "We have to get the work done. Sometimes we have to go without. Now get to work and help me get him ready."

49

John had had a bad night and was testy. Garven was about to tell the junior resident that he just could not make it on one meal a day and no sleep, unlike the resident giants stalking the halls, but he figured that he would sound like a wimp; so, he held his peace.

At five of seven, Dr. deCastro walked in, scrubbed and ready to go. They opened the chest with a midline sternal bisecting incision, taking care to avoid the "anomalous vein of Stanislowsky," as Dr. deCastro called the great innominate vein just beneath the sternum.

"I never heard of that vein," said Garven.

Dr. deCastro continued the dissection.

The chief resident, Devlin Peters, said, "We call it that because of one of our former residents. It seemed like every time he did a sternal split, he went right through the innominate, and we got a major hemorrhage. Every time he cut it, he would say in all seriousness, 'Must be an anomalous vein,' and the name sort of stuck."

The tumor was exposed with relative ease because of its huge size and different color from the surrounding normal tissues. The bright red, angry-looking neoplasm wrapped its ugliness around the esophagus and spread out over the leaves of the diaphragm. It had grown locally up the spine, paralleling the aorta and vena cava and their branches, large and small, and into the bottom and back of the lungs. The pleura looked like it had been glued to all of the nearby structures.

"Whew!" exclaimed John Parks, who was the second assistant. "That is a hill for a climber!"

"Indeed it is. I hope you wore your wading boots, boys. We're going to shed blood today," said Dr. deCastro.

To Garven, it seemed like the height of courage even to attempt to attack the angry red cancer, let alone to try and remove it all. He was not sure that he was much of a "climber."

DeCastro started to dissect the tumor off normal structures. Everywhere he touched, it bled. Garven and John manned the suction hoses with wide sucker tips, and Devlin tried to keep ahead of the bleeding with dry, absorbent surgical sponges. The suckers filled up jars, and the sponges were inadequate. Dr. deCastro pushed a long sponge that he called a "60," because it was that many inches long, into the bleeding site for tamponade and a rest.

"Start the blood, Axel," he called over the drapes to the anesthesiologist.

"Way ahead of you, Aldo. We're on our second unit. How many did your guys T&C?"

"Twenty units," answered John.

"Won't be enough," said Dr. deCastro. "Better get ten more."

"I already drew a tube," said the anesthesiologist.

DeCastro removed the compressing sponge and started dissecting again. Garven could see nothing from his position except bloody sponges and his sucker tip filling up. The operation was painfully slow, especially for Garven, who was the lowly third assistant. He knew he was not superfluous, however, because his sucker was as busy as the second assistant's.

The operation went on for three hours. The conversation was laced with cries from more suction, more sponges, more transfusions. DeCastro went patiently along, finding, tying, and cutting vessels, and electrocoagulating bleeders that flared up unexpectedly. He electrocoagulated vessels and tumor, causing smoke and a smell of burnt flesh. He made a small cut into the esophagus, and they had to divert from the tumor removal to suture the button hole.

The empty glass bottles from the transfusions were set down on the floor in order to keep an accurate count—this by decree of Dr. Lyons, chief of surgery. By two o'clock in the afternoon and more than fifty bottles on the floor, Garven was aware of the insistent pressure in his bladder. Devlin and deCastro took turns in going out for some juice and to relieve themselves; Garven and John, the underlings, had to stay on to keep pressure on the bleeding sites. It was in the tradition of considering interns to be "things" that the lowest men in the pecking order did not get to go out for food or calls of nature.

By five o'clock in the afternoon, there were an even 100 bottles on the floor, and it was almost impossible to walk anywhere.

Dr. deCastro turned to Devlin Peters and asked, "Think we got all of it we can?"

Garven prayed that the answer would be yes. His arms, legs, and bladder ached something awful, and he had a headache. The long day preceding this one was catching up with him.

"You can't get out any more tumor without transecting the esophagus, Dr. deCastro. And you'll have to take out a big section of the diaphragm. We'll never get that closed, and we would have to give this poor guy an esophogostomy and still leave in tumor. I think there comes a time when enough is enough," Devlin answered thoughtfully.

"I hate to admit it, but I think you're right. This guy will be dead in a couple of months. Tough," said deCastro. He surveyed the still vigorously bleeding operative site. "Okay. We'll bail out. Devlin, come and make rounds with me. We'll find out what that no-goodnick, Landers, the pediatrician, has been up to while we were in here. John, you and Garven stop the bleeding and close up. Call me in the office when you get done."

In so saying, he and Devlin stepped away from the table, removed their bloody gloves and OR gowns, and left the surgical suite.

"Call me in the office, my butt," sneered John when the two senior men were gone. "Stop the bleeding," he said sarcastically. "We'll be here all night. Aren't you glad to be the one who gets to suck hind teat, Garven, old 'thing'?"

Garven's heart sunk.

"All night?" he groaned inwardly. He knew his bladder capacity was not up to it. "Hey, look, John, before we do anything else, I have got to take a leak before I bust my pee bag, okay?"

John gave the intern a look of condescension and nodded toward the door. Garven had to pick his way through a tangled web of bottles and equipment going to and returning from the lavatory. He stopped off at the nurse's lounge and swiped three pints of milk that he downed one after the other. Doctors were not supposed to go into the nurses' lounge because they were notorious for stealing food, and they might embarrass a partially clad nurse. Since there was never any food in the doctors' lounge, a locker room that did not merit the title, "lounge," that was just one more rule that was universally ignored. Garven felt immeasurably better when he was finally back in position across from John.

At nine-twenty in the evening, the bleeding seemed finally to be under control. There were 112 bottles on the floor. John looked all in.

"Think I'll go see a man about a horse myself. Hold down the fort, Garven. Don't you dare move anything and get it bleeding again."

"Not on your life, boss," Garven assented.

They put in the last skin wires at 9:55. There were now 114 bottles on the floor. Garven's gown and his scrubs were completely soaked with blood—as much as if he had had a bucket of the living fluid poured on his chest. He could feel the stickiness on his skin, especially on his genitalia. His armpits were wet with sweat. He felt dizzy and unsteady on his legs, and his thinking was fuzzy.

Garven and John got the patient settled into his ICU bed. John called Dr. deCastro and gave him a progress report, then sat by the patient's bedside, prepared to spend the night with him. Garven headed back to the ward.

It was 10:35 when he walked back onto the floor.

Don Landers was waiting at the door. He was furious.

52

"Did it really take that much time, Garven? I mean, have you had a shower and dinner and everything?"

"Do I look like I have, Don?"

He felt like punching the guy in the mouth, but if for no other reason, he refrained because he was so tired.

"I'm sorry. I know it's just as tough for you as it is for me. It's only that I never bargained for anything like this. I thought they had to be kidding when they said we would be on for thirty-six hours and off for twelve. We've been at this for forty." Then he laughed as he realized, "And this is your night off."

Garven was too weak to find humor in anything.

"What's left, Don?"

"I have to go to the ICU. Everybody but your fresh post-op has turned sour, and John needs help. You have two workups, then you're done."

"Great," sighed Garven.

And so passed young Dr. Wilsonhulme's first day in surgical training, forty-two hours long. He was sure of only one thing that he had learned—never wear underwear to work; he had thrown his away as soon as he had gotten into the dressing room after the case.

CHAPTER
Seven

On Monday of the third week of his internship, Garven ate supper with John Parks in Garven's dorm room. Michael Dortmund, Garven's roommate, came from a well-to-do family; at least, they had enough money to give him a small black and white television set. Garven and John were watching the end of *General Electric Theater*, hosted by Ronald Reagan.

Garven thought that this was the best time to bring up the subject that had been troubling him. "John, I have a problem."

"Um hmmh," said John, munching down his Twinkie. "So what's the matter?"

"I'm supposed to get married."

"Knock somebody up?" John asked matter-of-factly.

Garven laughed. "That's not the problem. The trouble is that my fiancée and her mother have scheduled the wedding for next Saturday."

"Yeah, my friend, that's a problem. Whatever possessed you?"

"I had no idea that it would be so tough to get a little time off," Garven said. "I'm willing to take call for the entire week, and Don will trade for two days. That's more than fair."

"'Fair' doesn't have a whole lot to do with it. First off, nobody is tough enough to take call for five days straight. And most important to you, Lyons has a hard and fast rule: no extra days off for interns; sets a bad precedent and all that. He'll never go for it. He doesn't think interns—or residents, either, for that matter—should be married," John told him.

"Man, what a problem," Garven sighed. "I'll have to try. Wish me luck."

54

The two men finished their meals and left for the clinical ward before Reagan came on for his closing statement on the TV program.

Dr. deCastro gave his permission, and even Dr. Lillornan allowed himself to be persuaded to let Garven have the weekend off since he was doing so well on the service.

"But," Dr. Lillornan said, "you can't do it without getting the chief's permission. I wish you luck. You have about as much chance as the proverbial snowball in hell."

Garven got an appointment with Dr. Lyons by promising that it would be very brief. He presented his case to the chief of surgery.

"I will only be gone for two days. I'm going to fly over to Phoenix and back. Nobody will have to do anything extra. I mean, it's been worked out to be more than fair."

Dr. Lyons was in a hurry.

"You know my opinion about married interns, Dr. Wilsonhulme. You don't need to be married. That's what back stairs and student nurses are for. The answer is no. If she's the right girl, she'll be happy to wait until you finish your residency. Now, I have work to do. If you will please excuse me."

The chief of surgery stood up and walked over to his inner office door to let Garven out.

It was clear that there was nothing more to be said.

On Tuesday, Don Landers and John Parks both asked Garven what the "old man" had said.

"He said it was okay," Garven lied.

He was betting that Lyons would never know about a little ripple in the chest cutter service.

"Great," said Don. "I am going to sleep for the next five nights and try and make up for my chronic exhaustion."

Both John and Garven rolled their eyes back in their heads.

It was murder. One day on intern surgical call was difficult. Five days were murder. On Saturday morning, Garven was a zombie. He did not even dare to try and drive his car to Los Angeles International Airport to catch his flight. He used a portion of the money the Fletchers had sent him for his travel to take a cab.

Fortunately for the whole production, no one paid much attention to Garven, the groom. He stood up as custom demands, and fortitude permitted, and his bride glowed with happiness. Even her father seemed genuinely happy for Elizabeth. The wedding was lavish beyond Garven's wildest expectations—live bands, imported orchids, the best champagnes. Garven scarcely noticed. He did, however, pay attention to the wedding gift from the elder Fletchers—a ten-thousand-dollar check. His mother gave them a mix master. Against his better judgment, Lyle, Ray, Bubba, and E.D. were invited. As expected, they got roaring drunk and had to be helped out. Garven lapsed into a stupor as soon as he and Elizabeth stepped into the Camelback Inn to spend their first night of wedded bliss.

Garven gave a reasonable, but uninspiring, performance at the consummation the following morning. He enjoyed the sumptuous breakfast in bed more, if the truth be known. He and Elizabeth made plans for her to take a suite in the Beverly Hills Hotel. Like it or not, he would have to stay in the dorm most nights. They flew back together to LA. She rented a car to get him back to the dorm Sunday night, so he could take call.

The cardiovascular-thoracic service rotation was a month long, like all of the internship rotations. Dr. Lyons got wind of Garven's having disobeyed him and would have come down hard on the young intern during the last week of July when he heard the facts had he not gotten a far more serious problem to deal with in the heart surgery program. Garven was peripherally involved.

G.V. Lillornan was a famous, if not altogether competent, cardiac surgeon. He had great courage when it involved other people's bodies and took on cases that others would have rejected. Around the LA basin, the internists and cardiologists held back their patients from surgery until they had one foot in the grave and the other on a banana peel. The result was that heart surgery mortality was forty percent around the country and approached seventy percent under Lillornan's knife. His argument was that he got the sickest of the sick cases, but that he did as well as anyone when he had a decent case. The problem Garven witnessed was on such a "decent" case.

Margaret Trumbell was a very pretty seventeen-year-old cheerleader at Los Angeles High. She came in on the charity service because she was found to have a heart murmur. A surgically-minded resident admitted her to the surgery service rather than the usual practice of being admitted to cardiology. As a result, she became Dr. Lillornan's patient by the luck of the draw on the day that he was the attending surgeon on call. The girl's only complaint was that she had begun to tire a little more easily. Her only physical sign was a murmur. Margaret was found to have a ventriculo-septal defect, a VSD— congenital hole in the heart— on her workup.

56

Dr. deCastro and Devlin Peters argued with Dr. Lillornan that the patient should be treated conservatively since her signs and symptoms were so minimal. He heard them out, but being the world famous and senior heart surgeon at the institution, he overruled the two naysayers.

"Margaret is the perfect candidate for surgery. She is young and healthy, unlike our usual train wrecks. This girl is going to deteriorate, and now is our chance to patch her up safely."

DeCastro and Peters assented reluctantly.

"So, Peters, get her on the pump by nine on Thursday. I have to be in Chicago to present a paper to the American Society, but I leave on the early flight that morning. I'll be back to plug up the hole before nine. No fail now, Peters. I have a devil of a day on Thursday. I have to be done at noon. The Greek patients will be coming to the hospital then, and there's going to be a little press ceremony to welcome them."

The Greek heart patients were a group of people from the Greek Islands who were being sponsored by a rich benefactress, and one neither Dr. Lillornan nor the hospital could afford to offend.

Garven had a hard night before the surgery and was awake for most of it. In the rare periods when he was unmolested, he slept in the cardiac surgery ICU between two fresh multiple valve replacements and listened to the audible clicks coming from the patients' chests. In the morning of the operation, Garven was second assistant. The anesthetic induction, intubation, sternal split, and placement on the cardiac bypass apparatus went off without the slightest glitch. Margaret was on the pump by eight-thirty in the morning. Devlin Peters was very good. He planned to practice cardiac surgery exclusively and had arranged a preceptorship with Russell Nelson in Salt Lake City. Dr. Nelson had and deserved the best reputation in the western United States. Devlin took the utmost care. In anticipation of G.V.'s imminent arrival, Devlin had dried up every bleeder and changed the wound drapes so it would look pristine. Garven was fascinated to look into the girl's chest cavity and to watch the heart pulsate.

"Call G.V.'s office. Tell him we're ready in here," ordered Dr. Peters.

The circulating nurse left for the OR office. She was back in five minutes.

"No answer," she said.

"Oh yeah; it's not even nine. His secretary isn't even in," Devlin said. "Give me a wet towel. I'll cover the wound. We'll wait for the boss."

There was a quiet space.

Devlin turned to Garven. "Do you know everything there is to know about VSDs, Garven? You've been on the service long enough to be an expert."

"You bet your sweet bippy," Garven said.

He was feeling cocky after a fourth of a night's sleep and a day of broken study on ventriculo-septal defects from the textbooks and even the journals.

Devlin and John Parks laughed.

"So entertain us," Devlin said.

Garven took half an hour to tell the two surgeons, the anesthesiologist, and the two nurses everything he knew about holes in the heart. They were a rapt audience; for the surgeons, it was a good review, and Garven did a better than passable job. For the nurses and the anesthesiologist, it was information that no one deigned to share with them most times. Garven came off looking good.

"Call him again," Devlin asked the circulator after Garven finished.

She did. This time, she reached the secretary, who did not know where G.V. was if he was not in the operating room.

"Hey, Devlin," said Dr. Johnsson, the anesthesiologist, "I don't want to be picky, but this is adding to her pump time. I don't particularly like it. Know any secret numbers for him? We need to get going."

Devlin sighed. "Take over, John," he said to Dr. Parks. "That means don't do anything, incidentally."

He took off his gloves and strode out of the room.

John said to Garven, loud enough so the rest of the OR crew could hear, "Hey, Garven, you hear about the doctor and his wife who weren't getting along?"

"Nope," said Garven, willing to be the straight man.

"Well, it seems they had a fight one morning before he left for the OR. He said a lot of nasty things and finally concluded with, 'You're no good in bed, either,' slammed the door, and left for work. Along about two in the afternoon, he had an attack of conscience and called his wife to apologize. It took ten rings for her to answer.

"'What took you so long to answer?' the doc asked her.

"'I was in bed,' she told him.

"'At two o'clock in the afternoon? What were you doing in bed this late?'

"'Getting a second opinion,' she said.'"

They all laughed.

"Did you hear about the new Japanese restaurant in the valley?" asked Dr. Johnsson. "The one owned by the Japanese attorney?"

They all said no.

"It's called So-Sumee," the anesthesiologist said, deadpan.

The scrub nurse said, "I heard about two psychiatrists who happened to be friends. They hadn't seen each other for a while. The first shrink says to the other, 'You're fine. How'm I doing?'"

They started to chuckle.

Devlin came back into the room. His face was serious. Garven looked at the clock—nine-twenty.

"Can't get him," Devlin said. "I even tried the special never-to-call-except-in-an-emergency number, and she told me he was in Chicago."

"You can't be serious," said Dr. Johnsson.

"'Fraid so," said Devlin.

"I'll call his hotel in Chicago," said the circulating nurse. "I'll get the name of which one from his secretary."

"Parker House," said Devlin. "That's as good a place as any to try."

"Checked out at five o'clock in the morning," came the answer after the call.

They waited fifteen more minutes. Everyone was getting nervous. The pump time was getting to be too long.

Dr. Johnsson said, "We need to get Aldo down here. We can't sit here with the girl's chest open and her on the pump. Mary-Alice, get on the horn and call Dr. deCastro."

The circulator turned to leave.

"Won't do any good. He left for the international conference in Berlin this morning. He's somewhere over the Atlantic about now," said Devlin.

For the first time, there was a note of concern in the unflappable chief resident's voice.

Before he had to say anything, an orderly brought in a note. Mary-Alice read it aloud.

"From Dr. G.V.," she said. "Am in Denver. Bad weather so route had to be changed. Keep her on the pump. Do not do the case or close up. I'll be there before eleven."

"Eleven!" ejaculated Dr. Johnsson. "She will have been on the pump for nearly three hours by then!"

"She's young and healthy; she'll do all right," Devlin said confidently.

He wished he felt as confident as he sounded.

Garven was aware of the stress being suffered by the two surgical residents.

"Okay, eleven. If he's not here then, you either close up or do the case yourself, Devlin. That's plenty long enough to be on the pump."

It was five after ten then.

Devlin lavaged the chest cavity with sterile saline, had the nurses check the patient's temperature—which was a little low—and to make sure the ACE wraps on her legs were all right. That passed five minutes.

"Know any lawyer jokes?" he asked.

Dr. Johnsson said, "Sure. There were two lawyers who had a gorgeous secretary. She got pregnant, and it was unclear which of them was the father. Being honorable men, they formed a 'Father Partnership' and agreed to set up a trust fund to care for the baby. On the day of the blessed event, one of the lawyers sat out in the hall and waited nervously for the baby to come. The other couldn't stand the stress and went outside on the hospital grounds for a smoke. He told the first lawyer to come and get him as soon as there was news. In an hour, the first lawyer came out to the grounds and found the second. 'Why the long face?' asked the second attorney.

"'Well,' he said, 'I have bad news. I hardly know how to tell you.'

"'Go on. Tell me. What's so terrible?'

"'We had twins,' the first lawyer said with a very sad expression. 'It was terrible... Mine died.'"

Garven had been involved with the medical profession long enough to have absorbed some of the venom that doctors feel for lawyers.

He said, "I know a story about neurosurgery that applies, want to hear it?"

"Sure," the bored OR crew said. "Nothing better to do."

It was ten-thirty.

"Okay. A guy was involved in a terrible car accident and suffered massive brain injury. The neurosurgeon told his wife that the only thing he could do for her husband was to do a brain transplant.

"'How much would that cost?' the woman asks.

"'Depends on the kind of brain you get,' he told her. 'For example, you can get a pound of brain surgeon's brain for about $15,000, of truck driver's brain for about $20,000, or of orthopedic surgeon's brain for around $50,000.'

"'I have always had a secret desire for my husband to be an attorney,' says the wife.

"'I can do it,' says the brain surgeon, 'but it'll cost you two or three hundred thousand for a pound of attorney brain.'

"'That's terrible. Those rotten lawyers; they always overcharge!'"

"'No, no, lady, you misunderstand. This time it's not their fault. Have you ever thought how many lawyers it takes to come up with a full pound of brain?'"

The crew had a good laugh.

60

There was an awkward silence now. The circulator tapped her finger on the tabletop where she was keeping her records.

"It's eleven. Where is he?" demanded Dr. Johnsson.

The orderly came into the room, bearing another message, as if in answer to the query.

"Engine trouble on the plane, will be there in another hour. Dr. Peters, hold the fort until then."

"Devlin, this is the wrong thing to do," said Dr. Johnsson flatly. "You have to close up now or do the case. I'm worried that we'll have trouble getting this kid off the pump as it is. You have to decide."

"Have you any idea the position this puts me in, Dan?" asked Devlin. "Lillornan isn't a forgiving guy, in case you hadn't noticed. He'll crucify me if I steal the case, and everybody will be on me if I just close up. I'm caught between a rock and a hard place."

There was genuine pathos in his voice. Everyone knew how much he wanted the recommendation from Lillornan to round off his credentials for heart surgery.

"Comes with the territory," the anesthesiologist said quietly.

Dr. David Stark, chief of neurosurgery, chose that moment to walk in and to ask if he could see what heart surgery looked like. It was commonplace for surgeons, as a friendly gesture, to come into the operating rooms of their colleagues to see them at work. Devlin took off the sponges covering the heart.

"So, what're you guys doing now?" Dr. Stark asked. He thought it odd that there was no activity. "Are you ready to go after the defect?" he asked.

He knew the girl's diagnosis from the posting tag on the door to the operating room.

"Well, there's been a little delay," Devlin said quickly. "We're waiting for Dr. Lillornan."

Dr. Stark looked at the worried faces and at the clock. "What time did you start this case?" he asked.

He was less buoyant now.

Dan Johnsson was more than worried now. He was angry. The anger Loosened his tongue.

"Eight o'clock. She's been on the pump since eight-thirty."

"It's nearly twelve-thirty, Dan. What's up? Isn't this Lillornan's case? Where's he?"

Devlin wanted to defuse the potential problem before the full information could be noised about. "Well, Dr. Stark, G.V. is…well, he's…" he stammered.

61

Dan Johnsson said it straight out, "He's in Denver. He was in Chicago when this thing started. He doesn't want Peters here to proceed. Puts the residents and me in a rotten position, if you ask me."

"I thought you couldn't leave people on the pump all that long," said Dr. Stark. "How long is it safe to leave them?"

"Couple of hours," said Dr. Johnsson. "We're getting well past time."

Dr. Stark was a full professor at the University of California. He was known as a super hardnose who put the needs of patients first, and did not care if some resident lost his job for a misbehavior or a mistake. He recognized that this was a more politically delicate situation. That did not faze him for more than a minute.

"Are you the chief resident?" he asked Devlin.

"Yes, Sir," Devlin replied. He was pale.

"Do you know who I am?" Dr. Stark asked.

"Certainly."

"Then, on my authority, you are to close the chest and get this girl out of here while you still can. Do you have a problem with that?"

"Well...look, Dr. Stark. Dr. Lillornan's my boss—"

"I can have Peter Lyons over here inside half an hour. Is that the way you want to go? I, for one, don't think any more time should be wasted." Dr. Stark's eyes, over his mask, were implacable.

"Ah, man, what a terrible position," Devlin said with a sigh. He knew that he would be the loser no matter what happened. "Dan, let's get her off the pump. Rachel, get the sternal wires ready. John, go down to the femoral tubes and get ready to get them out. Okay, Dr. Stark, we're going to close."

"Good boy. What's your name, doctor?" Stark asked.

"Devlin Peters, Sir."

He turned his attention to the business of getting the patient off the table.

Dr. Stark left. Getting Margaret Trumbell off the pump was much easier said than done. Her heart was flaccid and weak after the long period on the bypass. She fibrillated—ventricular fibrillation, a useless fluttering of the heart—every time they tried to put her on her own natural mechanisms and had to be defibrillated and heavily medicated repeatedly. Finally, in desperation, Devlin gave her a large dose of epinephrine and digitalis, which made her heart race, but overrode the fibrillation long enough to get her off the pump. The team rushed the girl into the PAR. She fibrillated again in the post-anesthetic recovery room and then went into a full arrest. They could not get her back again despite everything they did. The girl could as well have died in the operating room, but there is an implicit and even explicit rule that no one is supposed to die in the OR. Somehow, it was better for records or something if the death occurred in the PAR or the ICU.

The following day went along, business as usual. Garven had to open the chest wound on the man who had received the 114 units of blood for the attempted removal of his esophageal malignancy. The substernal space was a sea of pea-green pus with a sewer stench familiar to everyone.

"Pseudomonas!" the nurses gasped as Garven collected a sample for culture and started to clean it up.

Garven and John came into the ward to find a neat new tracheostomy on the derelict who had been having the DTs on the ward and who screamed all night long. The neurosurgery ward was right next door, and their resident was suspected of doing the procedure to keep the derelict from making so much noise that he could not sleep. It was never proved. Friday was pretty much like that all day. The grand finale came at rounds.

The residents and Dr. deCastro finished formal rounds at eight o'clock. Garven was off and had only three H&Ps to do before he could leave and spend a little time with his neglected wife. The last thing Garven did before he closed his eyes was to add the Lillornan/Margaret Trumbell saga to his growing list of staff offenses in his notebook.

Dr. Lillornan stormed into the residents' quarters where the group had just finished discussing the last patient. He was livid with anger.

"Dr. Peters!" he shouted. "Would you like to tell me why it is that you killed my patient, my perfectly healthy, young girl patient?!"

Devlin took a step backward as if he had been slapped. "Dr. Lillornan, I…uh, we…uh did the best we could. She was on the pump all day. Did you get the information about Dr. Stark coming in?"

He was pale and looked as if he would faint.

"You miserable, insubordinate imbecile," growled Lillornan.

"Hey, hold on a minute," interjected Dr. deCastro.

"Shut up. This is none of your business, Mr. Assistant Professor. I will handle this, if you please."

Lillornan was well past the reasonable stage; he was furious.

"Dr. Lillornan—" started Devlin again.

Lillornan stopped him short. "You're fired. Get out. Don't let me see you on my ward again. You are an incompetent nincompoop. You have no business in cardiac surgery!" He was yelling.

63

"And neither do you. Neither do you," Devlin growled, having been pushed beyond his capacity to endure. "We'll see what the surgery committee has to say!"

The two men stormed off in different directions. There was a hearing, Garven learned later. Dr. Stark from neurosurgery insisted on presenting what he had seen. A cardiologist was called in to describe the cardiac condition, against Lillornan's vehement protests. In an unheard of, unprecedented decision, the committee stripped Dr. Lillornan's operating privileges completely. They could not take away his university tenure, but they added insult to injury by dropping him from all of his committee positions. Devlin Peters' firing was left in force. He got a job as a solo practitioner in general surgery in Nevada, according to scuttlebutt from some of the nurses who had thought a lot of him. Before the year was ended, Garven learned that Dr. Lillornan was made chief of surgery with an endowed chair at the University of Upstate New York. The lesson for Garven was about justice, medical academic style.

CHAPTER
Eight

The food was so good and the bed so comfortable at the suite Elizabeth had taken at the Beverly Hills Hotel that Garven stayed with her as often as he possibly could even though it proved to be inconvenient to have to travel. Besides the obvious benefits of staying in the Beverly Hills Hotel, Elizabeth was sympathetic and gave excellent back rubs. She had taken a position as a docent in the UCLA Museum of Art to fill her time. The controversy over Dr. Lillornan was intense enough that Dr. Lyons never got around to chewing Garven out for getting married.

The rotation for August and September was on general surgery. The general surgery division was very large and was divided into four services, named unimaginatively, A, B, C, and D. Garven was assigned to Surgery B, headed by Homer Ashworth, associate professor. Having learned his lesson on July first, Garven showed up on ward 6-B at five o'clock in the morning to be sure that he was not accused of being lazy and late on the day he started his tour.

The ward was entirely similar to the cardiovascular-thoracic ward he had just left. By now, the patients were starting to look alike as well. Garven sat in the nurses' station and read over the charts: appys, gall bladders, stomachs, bowels, and cancer—the bread and butter of surgery.

The Surgery B house staff were all on the floor by six. Garven introduced himself and met the others—senior resident, Todd Douglass; Dick Atkinson, junior resident; and the other intern, Tommy Wright. Dick handed Garven the scut list; it was Garven's turn to be on the ward and Tommy's turn to go to the OR. Garven had a pang of jealousy because Tommy was going to get to do an appendectomy, and Garven had yet to hold a scalpel.

Garven cleaned the pus, put down and in the tubes, did the admission workups, and hunted the X-rays. He did two cut-downs. On the first, he made his incision half an inch off the mark and could not find the saphenous vein in the ankle. After he floundered around and commented more than once that the guy must have had anomalous veins, the charge nurse, who was helping him, mildly suggested that he try more laterally. Garven had learned better than to ignore the advice of good nurses and extended the incision. He made quick work of finding, dissecting out, tying off the distal end of the vein, cannulating the proximal end, and establishing a good access to the patient's bloodstream. He had not left the patient's bedside for as much as ten minutes when the nurses' aide reported to him that the tube had fallen out.

There was blood all over the bottom of the bed, and the patient was nearly hysterical at the sight of it. Garven calmed him down and opened the wound. He had forgotten to secure the proximal end of the vein to the cannula with a ligature. He was lucky enough to be able to reinsert the tube. And he only wasted half an hour.

There were fourteen admissions. Garven worked doggedly away at getting their H&Ps done, orders written, and labs drawn. He had done ten of the fourteen by seven o'clock, when the rest of the house staff and Dr. Ashworth assembled in the residents' sleeping room for evening rounds.

He was particularly pleased because, in the course of his day's work, he had found himself an appy. Curly Mae Bosworth was a thirteen-year-old Negro girl who had been sent up from the "muncy room" with a case of "stobbin' pain in the 'domen and outward fever." Everything was classical—pain, point tenderness, and rebound in the right lower quadrant of her abdomen— McBurney's point—except that she did have a fairly significant anemia. Garven had his first real case to do. She did not seem too sick and could be put on the schedule for the following day. She made the work of the day worth the effort.

When it came time to present her to the other doctors, Garven gave the history, physical findings, the fact that she had an elevated white count, and the diagnosis in a couple of minutes, straight, simple, and to the point.

"What about her periods, Garven?" asked Dr. Ashworth.

Garven had forgotten to ask. He thought he could probably fake it; after all, she was only thirteen years old. However, he figured that the question

66

must have some basis, so he admitted, "Sorry, I forgot to ask. Or if I did ask, I didn't write it down."

"Did you do a pregnancy test?"

Now what did that have to do with anything? She had classical signs and symptoms of appendicitis.

"No. It never occurred to me," he said with a perplexed frown. "She's only thirteen."

"What's the differential diagnosis?" asked Todd Douglass.

"Appendicitis, maybe ruptured ovarian cyst," Garven said thoughtfully. He really did not think she had a ruptured ovarian cyst. "Maybe mesenteric lymphadenitis."

He had no way of ruling out the benign but uncomfortable inflammation of the lymph nodes of the tethering structure of the bowel.

"Or tubal pregnancy," blurted out the other intern, Tommy Wright.

And the reason for the questions about her menses dawned on Garven.

"Yeah, that's right. I didn't think of tubal pregnancy. She's only thirteen; so, I thought—"

"So find out. If it's an ectopic, we'll have to go tonight," Todd said. "Ask her, and kill a rabbit. Call Dick as soon as you know."

Directly after rounds, Garven ordered the pregnancy—rabbit—test. He went right to Curly Mae.

"Curly Mae," he asked, "when did you last menstruate?"

Curly Mae looked at Garven, bemused. "Say, whaa?" she asked.

"When was your last period?"

Another questioning look.

"Just a minute, I'm going to get one of the nurses."

Garven found one of the Negro nurses' aides to help with the communication.

"Hey, chile, how is ya doin'?" asked the aide.

"Now that you ast, not good. Not good at all. I has a powerful spasm in my 'domen. Think I gots the toenail poisonin'."

"When was the last time y'all dropped ya roses?" the aide asked.

Garven had told her what he was trying to find out. He had no idea what the two women were talking about.

"I realized when I wuz ten, and, let's see, I come after that until…had a few clarks in my pajama 'bout two munce ago, I reckon," said the girl. "I nevah come sick aftah that."

"Were y'all's monthlies reg'lar 'fore that?"

"Yas'm."

67

"You been messin' 'roun', Curly Mae?"

The answer came in the form of a shy look down at her feet.

"Think y'all are frangrant?" the aide continued.

"Mebbe. Don' think so, though. We done it durin' the day."

"Ever had the purse tubes, Curly Mae?"

"No, Ma'am. But onct when I wuz eleven, I hadda have the doctahs in jim clinic dial and correc my womb."

"Was that for a miscarry, girl?"

"Mebbe."

Garven interrupted. "Ask her about the anemia, if she knows anything about that."

It was worth a try, he thought.

"Y'all got the low blood, girl. Anybody ever tell you 'bout that?"

"Yas'm."

"What did they say, Curly Mae?"

Garven asked to rush the laborious communication along. She looked at him as if he were an interloper on her conversation. He backed off. He continued to take notes, so he could ask the aide questions when she and the patient were finished.

"So what'd the doctahs tells you?" asked the aide.

"Said I had the sick as hell anemia. That's the natural fact."

She was proud to remember all of that. Garven understood that much. She had sickle cell anemia.

They left the girl. Garven asked the nurses' aide, Sophronia, for an interpretation of the parts of their language that he had not understood. The thread of the conversation had been: Curly Mae had a bad pain, a spasm, in her belly and thought that she had ptomaine poisoning. Her last menstrual period was two months previously, and she had been regular ever since her menarche, or onset of menses, at the age of ten. At the time of the menstrual period two months ago, she had had a few clots in her vagina, but it had not been a regular period. The girl had been having unprotected intercourse, presuming that having coitus during the day was a protection, and had had a D&C—dilatation and curettage—in the gyn clinic. It had taken an explanation on the part of the aide to convince Curly Mae that D&C did not refer to "where Washington is at." At least as important as the history of the pregnancy was the presumptive fact that she had the serious anemia of Negroes—sickle cell anemia.

The pregnancy test was positive.

When Garven told Dick the results, Dick said, "We've got to crack her belly. She probably has an ectopic, and we have to get it out before it ruptures. You can do a prophylactic appy. I assume you're on tonight, right?"

"Yep."

"Give her a couple of units, and I'll go down and get her on the schedule."

"Uh, I hate to bring this up, but isn't she a gyn case?" Garven asked tentatively.

"Technically," Dick said. "But you'll never get to do anything if you give away surgery for such a light and transient reason as the rules. Besides, the gynners operate like panda bears playing with themselves. You wouldn't want nice, little ole Curly Mae to fall into their hands now, would you?"

Garven certainly would not wish any such thing on the girl for whom he felt such fondness and responsibility. It turned out to be a pregnancy localized in the Fallopian tubes as he had predicted, which made Dick happy because he had a chance to do a little bigger case, and it turned out well in the end for Garven because he got to do his first appendectomy.

By a sort of a fluke, Garven got to do the biggest case of his internship career two days later. Actually, it took two flukes and a stretch of the truth. Alice Kendall was a private case of Dr. Ashworth. She had an obvious breast mass with skin dimpling that was highly suggestive of a carcinoma. Todd had Dick schedule Mrs. Kendall as first case—biopsy and possible radical mastectomy—with Dick as first assistant to Dr. Ashworth and Garven as second. That meant that Dick, the junior resident, would do the case, with Dr. Ashworth teaching. Garven read everything around about breast surgery and all but memorized the descriptions in Schwartz's *Principles of Surgery* and Cutter's *Atlas of Surgical Technique* on the procedure of doing a radical mastectomy, knowing that he would be the target of hundreds of questions, and he wanted to be prepared to ace everything thrown at him.

Dick and Tommy were on call the night before and were involved in an emergency gunshot wound to the abdomen when it was time to start the first case. Garven did all the positioning and prepping for the breast case. Mrs. Kendall was ready when Dr. Ashworth entered the OR.

"Good work, Garven," the senior surgeon said. "Where's Dick? I thought he was supposed to be first assistant."

"He and Tommy have a GSW. Went through big stink. They'll have to do a colostomy. Looks like several small bowel punctures, too," Garven said.

"How about Todd?"

"He has a big case, resection of an abdominal aortic aneurysm. He's already in there."

"Who is going to help him?"

"Tommy was supposed to, but now I guess he'll have to get a couple of medical students."

"Okay. I guess you got the black bean. You have to be alone with me. You have just been elected first assistant," Dr. Ashworth said with a smile. His smile was a little weak. He had been fighting the flu all week.

Dr. Ashworth did the biopsy. He cut a generous ellipse of skin over the mass and dissected the fatty portion of the breast all around the mass to provide a margin of hopefully tumor-free breast fat. The specimen was sent out to the surgical path lab for a frozen section. They covered the wound and waited.

Dr. Ashworth looked somewhat pale and was sweating under the warm operating lights.

"You look like you feel terrible," commented Garven.

"I look like I've been dead for three days, and I feel worse," said the professor.

Dan Johnsson, the anesthesiologist, asked, "What are the chances that this one is benign?"

"Nil," said Dr. Ashworth. "She has a couple of palpable nodes in her axilla. The biopsy is just a formality."

"It always seems like it takes forever to get back the frozen. I think those guys don't even get to work before ten. I knew I should have been a pathologist," Dan said.

"You remember the difference between an internist, a surgeon, a psychiatrist, and a pathologist, don't you?" Dr. Ashworth asked, knowing that it was an old joke.

Garven had not heard it.

"An internist knows everything and does nothing. A surgeon knows nothing, but does everything. A psychiatrist knows nothing and does nothing. And a pathologist knows everything, can do everything, but he's too late."

Not to be outdone, Dan asked, "Did you hear about the internist, the psychiatrist, the surgeon, and the pathologist who went duck hunting?"

"No," chorused the doctors and nurses.

Telling jokes helped to pass the time, and waiting for the frozen section was a drag.

"Well, it seems these guys were waiting behind a blind all morning for the flight of ducks to pass over them. Finally, they heard the sound of bird wings overhead, a distance away. The internist stood up, strained his eyes, and fretted, 'Are they ducks, or geese, or swans, or loons?' As he fretted, they flew by, and he failed to get off a shot.

"The psychiatrist leaned out and debated, 'Should I shoot or should I not shoot? How will I feel? What will they think of me?' And the flight of birds passed him by as well.

"The surgeon jumped up and started to blast with his shotgun. Several birds dropped out of the sky. He exclaimed, 'Were those ducks?' Then he turned to the pathologist and asked, 'How about you going out and fetching a couple and tell me what they were?'"

The surgeons laughed most heartily at the joke about their stereotypical characters.

The frozen section came back positive—ca of the breast. Dr. Ashworth picked up the scalpel and, realizing that he had not yet marked out the incision on the patient's breast, quickly set it back down. He did so too quickly and cut his own left thumb a rather nasty laceration. He swore and stepped away from the operating table to compress the bleeding site. He changed gloves, but the blood continued to seep into his glove. Finally, he decided that he did not feel good enough to fight it.

"Garven, I am just not up to this case today," he said. "Where are Todd and Dick?"

"They're both operating."

"Can't you take one of their places; so, he can come in and do this case? It's a good one."

"I don't think so, Dr. Ashworth. Their cases are resident level; the interns aren't ready for them." Garven knew perfectly well that he could bail Dick out of the GSW and help with the closure while the junior resident could come over and do this great case.

Dr. Ashworth considered for a moment. He had more than a sneaking hunch that Garven was exaggerating, but he rather liked the young man's moxey. It reminded him of himself a few years ago. *Garven Wilsonhulme is a true-born surgeon*, he chuckled inwardly. "Hey, Garven, you ever done a radical mastectomy?"

Garven did not hesitate for an instant. "Two," he said. "And assisted on half a dozen others."

There was not the slightest hint of self-doubt or indication of anything less than the whole truth and nothing but the truth.

Homer Ashworth truly was feeling punk then. It rather tickled his fancy to give an intern a really great case.

"Okay," he said. "You do it. I'll assist."

Garven turned to the scrub nurse.

"Andrea, get me the methylene blue, please."

He broke off a swab stick and dipped the sharp fragment into the opened vial of blue dye and marked out a generous incision line across the patient's breast.

"Garven, I prefer a vertical incision," said Dr. Ashworth.

Garven said, "My reading indicates that the transverse incision heals better and with a lower frequency of infection or dehiscence. I'd like to do it this time."

He was firm. More than a mere preference, it was a small test of who would actually be the surgeon. To be the surgeon is more than who does the cutting; it has to do with who makes the decisions. That subtlety did not escape Dr. Ashworth.

"Okay, Garven. It's your case. Do it your way. I have to admit that my real reason has more to do with tradition than with good objective data. Go ahead."

Garven ran the material he had read the night before through his mind as a review. The pages of the surgical textbook were remarkably clear in his memory. He should have been afraid to tackle such a big case without adequate experience, but he was not. He felt as assured as if it were a daily occurrence for him. There flashed through his mind what Dr. Cartral in medical school had had to say about surgeons, "Always certain. Not always right, but always certain." He did not let self-doubt interfere. He took the knife in hand and made the incision.

He and Dr. Ashworth worked well together. Garven's hands were surprisingly sure despite his unfamiliarity with the role of surgeon. Dr. Ashworth clamped and tied off bleeders and kept the field dry. He made Garven look good—the primary role of a good assistant. Usually, senior surgeons made lousy assistants because they were always trying to get the knife. Ashworth was the exception. Garven was slow despite the excellent assistance, and he knew that the staff man was having to bite his lip to keep from taking the scalpel back. Some of Garven's ties slipped off and, therefore, he lost more blood than a better surgeon would have done. However, all in all, he knew that he was doing all right.

"Okay if I use the cautery to cut the muscles?" he asked.

Eastern purists would not hear of using the cutting cautery instead of the classical scalpel cut followed by tying off encountered bleeders. Garven was unsure where Dr. Ashworth stood.

"Sure, we want to get done with this case today," Dr. Ashworth said as a mild dig.

Garven got the hint. He put a large clamp under the fibers of the pectoralis major and lifted them up. Then he applied the cautery blade and began to burn his way through the heavy muscle fibers. He was a little overcareful about bleeders and created a smelly smoke. The nurses snickered. Dr. Ashworth bit his lip and said nothing. His eyes smarted a little from the acrid smoke.

Todd Douglas walked into the OR as Garven was finishing his hot-knife transit through the pectoralis minor muscle. The smoke hung like the smell of cordite in the room.

"Having a little BB cue?" he asked Garven.

Garven felt a little sensitive, and nodded with a wan smile.

"I've been done for fifteen minutes. Is this the same case, Homer?" Todd asked, being cute.

"Um hmmh," answered Dr. Ashworth. "Did you do the closure on the 'rism?" he asked, giving a little tit for tat back.

"Touché," said Todd.

He had finished only his part of the operation on the aneurysm. His assistants would be another hour on the complicated closure.

Garven gingerly dissected around the fat and the several hard lymph nodes in Mrs. Kendall's axilla. He put a clamp across the uppermost segment he could reach and another across the axillary tail of Spence portion of the breast tissue.

"Big Mayo scissors please, Andrea," he requested.

She was holding a scalpel in her hand in anticipation of his request.

Before the scrub nurse could hand Garven the instrument he had asked for, Dr. Ashworth said to her, "Give him what he needs, not what he asks for."

Andrea gave Garven the scalpel.

"That's what I wanted," Garven said and laughed.

He knew Dr. Ashworth's preference for the precision of the blade over the speed of the scissors.

"You going to do the oophorectomy, Homer?" asked Todd, who was still kibitzing.

"Sure. Standard indications—can't hurt, might help, organs are present, and Garven hasn't done one for a while. She's too old to have ovaries anyway."

He was joking. It was standard practice to remove the ovaries when axillary nodes were present. Dr. Ashworth had warned Mrs. Kendall pre-op of the possibility.

"I thought those rules just applied to uteruses," said Todd in the same jocular vein.

"Nope. It's a fundamental rule of surgery. Sort of like 'to cut is to cure.' I hope these pearls will help you, young man," Ashworth said to Todd.

"This is me writing them down in my pocket Bible," said Todd and mimed the action of writing in the little notebook full of cheat sheets and things to remember that almost every intern and resident carried.

The large specimen of breast tissue, cancer, fat, muscles, and lymph nodes came out in one piece, and Garven plopped it into the steel pan on Andrea's Mayo table.

"Good job, Garven. You might be a surgeon one day yet," the attending surgeon told the intern.

"Thanks a lot for the help. Thanks for letting me do the case. It was a great case," Garven said.

"We're not done."

"Speaking of that, Homer, how about letting Dick snatch her 'nads. He had to come in and do the closure on my case, and he's feeling picked on," Todd said.

"You'll have to ask the surgeon, Todd. See what Dr. Wilsonhulme wants to do."

Todd looked meaningfully at Garven.

Garven was very strongly inclined to tell him to stuff it. This was his case, but he knew he had better not press his luck if he ever wanted to do another case on this service.

He said, "Sure. Good old Dick. Wouldn't want him to feel left out."

Dr. Ashworth laughed out loud at the sour expression in Garven's eyes above his mask. This kid was going to be a real surgeon; he had the basic selfish, cocky, and ruthless personality for it.

CHAPTER
Nine

Garven was rewarded for his pragmatic largesse about two weeks later. Dick, the junior resident, by rights, got all gall bladders. On that morning, Dick was tired and said he had done enough gall bladders for a while. He told Garven that he could do the case; they had a hot gall bladder in a forty-two-year-old, fat white woman, typical patient with cholecystitis and stones. Garven was too excited to sleep the night before. This would make all of the lab scut, pus cleaning, late hours, and demeaning comments worth it. He was awake anyway; so, he poured over his surgery texts—*Cutters*, *Schwartz*, and the huge *Allen, Moore, and Rhodes* tome, just for completeness' sake. It was overkill, but he was ready.

Garven brought his *Schwartz* text into the OR, open to page 1104; he had no false pride. He and Dick prepped the patient. It was the rule on the general surgery service that the house staff did the scrubbing and preparation of the skin, so they had no one else to blame if there was a post-op wound infection. Garven held the scalpel over the large expanse of white abdomen.

"Kocher or Courvosier?" he asked Dick.

"Kocher," said Dick, indicating his preference of incisions.

Garven cut a deep, oblique right upper quadrant incision through both layers of skin and watched the yellow-white fat bulge into the opening. There was very little bleeding, and the skin edge veins and arteries were controlled with cautery and application of skin clips and a skin-edge towel. He carried the cut down to the strong abdominal fascia. It was now a fairly significant trench with greasy slick edges. Dick placed large, self-retaining retractors so they could see the depths. The incision went carefully through each layer—fascia, rectus abdominus, and oblique muscles—until the nearly transparent peritoneum was exposed.

"Don't cut it with the fascia and muscles," Dick had instructed. "I like to get the peritoneum closed separately."

The two of them put clamps on the tough lining of the abdominal cavity and lifted it up into a tent; then, Garven nicked it with his small, curved #15 blade, an incision just big enough to allow the insertion of his index finger. Small bowel kept trying to peek its way through the opening. Garven fumbled to get it out of the way. He was getting frustrated.

"Can you stand a little advice?" asked Dick, who was getting a little frustrated himself as he watched the intern.

It was a hundred times easier to do the case himself than to watch or to assist the inept beginner. He was sure that he had never been as clumsy as Garven when he was at that stage.

"Maybe," Garven said.

He had thought he had the technique down cold, and it ruffled his feathers to have Dick wanting to make suggestions.

"Or would you rather make this into a 'career' case, as opposed to an 'all day' case, a lesser insult?"

"So go ahead. I'm not getting anywhere," Garven said ill-naturedly.

"Put a sponge stick down in there and push the guts out of the way."

"Why didn't I think of that?" Garven asked.

He was feeling a little more humble and teachable now. He did have something more to learn, he had to admit to himself.

He kept his finger under the peritoneum to prevent any chance of cutting a hole in the intestine. He was successful at that, but did nick his glove and had to change. That was not such a big deal. The large incision gaped open and the pile of guts wriggled below.

Dick pried open the edges of the wound with handheld retractors.

"How do you want to treat the wound edges, Garven?"

Garven was ready for that question.

"Towel and some towel clips, Andrea," he requested. He put out his hand without looking at the skilled assistant.

She was a very good scrub nurse; if she did not actually anticipate the surgeon's need, she commanded a view of all of the pertinent instruments, and was able to lay the requested tool in the surgeon's hand with alacrity.

76

Garven laid the towels over the wound edges and got rid of the annoying slick fat. Moving the intestines around proved to be considerably more difficult. He pushed them and held them, but more kept creeping around his fingers and palms to obscure his vision.

"They're slick as snot on a doorknob," he complained to Dick.

The junior resident held back, enjoying the show of Garven fumbling with the greasy guts.

"So help me," Garven finally requested, exasperated at his own efforts.

"Sure. Thought you'd never ask," Dick said.

He laid a large, saline-soaked sponge cloth over a mound of writhing intestines and swept it back and toward the left, and held it in place with a large Deaver retractor. He did the same thing on the lateral side of the opening.

"Voila!" he said, and indeed, there was the engorged gallbladder peeking up from under the liver. And there was no annoying mass of intestines in the way to obscure vision and to limit work space.

"Oh sure," Garven said. "Anybody can do it without the guts in the way."

He gave a self-deprecating laugh.

Garven got a large, striated clamp from Andrea and put it firmly on the ampulla of the gallbladder, and retracted down and to the right. Dick readjusted his retractor and moved the duodenum more firmly out of the way. The thickened gall bladder was closely applied to the underside of the liver by adhesions. Garven snipped and dissected them away with all of the excessive timidity of a novice surgeon.

Dick thought he would go crazy.

Finally, though, Garven had both the cystic duct, leading from the gall bladder to the common bile duct and thence into the duodenum, and the cystic artery identified and free.

"Want me to get the artery?" Dick asked.

"Please," Garven said.

"Andrea, hold this retractor," Dick directed the scrub nurse.

She took a firm hold on the retractor holding the duodenum.

Dick cautioned, "Not too hard now."

Andrea rolled her eyes. She had been working in surgery when this one was still in knee pants.

Dick cross-clamped, tied, and cut the cystic artery. Garven put a clamp down into the deep wound.

"Make sure you get it down low. Don't stroke the duct or the ampulla before you get the clamp on."

"I know that," Garven said, a little snappishly.

He did know that, and resented being reminded of the things he did know. He deftly applied the clamp, then ran his fingers along the duct, from bottom to top, and satisfied himself that there were no stones in the cystic or common bile ducts.

"Think we need a 'gram?" he asked.

"Is the pope Catholic?" Dick retorted.

Cholecystograms were standard.

"I don't care if you think you can't feel a stone; do the 'gram. And we'll put in a T tube, too. I'm a belt and suspenders guy. And if you know what's good for you around here, you'll do it every time, too."

Garven put in the T tube into the cystic duct and instilled the iodine contrast as the X-ray tech took a picture. Garven was pleased that they got a good picture on the first try. He ligated the tube in place. Removal of the gall bladder involved cutting it away from its peritoneal mesentery and the adhesions, but that was relatively easy. He did not nick it, and the clamp on the proximal end of the cystic duct stayed in place, so there was no leakage of bile into the abdominal cavity, a definite "no-no." Dick made a stab wound to the far right of the upper quadrant of the abdomen and pulled the T tube up through the opening. Garven laid a flat latex drain into the gallbladder bed, and brought it up through the same opening. They closed the wound with a multiple-layer closure.

The case took three hours, considerably longer than world record time, but it was deserving of the "good job" Dick had pronounced when they were finished. For a first effort by an intern, it wasn't half bad, if Garven did not say so himself. He followed his patient with greater concern than he had done for any patient before. He felt a very proprietary interest, and had begun to know how a surgeon feels. He liked the feeling, even though it made him feel on edge most of the time. It was more than the old house staff dictum of "he who ops, post-ops." This lady was his patient, his own patient.

Garven did a vein stripping with Todd Douglass. Todd let Garven do the surgery, but insisted that he understand that this, like all cases, was a serious operation and not to be taken lightly.

"We used to have two more staff men on the service. You probably heard of Danforth and Eichnel."

Garven had. "They're just researchers, aren't they?" he asked.

"Yeah, that's all they're allowed to do. Lyons won't let them near a patient. Ever hear why?" Todd replied.

"Nope."

"Well, there was a very famous case around here. Probably the first malpractice case in the history of the hospital. Those two coo-coos were the junior staff men on B. They were bored with the standard stuff, especially since they only got to do the easy cases. Anyway, one day, the two of them were doing a vein stripping. To make it more interesting, they made a bet about which one of them could do his leg the fastest. Danforth was on the right, and Eichnel was on the left. They set off like banshees, blood and fur just a flyin'. Halfway through the case, Eichnel discovered that he had been dissecting out the femoral artery, and Danforth found out that he had been working on the femoral nerve. Ruined the patient—and they never did get at the varicose veins."

Garven laughed at the improbable story. "You sure that really happened, Todd?" he asked.

"You betcha. That's been in the hospital rumor mill for years. I checked it out with Tindall Drummond—he was one of Lyons' first residents—he swears it was the gospel," Todd said, completely serious.

Garven still shook his head. He was pretty sure that most of the apocryphal heritage of Osterlund Memorial was either complete crap or only slightly diluted. Still, they made for great stories.

Surgery clinic teemed with the usual problems, the usual questions:

"Is you the doctah what's been waitin' on me? I been here mos' all day."

"Say, looky here, thattsa gonna hurt."

"The pain starts here; then it whips on 'round thissa way."

"Y'all gotta gimme somethin' for my pain."

"Pills don' do no good, doctu. I needs a shot."

"Don' y'all think mah fren' heah *need* a shot, doctu?"

"Darvon? Darvon don' do me no good. I needs a shot."

"Ya'll gonna do whaa?"

"Is it agonna hurt, doctah?"

"Y'all ain't gonna stick me with that needle is you?"

"Wait a minute! Wait a minute!"

"Now, don' treat me rough!"

"Aie, ya, ya, ya, ya! Ah felt that! An' ya'll said it wouldn't hurt at all."

"Straighten up honeychile an' let the doctah works on you. You actin' like a baby!"

"Well awright then, if that's the way y'all gonna be, not givin' a man a shot, not fillin' his nerve pills. Ah am gonna see mah private doctah. How you like that?"

"Mah nature as been bad lately. Y'all think y'all can do somethin' about mah nature whilst Ah'm heah?"

"Well, Ah takes two white pills in the mornin' and one yella one of an evenin', or is it two yella pills in the mornin'? Anyhow, Ah got to feelin' so good Ah done stop takin' mah high blood pills."

"Well, now Ah couldn' jus' tell the nurse wha' really happen' now, could Ah?"

"No spik the English."

"Ah done been hit upside the head. Kin ya'll write me a excuse foah work?"

"Ya'll done gimme these suppository things with the silver metal cover on 'em. Ah done jist what ya'll said. Swallawed 'em down even though that metal stuff hurt mah 'froat. Was worthless, too. Might as wella shoved 'em up mah ass foah all the good they done!"

On his next to the last day in general surgery clinic, Garven was able—not by any intention of his own—to contribute a footnote to the history of the place. The residents told him he had to go and see the case in the next cubicle—a bad set of hemorrhoids. Garven saw it as a chance to get another case for himself before he had to leave for his next rotation. The residents had kind of funny looks on their faces, but Garven was too busy to pay them much mind. He figured they had just gone a little crazy from overwork and that the situation was normal, SNAFU, as the WWII vets described it, and he ignored them.

He stepped into the cubicle and found an unclothed young man lying on his abdomen. Garven introduced himself, then put on a pair of latex gloves. He always gloved both hands because you could never be sure what the people who came to the clinic might have on them, then he squeezed out some K-Y jelly on his gloved forefinger. The hemorrhoids were large and angry looking, obvious pre-surgical specimens. The rectal exam was required for completeness' sake.

Garven inserted his finger, felt around the anus and lower rectum for masses or abscesses, and pushed harder to feel the prostate. Here, again, his fingers were a little too short to make it easy work. He had to push a little harder. Shortly, he heard the young man moaning, and he looked at his face to see if he was hurting him. The moaning intensified. The young man's face was the very picture of pleasure, nearing sexual climax pleasure. Garven whipped his finger out and jumped back as if he had received an electric shock.

80

He heard several snickers coming from the partially opened cubicle curtain. Garven whirled around and caught a glimpse of the faces of the residents, contorted with poorly controlled laughter. He stormed out of the cubicle.

"You knew he was a flaming queer, didn't you guys?!"

They could not stop laughing long enough to protest their innocence, although later, they all swore that they had never seen the guy before. Garven never did hear whether or not the patient got his hemorrhoidectomy.

Garven was on general surgery for two full months, August and September. During that period, he was on call thirty of the sixty days, worked an average of one hundred twenty hours a week, and was home to see his wife only thirteen of those days. He did—as surgeon—two gall bladders, six inguinal and two abdominal hernias, one big-wound hernia, one radical mastectomy, one tracheostomy, one vagotomy and pyloroplasty for duodenal ulcers, four below-the-knee amputations for gangrene, five vein strippings, an even dozen appendectomies, thirteen hemorrhoidectomies and excision of perirectal abscesses, ten tonsillectomies and adenoidectomies, more cut-downs, paracenteses, heroin addict leg ulcers, and skin biopsies than he could keep up with.

He had learned to be efficient in getting the work done. Interns had to run the ward, do CBCs, hemoglobins, hematocrits, potassiums, stool guaiacs, make up the IV solution bottles, start the IVs or cut-downs even when there were no veins left, find the X-rays, and tend the patients' wounds and bladders, and put tubes in every orifice, real or surgically created. He could make a more-than-reasonable diagnosis, institute a quick and efficient workup, and do excellent post-op care on all of the bread-and-butter general surgery cases. If he had not been so chronically tired, Garven might have taken stock and found that he was becoming a pretty decent doctor, and had made significant strides toward being a surgeon.

He had lost weight—pounds he could not afford—Elizabeth pointed out every time she saw him. She complained that he loved medicine more than he did her, and Garven did not try to explain. He was to start plastic surgery on the first of October. Plastics were reputed to be a vacation tour. Garven looked forward to the rotation to improve his chances of survival.

81

CHAPTER
Ten

Harry Chang, the other intern, was already on the plastic surgery ward when Garven arrived. Harry had a reputation of being a real red hot, a case stealer, and very smart—and Garven knew that he would have his work cut out for him to shine on that service. Harry and Garven already knew each other.

"Ready for your rest up, Garven?" Harry said when Garven walked onto the floor.

Harry was looking at a very sick patient, located near the nurses' station, as usual.

"I've heard that, too. I'll wait and see. Most of those kinds of rumors turn out to be some kind of cruel joke. We'll probably work ourselves to death and then tell the next set of 'terns that it was a breeze. We're a cruel lot," Garven replied.

"I checked with some of last year's interns. They said that plastics are just general surgery done slower," Harry stated and smiled.

"Hi, guys," came a voice from behind them.

Garven and Harry turned.

"I'm Aaron Knight, chief of scut work here. I'm a general surgery resident, really, but this is my plastics rotation. This is my third month. I can hardly wait to get back to being a real surgeon—one more month."

The three young men shook hands.

"Before the world famous plastic surgery team arrives, I'll tell you where the bear sleeps. It's different here than on general. First of all, don't write a bunch. In fact, I don't want to see an H&P longer than four lines. I am responsible for all of the charts—like those ones you don't do the discharge summaries on, which is a capital crime, incidentally. If I have to turn a page, you fail the rotation."

"Sounds like my kinda place," Garven beamed.

"Next rule is that you have to go out and find your own surgery, except for what comes in from the ER on the night when you're on, and you usually have to fight me or the ER 'thing' for the case. So get out and convince all the little girls that their noses are too big, and their boobs are too small, or if you are on real good terms, that they could do with a tummy tuck. What you bring in from clinic is yours, too. So never say it's 'just a mole.' There's no such thing as 'just a mole'! All skin lumps are to be considered cancer until proven otherwise. Here, we follow the adages of 'when in doubt, cut it out, and to cut is to cure' to their logical and blessed extremes."

The rest of the team walked on to the ward and summoned the two interns and the junior resident. Garven thought he had died and gone to heaven. The scut list was only twelve items long, divided between the two interns. Garven and Harry flipped a coin. Garven won and went to the operating room while Harry did all of the scut in two hours, had a nap, and caught up on his reading. It was a miserable day for the Chinese man, who was used to living at a caffeine-enhanced staccato pace.

Garven had a fairly good day. The first two patients were sisters, sixty-three-year-old spinsters who wanted to have breast augmentations. It was not theirs to reason why, Dr. Withers, one of the two staff men, told him. All went smoothly until they were fitting the prosthesis into the last of the four breasts. Garven punctured the silicone bubble of the implant with a clamp as he was trying to smooth it out against the chest wall. The silicone gel oozed out into the surgical pocket.

Dr. Withers looked at Garven as if he had caught him drowning puppies.

"Go sit in the corner," the head of plastic surgery ordered.

Garven looked at the man's eyes to see if he were serious and decided that he was. He sat in the corner. In a few minutes, he felt silly, as if he had on a dunce cap.

He asked, "Do you want me to leave, Dr. Withers?"

"No, I want you to sit in the corner."

The professor always had his errant house staff men sit in the corner. It was an educational experience.

The next patient was a sixty-year-old man named Hopper. Lemonjello Hopper (pronounced Lay-man-jel-o). He had the most grotesque face Garven had ever laid eyes on. The center of his face was gone. There were no eyes, nose, upper jaw, or cheeks. From the eyebrows to the tongue, everything had been surgically removed. Garven could see the back of the nasal passages as they entered the pharynx, the uvula, and back half of the palate and the base of the skull.

As they scrubbed their hands, Garven, who had been reinstated from his dunce chair, asked Dr. Withers, "What happened to Lemonjello? Was he hit by a grenade?"

"No, Garven. He had an absolutely enormous neglected basal cell carcinoma—a rodent ulcer—that had eaten away and into the entire middle of his face. He did not present himself here until he no longer had eyes or a recognizable nose, and his teeth were falling out," Dr. Withers replied.

Garven glanced at the professor's face. It was entirely matter of fact.

"I take it he must not be too swuuf," commented Garven.

"I think you could say that," said Dr. Withers as he finished scrubbing.

With Garven's inexperienced help, Dr. Withers rotated an attached flap of the latissmus dorsi muscle up under the shoulder and into the hole in Lemonjello's face. The flap occupied only one-half of the defect. Great care was taken not to crimp the blood vessels to the flap as it was turned into a direction opposite from its normal orientation. The previous surgical bed was healthy, full of pinkish granulation tissue—proud flesh—and the flap fitted perfectly and appeared to be healthy when they put in the last sutures. Garven closed the muscle donor wound.

Between cases, Dr. Withers had Garven accompany him to a "reunion," as he described it. They went up the back flight of stairs one floor and down the hall to Dr. Withers' office. The office suite was elegant, an oasis of cleanliness and opulence, set in a sea of dirt and dilapidation, which was the hospital at large. There were original oils on the wall, an inch-thick carpet on the floor, Queen Anne desks, chairs, and tables, and they were not even bolted to the floor. In the rest of Osterlund Memorial Hospital, there were, for practical purposes, no chairs or tables, unless you counted the hardwood benches in the main waiting hall. The Osterlund patients had stolen the furniture and the replacement furniture so many times over the years that the county commissioners instructed the administration to let the patients and visitors to Osterlund sit on the floor. They had been doing so for over ten years.

"Like it, Garven?" asked Dr. Withers when he saw the young man looking about in a combination of wonder and covetousness.

"I can't believe that there is such a place in Osterlund. I bet you don't even have to bring your own can of Raid bug spray with you when you come in here."

Dr. Withers threw his head back and laughed out loud.

"I never quite thought of it that way. But, no, that is not something we have to do here."

Garven looked about with undisguised lust.

"So c'mon inside, and we'll see why I asked you to come over. I think you'll find this interesting," said the boss.

They walked into the inner office.

In addition to two attractive secretaries and several unremarkable spouses of both genders, there were thirteen of the most peculiar human beings Garven had encountered. Some of them were talking, some were listening. What they all had in common was that they had no faces. Only one person (a man?) had an eye. Their tongues waggled like large, red worms out of holes in the lower part of their heads. Where there might have been faces, there was a bland mat of hairless skin, a blank.

"Come in and meet my 'bullet heads'," Dr. Withers said.

Garven felt very uncomfortable, like he was going to have nightmares over this. He did not have a clue what he might say to them.

"This is my first 'bullet head', Dr. Wilsonhulme," Dr. Withers said by way of introduction.

The person extended a right hand, and Garven shook it. It was a man's hand. The person laughed—at least, Garven took the tongue movement for a laugh—at the professor of plastic surgery's characterization.

"These are all my 'bullet heads'," Dr. Withers said as he gathered them to him.

Almost as strange as the appearance of the people, who really did look, for all the world, like bullet heads, was the great affection they had for the eminent surgeon. The thirteen patients and their spouses all made it a point to give him a hug. A few of the spouses shed tears. By the movements of the 'bullet heads', it was possible that some of them were feeling the same level of emotion.

When they had toasted the unique group and the doctor had caught up on the family news from each couple, he and Garven trotted back down to the OR.

"How many are there?" Garven asked.

"Fifteen."

"That's pretty good that thirteen of them were there for the reunion," Garven said. "How about the other two?"

"One moved to Connecticut, said he was going to be in a circus. I don't think that's really true, but he had the best sense of humor of them all."

"I can't imagine living at all, let alone having a sense of humor," said Garven, giving his head a little shake of wonderment.

"It is a tough go. But when you consider the alternative..." Dr. Withers let his voice trail off in emphasis.

"What about the fifteenth one?"

"Committed suicide. Put a shotgun right in the middle of the graft site," Dr. Withers said unemotionally.

After the visit with the bullet heads, they did a repair of a nose. Garven thought the young woman had a perfectly fine nose pre-op, but Dr. Withers told him that she was a model and had to have a perfect nose.

"You will also note the perfect chin, breasts, bottom, and tummy—all thanks to the miracle of modern medical science."

Garven had to admit that the girl was as nearly perfect as a Grecian statue.

The next case was a face-lift on a sixty-six-year-old woman, Doris Pendleton. Dr. Withers moved swiftly and without a single wasted motion. It was visual poetry. The wrinkles and age disappeared as the sagging skin was pulled taut and firm across the dissected bed of the face. Dr. Withers made a dart here, clipped off an excess millimeter there, and fitted all of the parts into perfect contour and harmony. Garven thought that there was a great deal more to cosmetic surgery than the general surgery detractors had indicated. Although he remained unshaken in his resolve to go into neurosurgery, Garven bandied the thought about considering the advantages of plastic surgery.

The last case was a reconstruction mammoplasty. The woman was young, thirty-five, and had had simple mastectomies for removal of breasts full of benign but suspicious lumps after more than a dozen biopsies. The nipples had been taken. Dr. Withers complained about that privately to Garven. He said scathingly that the surgery had been "done at St. Elsewhere's." He did not have to add that it had been done by a private surgeon, one of the despised LMDs. In the town versus gown controversy, there was no doubting where Dr. Withers stood.

The mammoplasties went well; there was enough skin to allow the prosthesis to be placed against the muscular wall of the patient's chest. The problem came, as it always did, in trying to fashion a suitable nipple.

"We have a few choices, and none of them have been found to stand up very well; we can use a skin mound, a piece of Silastic, a segment of ear cartilage, but, I repeat, nothing works well."

Garven had done the admission H&P. He recalled that the woman had multiple large-skin polyps, really large ones.

86

"I have a thought, Dr. Withers. You can write it off as weird, if you want."

"Out with it, Garven. At worst, I can have you go back into the dunce corner."

Garven told the professor about the polyps.

"Let's have a look," Dr. Withers said. He was nothing if not innovative. "Perfect!" he exclaimed when he found a particularly plump one. "More perfect!" he said with even more enthusiasm when he palpated a second one, nearly identical to the first. "I'm not sure if there is such a thing as 'more perfect,' but for this great occasion, we have a perfect right to use the phrase."

Dr. Withers showed Garven how to take off polyps. He simply tied a garrote around the neck of the lesion and strangled off its blood supply, then snipped it off. It was bloodless surgery. The polyps worked admirably, standing out like little buried nipples. They had exactly the right size and texture. Dr. Withers was most pleased with his work that day.

He accorded Garven the compliment that, "I guess we don't have to put you in the dunce chair anymore today."

That was about as complimentary as the famous plastic surgeon could be.

They finished surgery at the gentlemanly hour of six o'clock. Garven wondered if he would have to turn in his intern credentials, getting off that early. Dr. Withers and Garven walked up five flights of stairs to the ward. The professor was a health enthusiast. There, they met the other staff man, Porter Clement; the chief resident, Tom Bird; and Aaron Knight. Rounds went quickly. Not only did the plastic surgeons not care for lengthy chart write-ups, but they were parsimonious with spoken conversation with their patients in the evening.

One of the first patients they came to was Doris Pendleton, the face-lift of earlier in the day. The house staff picked up through the hospital grapevine that the woman was among the richest in California. Her husband was *the* Carey Pendleton, producer of Hollywood musicals. Dr. Withers presented Mrs. Pendleton's face. It had not yet begun to swell and looked youthful and serene without care wrinkles.

"Splendid," said Dr. Clement. To the patient, he said, "You have had a masterful job done. You are ready for your husband's pictures."

Garven thought he was troweling it on pretty thick, but she seemed to like it.

"Thank you, Dr. Clement. Dr. Withers, I looked at the mirror. I am so pleased. I am less interested in getting into movies than I am in keeping my husband from straying to the casting couch," said Mrs. Pendleton.

As she spoke, Garven detected something amiss.

So did Nigel Withers. His facial expression never changed from his standard mannequin half smile.

"Please show me your teeth, Mrs. Pendleton."

She moved her face to accommodate the doctor's request.

"Good," he said as half of the woman's face moved up, and the other half remained as immobile as if it were made of plaster. "We'll see you in the morning," Dr. Withers said and led his entourage toward the door to her private room.

"But...she's..." Garven started to blurt.

Dr. Withers stopped the words before they could be uttered by a glacial look. The physicians stepped swiftly into the hall.

Dr. Withers said nothing more about Mrs. Pendleton's facial paralysis until Garven spoke up again when they were well out of the patient's earshot.

"Aren't you worried?" he asked.

"Not worried," said the professor. "Concerned, perhaps, but not 'worried.' Surgeons are never 'worried.'"

They finished rounds at seven-thirty. The surgeons began to disperse. It was Garven's night off; so, he started down the hall to leave.

"Garven," Dr. Withers called.

Garven turned to look back.

"Come with me to my office, please. It's important."

They walked through the hallways and down the stairs without talking. Garven sensed that something was up. When they were in Dr. Withers' inner office for the second time that day, he stood in front of Garven, who was substantially shorter and smaller than him, and placed both hands on the young man's shoulders. He looked directly into Garven's eyes.

He said, "You may not be aware of this Garven, but I am a born-again Christian. In keeping with my deep religious commitment, I want to let you know that I love you, young man."

Garven was shocked. He had never been accosted by a homosexual before, and that was the only thought that he could muster in the strange circumstance.

Dr. Withers waited until he knew that he had Garven's undivided attention, then he said, "I love you, Dr. Wilsonhulme, but..." and here he paused again for effect.

Garven was waiting for the other shoe to drop.

"You had a serious *lapsus linguae* this evening. You talk too much. YOU TALK TOO MUCH!"

The latter sentence was screamed. Garven jumped an inch off the floor and backward. He blinked. The next sentence dripped with venom.

"If you ever say another word to one of my private patients, you will be nothing more than a historical footnote around here!"

It took Garven half a minute to figure out what had brought on this outburst. Then he recalled his abortive little speech fragment in Mrs. Pendleton's room. Dr. Withers' face was deep red, and he was clenching his teeth to keep from…what? Exploding? Biting Garven? Garven did not feel the slightest urge to test the man.

He said very meekly, "Yes, Sir."

"Get out," said the chief of plastic surgery, and Garven got out.

He only told his wife part of the day's story.

The following day was Garven's turn in the clinic and to go to the ER for screening call. If anything serious came in, he had to call the resident. The clinic was full of moles, and lumps, and crooked noses, and wrong-sized breasts and FLKs. There were a dozen special funny-looking kids coming in that week. They had Crouzon's craniofacial dystosis, and the world's foremost expert, Dr. Paul Tessier of France, was coming as a guest professor to give lectures and to do some operations on the unfortunate children with flat faces and extremely wide interpupillary distances. Garven and Tom Bird saw a particularly homely woman together.

Tom was very patient.

The woman said, "I want a face-lift."

She had very few wrinkles, and was no more than forty years old. She had an unpleasant, demanding way of expressing her wants.

"We can do that," Tom said.

"What about my eyes?" she asked, almost defiantly.

Her eyes were slightly crossed and dull. There were very small bags beneath the lower lids.

"Okay, no problem," Tom answered.

"I don't like my ears."

She looked at Tom with a challenge.

"We can fix them."

"I hate my big nose."

It was big. It was ugly, too.

"We can do a rhinoplasty," he said.

"I have a little, weak chin."

She had a big, weak face.

"We can do a chin implant," Tom told her.

She seemed to have run out of complaints about her face. Tom went on to explain each of the procedures in detail, telling her about the potential hazards and complications. He had the photographers get multiple views of the patient's face.

As they waited for the next patient, Garven asked Tom if he was really able to make that homely woman into the beauty she envisioned.

"Oh, good grief, no. Nothing is going to make that woman look better. She is truly ugly. You know what they say, 'Beauty is only skin deep.' But I'm here to tell you that ugly goes clear to the bone."

Garven had been itching to ask Tom a fundamental question. He was concerned about how his chief resident would take it, but this seemed like an opportune time.

"Tom, how do you really feel about cosmetic surgery anyway? I mean, do you ever have a little nagging doubt that it might not be altogether legitimate, this business of doing what these silly, vain women want?"

"You mean, 'pandering'?" Tom asked.

His face was smiling.

"I didn't say that. But do you really think you do anything for them, make them better?"

"Absolutely. They get a new lease on life. Stay around long enough and you'll see a passel of pleased persons," Tom said.

Garven rolled his eyes back.

"Really, be open minded. Plastic surgeons are great guys. And they have their share of troubles and are sensitive to the needs of their patients, not just money," Tom said.

"You mean guys like you?" Garven said with a laugh.

"Maybe not me," Tom said, "but did you hear about the famous plastic surgeon who hung himself?"

It took Garven a second or two to catch the punch line, then he laughed at Tom and at himself.

Their patient was scheduled for the first of her three operations the following morning. She was to be first on the schedule, to be followed by a tummy tuck because those two operations would not take long, and the team would have the rest of the day to do the first in the series of Crouzon's patients.

The next patient in the clinic was a young man, age nineteen, who was sent over to the clinic from the emergency room with a broken nose. He had been

90

at football practice. His mother and two sisters accompanied him. Tom and Garven reviewed the X-rays.

Tom said to the boy and his family, "This is Dr. Wilsonhulme. He will be taking care of you today. He is a broken nose specialist."

Garven knew that that was not only an exaggeration, but that he barely knew what to do. He had a hurried conference with Tom out of the hearing of the family. Tom gave him the short course in straightening broken noses.

Garven put the nasal forceps inside the nose and his other thumb and index finger outside, and gave a mighty twist. The boy almost fainted with the sudden pain. His eyes filled up with water, but he was stoical and made no protest. The nose looked exactly as it had before Garven made his effort. Garven was too much of a humanitarian to do that again. He put a pledget of cocaine into each nostril and injected lidocaine until the nose was numb. For the next forty-five minutes, he wrested, twisted, instrumented, pushed, and pulled the stubborn fracture, but to no avail. The nose remained as crooked as it had when the boy came in from the ER. Both the doctor and the patient were sweating.

It was evident that he was not going to get anywhere with what he was doing. He left and found Tom.

"I can't get that nose back into place. It's like it was cemented there. I tried everything," Garven said.

Tom believed him. "Go see if the mother has a picture of him. Mothers always have a picture of their kids."

Garven looked at him quizzically. Tom went back to work, suturing a jagged facial laceration.

Sure enough, the mother did have a recent photograph of her son. She brightened up for the first time when she produced it. The picture was of a dull-eyed young man standing next to his motorcycle. It was a good, clear photograph of the boy's face, including his very crooked nose.

"Why didn't you tell me he had a broken nose before, that it was as crooked as a dog's hind leg?" he demanded of the mother.

The boy was listening, along with his two sisters.

The answer was classical, and Garven should have anticipated it.

"You never asked."

Garven put tape across the bridge of the young man's nose and sent them on their way.

Garven was on call that night. It was quiet until two-fifteen in the morning. He got a call from a young woman who had just delivered a baby.

"Can nursing hurt my breast enlargements?"

"No," Garven told her sleepily.

He resented the fact that that piece of information was not only given verbally to every patient having a breast augmentation, but that it was in the booklet.

The next call came at four a.m. It was from a woman who had a tummy tuck two weeks previously. She had a worried voice.

"Doctor, I'm Minny Crabtree. I had my stomach fixed a couple of weeks ago. I got a question."

Garven's thought was, *This better be important.*

"Can being pregnant ruin my nice stomach?"

"It sure can. You were supposed to have made the decision not to have any more children before you decided to have the operation. Didn't they tell you that?"

"I think so."

"How far along are you, Mrs. Crabtree?"

"It's miss. I mean, just Minnie. Let's see..." There was a pause, then she added, "About twenty-five minutes." She said this with a note of genuine sadness in her voice.

Garven decided that you didn't have to be crazy to have plastic surgery, but it probably helped.

The next day, he and Tom Bird were in the operating room. The face-lift was routine and quick. Dr. Bird was very smooth with his hands. The tummy tuck had one hitch.

The surgery was almost done when Tom said to Garven, "I screwed up."

"What happened?" asked Garven.

"I forgot to measure how far to put the belly button up on the abdomen. I have to figure out a way to get it right. People are very touchy about their belly buttons." He thought for a minute or two. Then, he had an idea, a plan.

"Hey, Dixie," he said to the circulating nurse in the room. "How about you measuring the distance from your pubis to your belly button?"

Dixie looked at the chief resident very suspiciously. No nurse liked to be the butt of the residents' practical jokes, and Dixie had been around long enough to smell one in this request.

"What for?" she asked.

Tom explained. Dixie still did not look entirely convinced, but she took the metal ruler and walked to the corner of the room.

"Don't look," she demanded.

92

Dixie undid her pants, stuck the ruler into the opening, and, with as much dignity as possible, measured the distance from the top of the pubis to the navel. She called out the figure to Tom. As she was removing the ruler from her opened scrub pants, Dr. Clement, the attending staff man walked in. He gave Dixie a curious look, and she all but admitted that something hinky was going on by blushing scarlet. The room erupted into laughter at her expense. Dixie laughed louder than anyone when she finally got her pants retied.

If Garven had expected to go home early, or even at a reasonable hour, that night, which was his night off, he was sorely mistaken. The little girl with Crouzon's Disease was wheeled into the operating room at eleven-thirty a.m. Dr. Tessier served as operating surgeon and Dr. Clement was the first assistant. Tom and Garven tried to make themselves appear useful. Dr. Tessier performed a mid-face advancement, widened the space between the eyes, and built her a new forehead. The operation took seventeen hours. After the two professors went home, the post-op arrangements and vigil in the ICU took another four hours before Tom and Garven were satisfied that the little girl was going to do all right. It was six a.m. when Garven finally crashed on a gurney on the plastics ward.

The bandages came off in two days. The change in appearance was so dramatic and represented such an improvement in the girl's looks that the child's mother could not believe that it was really her. She had to hear her child's voice before she could be convinced. She wept for joy.

The same satisfaction came from seeing the improvement that took place when a baby's cleft lip or cleft palate was repaired. There were quite a few of them in the poor section of Los Angeles, Garven concluded by the time his tour on plastic surgery was over. The staff and residents did beautiful work to change the children from grotesque and frightening anomalies to attractive boys and girls with slight scars. The operations were done with extremely careful measurements so that there would be a precise and cosmetic closure of the defect. They took care to fashion a cupid's bow natural upper lip line instead of the crude repair of years' past that ended up with the child having a straight and unsightly lip and a mouth that was held in a permanent, unnatural soft grimace.

93

CHAPTER
Eleven

Garven was assigned to The Pit for the month of November. The house staff doctors in almost every big city charity hospital call their emergency room "The Pit" for obvious reasons. The Pit at Osterlund Memorial was huge and overwhelmingly busy. It was segmented into seven nearly autonomous divisions: medicine ER, peds ER, psych ER, ob-gyn ER, ortho ER, the triage desk, and the Emergency Operating Rooms—two of them—known to the staff as the EOR and to the patients from the community as the EOR-AH, a phonetic pronunciation.

The triage desk was the screening point for all comers to the "muncy" room, another phoneticism, and had the absolute final say concerning the disposition of incoming patients. The four autocrats who sat at that desk twenty-four hours a day consisted of three residents and a battle-hardened nurse. There was an internist, a surgeon, and a psychiatrist. The triage desk concept had been instituted by a wise University of California administration to prevent bloodshed among the interns, residents, and nurses working in the ER. The greatest instances of rancor came when an overworked intern thought that a patient had been "dumped" on him or her, or when an overzealous house staff doctor thought someone had stolen his or her patient. The triage desk obviated all of that. Like the internal affairs department of a police force, the triage desk workers were kept insulated from the rest of the staff. If you had an inch-thick crust for a skin, it was not a half-bad job.

Garven's first patient was violent. Two burly orderlies were holding him down when Garven entered into the man's curtain-enclosed cubicle. The man was yelling and blaspheming. He hurled inarticulate invectives at the young intern. His dif-

94

ficulty with communication stemmed not from his injury, nor from the alcohol he had imbibed, but from the fact that he had a generally limited vocabulary. He was the type who misspelled graffiti on the doors of men's room toilet stalls.

He had a nasty gash on his forehead from a fight with his girlfriend over who was entitled to the last swig of the Muscatel in their bottle. His age was indeterminate, but the dirt on his clothing and body were definitely old. Garven could not do a thing with him. He tried to calm him, to reason with him, and had to give up. He left the cubicle, walked to the nurses' station, and told the head nurse about his predicament.

"You must be new. Oh, that's right, it's the first. No problem, Dr. Wilsonhulme," she said, reading the name embroidered on his lab coat. "Get the deputies!" she yelled over the prevailing din in the EOR.

Shortly, two neck-less Neanderthals in uniform came to the desk.

"The guy in three is having trouble with his understanding of the rules," she said.

"No problem, Julia. We'll pay him a visit."

The two powerfully-built sheriff's deputies walked purposefully over to the cubicle. Garven gave a little shiver. He would just about as soon meet King Kong in a dark tunnel, he thought.

There were some noises in the cubicle that sounded like they came from inanimate objects, and there were a series of three yelps followed by a long series of moans. Intermittently, Garven could hear the gravelly voices of the deputies. Although he could not make out what they were saying, the general tenor of the voices was that of courtesy and calm.

Shortly, the two deputies stepped out of the cubicle and reported to Garven.

"He has had an attitude adjustment. He is looking forward to cooperating in every way."

When Garven entered the cubicle, the derelict patient no longer seemed drunk, was one hundred percent cooperative, and was absolutely docile.

Garven happened to ask Julia later in the day what the deputies did in the cubicle. She said succinctly, "We don't ask."

And that was the prevailing attitude throughout his stay in The Pit. Two deputies were present in The Pit three shifts a day. Julia told him that there was the police room for "customers" who could not be persuaded by the deputies. Garven could only imagine what had to go on in the police room. There was no way the emergency room could run without the deputies. In the history of Osterlund Memorial, there had never been a complaint from a doctor or nurse about the methods of the deputies.

The emergency room was the place that provided the most convincing evidence to Garven as to why he had chosen to pursue a career in surgery. From the triage desk, Garven watched three nurses' aides herd a derelict with brooms into the medicine ER. With the light at his back, the bum seemed to have an aura, a sort of glow about him. When Garven came closer, the nurses' aides shooed him away.

"That's lice and fleas you sees a jumpin' on ole Fred," one of them said.

Indeed, on somewhat closer inspection, he could just make out the tens of thousands of jumping creatures catching the light from the hallway. The aides pushed the old fellow—aged about thirty-two—into a tiled cubicle, located about halfway down the entrance hallway. It looked like a shower.

With difficulty, the hospital personnel induced the new medicine ER patient to take off all of his clothing and to dump it into a large paper bag that they promptly tied off with a length of stout string. While one of the nurses' aides took the bag of clothing to be incinerated, the other two gassed the naked man with DDT powder from the shower heads.

"Clean him up thoroughly before he sets foot in the ER!" the resident in charge shouted out to the two remaining aides.

"The usual?" they yelled back.

"Yeah, gasoline and a wire brush. Twice if you need to." the doctor ordered.

Others came in past the triage desk, "harkin' up clogs" (coughing up clots), or having "blind staggers" (dizziness after meals or upon standing), having the "DDTs" (DTs—Delirium Tremens), in "electric light trouble" (imbalance of the blood electrolytes), with "hepateetus," and with the "inward fever" (a truly grave illness).

The three most common complaints leading to admission to the medicine ER were "roaches of the liver," also known as "ferocious liver" (alcoholic cirrhosis of the liver), the combination complaint of "I gots the Typhoid-Malaria," which was almost any illness (exclusive of either typhoid or malaria), and "movin' miseries." Other common presenting complaints included: "Yaller janders," "vomikin'," "swimin' of the head," "sugarbetis," "spasm," "smotherin'," "newmonie fever," "Lucas" (SLE—Systemic Lupus Erythematosis), and the "hurries" (Montezuma's Revenge). Some wanted "Desperation Hach," the cure-all for every bowel disorder, and they all insisted that "aspereen" did not work, and that they had to have "penumcillium." It seemed to Garven that he was better suited to the blood and guts of the EOR for the time being and to surgery for the remainder of his natural life.

Also from the triage desk streamed legions of squalling children, their noses running, having "fitch" (fits) or "motorcycle ekalectasy" (psychomotor epilepsy) for the more sophisticated parents, or with obnoxious childhood exanthems like "missiles" or "chicken pops"—their skins all scabbed and splotched. The parents 'splained that their children had "henfection of the years" (otitis media), "bowels locked open" (or the green apple quickstep), were "corrupted" (nauseated, not a comment on outside influences), had the "cold rigors" (shakes), or the "brown cheeter" (bronchitis). A career in pediatrics was too terrible to contemplate.

It was not all that difficult for Garven to rule psychiatry out as a profession. Not that he stepped foot during his internship on the "bug ward," as everyone but the psychiatrists called it. The ambulatory hallucinators, confabulating drunks, and the Alzheimer's patients who passed by the triage desk and into the psych ER would have been enough to keep Garven away from any involvement in the treatment of mental illness. But it was the screamers who were the clincher.

There was even a special room for the screamers. It was located just to the right of the entry lobby of the emergency room. The screamers did not even have to stop at the triage desk; everyone knew where to take them. The patients who got to go to that well-equipped room included the skid row drunks from Hill Street and the low numbered streets of Los Angeles who came in with delirium tremens screaming about the snakes and spiders that were after them. The main cause of that phenomenon was the cessation of serious drinking for a few days. If there was anything that the working people in the ER did not advocate, it was that people quit drinking. It was a most serious complication, and one to be avoided. There were senile old ladies brought over from the nursing homes because they could no longer be handled. Some of the screamers were protesting about their psychotic hallucinations; some were preachers from Pershing Square. The worst were the drug addicts, especially those who had gotten into contaminated stuff. During one of the recurring riots, the scream room even got to handle one of the members of the Osterlund Memorial house staff.

It happened during the most recent riot. Los Angeles has periodic riots in which poor people protest the realities of the world, their oppression, and their impotent position by burning down their own homes and neighborhood businesses. When that phenomenon occurred during Garven's tour in the ER, the rioters' logic escaped him. He and the rest of the house staff were confined to the hospital for two full weeks while the local police and imported US Marines quelled the disturbance. The ER looked more like a war zone than usual, and all of the medical center's doctors worked themselves into near exhaustion dealing with the incoming wounded. The elective surgery schedule was suspended for the duration.

The medical staff began to get cabin fever, some fairly severely. A few sneaked out to local bars at night to relieve the tensions. Although they were of a different skin color than the majority of the prowlers on the streets, they blended in well with the denizens of the dark since they were dirty, unkempt, unshaven, and odoriferous. Since in the night all cats are gray, they were left alone to get drunk and disorderly like the populace they served.

On the last Saturday night of the month of November, Garven was trying to render aid to an accident victim, a man presumed to be another casualty of the now diminishing riotous conditions outside. He had a LaForte III facial fracture, and both of his kneecaps were smashed. Despite his caved-in face, the gentleman was alert and oriented. Garven wheedled out of him that his lover's husband had set upon him with a baseball bat. After cleaning him up, Garven was waiting for the facial X-rays to come back from radiology. It was then that he heard an unusual voice coming from the scream room.

"Mandel! Mandel!" the disembodied voice was calling.

Garven could see Dr. Mandel Simons walking down the hall past the door to the scream room. Mandel appeared either not to have heard, which was impossible, or to be ignoring the hollering of his name.

Garven got up and walked toward the scream room, curious.

"Hey, Mandel," he said, "somebody in there knows you."

Mandel laughed. He was not thrilled to have been recognized. "Some drunk or crazy. I don't know how he got my name. I figure if I ignore him, he'll go away."

The yelling continued, a plaintive call.

"C'mon, Mandel. You must be curious. Let's go peek in," Garven said.

Mandel followed along very reluctantly. It was one of his rules for survival never to go near the scream room. The nurses kept the room dark. That was unfortunate, the psychiatrists thought, because it was done in such a pleasant shade of pink. Some psychiatrist had done a study that indicated that the color pink was tranquilizing. For that reason, admission and holding rooms of big city ERs, jails, and prisons went through a fad of being painted pink. Garven and Mandel could hear the voice coming from one of the back gurneys, so they walked on into the room.

Their eyes adjusted to the dim light. The room was lined with gurneys on which were strapped an assortment of mental and physical derelicts, bound together by the common thread that they were unable to halt their screaming. It was like the anteroom of hell.

"Mandel! Help me. You know me! Help me, Mandel!" yelled the disheveled drunk on the gurney.

He was in four-limb leather restraints.

There was a glimmer of recognition on Mandel's part. He drew closer.

"Mandel, thank God you've come," the tethered shadow choked in a hoarse whisper. The voice came from a parched throat.

"Who is it?" Mandel asked, rather timidly.

"It's me. Ronald Haldermann."

"No."

"Yes."

"What are you doing in here, Ronald?"

"Who is Ronald?" Garven asked.

"Oh, sorry, Garven. This is Ronald Haldermann," said Mandel.

For some reason, Garven thought it might be Ronald Halderman.

"Oh yeah. He's a medicine resident. Here at Osterlund."

Now, what was wrong with this picture?

"So, what's going on, Ronald?" asked Mandel.

"Look, it's all a big mistake. I went out last night. The cops raided the bar and took us all to the drunk tank. Roughed us all up. It was terrible. I told them who I was, that I worked at Osterlund. I must have told them a thousand times that I was a doctor. Either they were deaf or they wouldn't listen. I tried yelling at them so they would know who I am. That's when they brought me here and tied me up. This is the most awful place on earth, Mandel. You have to get me out of here!"

He looked like he was going to get excited again.

"Calm down, Ronald. I will go explain to the nurses and to the psych resident if I can find one. There will probably be some papers to fill out. You should be out of here in an hour," Mandel told his colleague to comfort him.

"Oh no! I can't take it anymore!" cried Ronald.

But Mandel left to tend to the proprieties of getting his friend out of the scream room.

Garven stepped up to the gurney and undid the restraints, helped Ronald to his feet, and said, "Have a better day. See ya."

In this additional example, Garven recognized the fundamental differences between the internal medicine way and the surgical way. He preferred the way of the surgeons.

Garven spent a very happy two days with his wife between The Pit and the G-U service, his next rotation, as a reward for his two weeks of nonstop ER service. She considered this period to be her honeymoon.

CHAPTER
Twelve

On the first of December, his wife's birthday, Garven was on call on the G-U service. He did not get home to wish her a happy day, and he forgot to get her a birthday present. He had spent the day in the genito-urinary clinic, attending to uriniferous old men, and Elizabeth's birthday simply slipped his mind. The men had big prostates, BPH—Benign Prostatic Hypertrophy—and prostate and bladder cancer. They had sprinkling pot urethras from the ravages of late, poorly-treated gonorrhea and syphilis—better known as the "runnin' range" and the "bad blood." They complained of urgency, frequency, "pulse" (pus) in the urine, and pain so long, so repetitive, and so vociferous, that Garven could still hear them in his sleep, and that was part of why he could not remember his wife's birthday.

Garven had not expected medicine to be nice, or necessarily gentlemanly, but G-U clinic had been about as far from gentility as he could have found himself. He double gloved the entire day while he touched "blue-balls" or "corrupted grimes," as some called their buboes—enlarged groin lymph nodes of lymphogranuloma venereum—squeezed down green "purse" by massaging tender prostates, examined "love bumps"—euphemism for anal warts associated with venereal granuloma acuminata. Garven took extra pains to be sure his gloves had no holes in them when he changed the bloody catheters of old gents who had had "T.U. Auras"—TURPs, TransUrethral Resection of the Prostate—for BPH the week before. His sensibilities were not protected, but his workload was decreased by the old men with chronic bladder or urethral failure and who required permanent catheters through their penises and into

101

their bladders. These old hands at the procedures catheterized themselves. Lacking provisions for sanitary placement of the urethral tubes, they simply passed the used latex catheters through their mouths to moisten and lubricate them, then deftly reinserted them. Images of that activity diverted Garven's attention from the birthday present he intended to buy that day.

The most diverting reason and the strongest memory to come out of the day to interfere with Garven's attention to the fine details of civility and conjugal living was that this was transsexual day in the clinic. Transsexuals advertised themselves as being people trapped in a body that was the wrong gender. The most common entrapment was men who knew that they were rightfully women. Garven could not stomach that definition; he all but retched when he had to talk to and examine the patients. They were no more and no less than transvestites who wanted a sex-change Operation; so, their girlish clothing would fit better so far as he was concerned.

University of California Osterlund Memorial Hospital—UCOMH—had embarked on a major program to provide medical assistance to the unfortunate transsexuals, so they could have their sexes changed. There were more than two hundred of them—remember, this was California—and the university system was their court of last resort. The private community had a very brief flirtation with the idea of performing the incredible operations, and rejected it out of hand when the hospital staffs and nurses put up such a protest. In the vicinity of Osterlund Memorial, at a private medical center, a Japanese urologist was asked to give a report on the status of the sex-change operation revolution that was supposed to be sweeping the country. He had never done one of the operations himself and had no plans to do so. The medical staff at the private hospital was very predominately Hispanic-American in origin. After Dr. Shimitaki gave his talk, he was blackballed by the medical staff; he never received another consult because he was widely and incorrectly reported to be in favor of operations that went against God.

It was in that atmosphere that Garven saw the preoperative sex-change patients. All of them had been on estrogen therapy for two years, had had two counseling sessions with the urologist, Dr. Kensington—the only attending who would do the cases—had undergone regular psychotherapy, and had had breast implants. The one thing that all of the medical participants had in common was an unwavering conviction that such a medical problem as transsexualism existed, and that the two hundred plus people they were following had that cruel disorder. Garven thought they all—doctors and patients—suffered from some sort of mass delusion or hypnosis. The patients were plain and simple homos to him. But, given his position in the pecking order, he kept his opinions to himself.

It was disconcerting to examine men with hairy chests, deep voices, and opulent breasts. None of the women-in-evolution were content with normal-sized breasts. They all had to have the super sizes—double D and bigger—to be more than women. Garven well remembered Dr. Yosobuchi's breast lectures about supers, droopers, and super droopers. Most of them still needed a face shave every day. Garven dropped off to sleep that night with his last waking thought being that he was going to have to participate in two of those mutilating operations.

True to Garven's nightmares, the following day, the patient was placed on the operating table with effort by two orderlies, the intern, and the resident. He was big. He had a very ample bust, his nails were polished, and, in his long, suicide-blond hair, he wore a gardenia. It reminded Garven of some song, but he could not come up with the tune. Despite all these accouterments of femininity, the patient still looked like a man in drag, even naked.

The operation consisted of a penectomy, castration, and creation of a fleshy tunnel, a neovagina, between the man's anus and the empty scrotum that had been opened and curled over to look vaguely like labia majora. The last step was to place a plastic support prosthesis—a dildo—into the new tunnel to keep it open. The result looked to Garven like the man had fallen astride the tractor gears, but the patient, who had legally changed his name to Scheherezade, was ecstatic with epicene joy.

"It takes all kinds," Garven muttered to Jack Klusky, the senior urology resident.

"And we just serve them," Jack responded.

The second case was a failed sex-change, at least in the opinion of the patient. He-she had married, but was going through a terrible psychological down period because he-she could not have orgasms. Dr. Klusky saw the patient, Mrs. Dirksen—Nancy Dirksen—in clinic and heard out his-her soul's complaints with great patience while Garven squirmed in his chair. Examination revealed that the surgical opening created in front of the anus had closed completely with scar.

"Mrs. Dirksen, your neovagina has closed up because you failed to keep the prosthesis in there like you were supposed to do," Jack told him-her.

He-she said, "But, Dr. Klusky, you don't understand. How could you? You're only a man!"

Garven turned his head to the side so that he-she would not see him rolling his eyes.

"It was so, so icky!"

That certainly explained it all.

"We can't redo the neovagina. There's too much scar. What we can do—it's experimental—you have to know that, is bring a piece of your large bowel into an opening alongside the old neovagina. You will have to be willing to take some risk. It's a major abdominal operation, more than what you went through before," Jack told the patient.

"I am willing to do anything to save my marriage, to establish my femininity," he-she said.

Garven wondered if it would help if he stuck his finger down his throat.

Mrs. Dirksen was on the operating table for four hours. A segment of large colon was separated off with a vascular pedicle to sustain it. The internal portion of the bowel was over-sewn to make it a blind sac, then the sac was pushed through an opening in the floor of the pelvis and the opening sewn to the skin. If one did not look at it, the opening was something like a vagina by feel. The smell was peculiar; even the most enthusiastic proponents of the procedure had to admit.

Mrs. Dirksen had what is euphemistically described in surgical argot as a "stormy course." Garven spent the night with him-her in the ICU because he-she had a cardiac arrest in the PAR. In the postoperative period, Mrs. Dirksen had an intra-abdominal infection and had to be reopened, and to have a colostomy for ten days. At the end of the month, however, he-she returned to clinic ecstatic. He-she was having serial orgasms.

The operation was an "unqualified success," Klusky reported to the committee on human experimentation.

Garven thought, perhaps, that it could have been regarded as being more like, "qualified."

Garven only came to the attention of the chief of urology, Dr. Webster, once during the G-U month, and that was negatively. Webster had resected a cancer of the prostate so large that it had to be taken out through an abdominal incision. The more common route was through the penis. A tube through which cutting devises were passed was used to hollow out the gland. This one was too big for that.

At the conclusion of the operation, a tube was surgically placed in the bladder and drawn out through a separated stab wound in the abdominal wall—a suprapubic cystostomy. The tube was very carefully sewn into place because accidental removal required a fairly major operation to replace it. Garven had been the second assistant after the chief resident, Andy Nordstrom, who did the suprapubic cystostomy. All three men relaxed after the long operation. Andy started to remove the drapes.

He did it with a flair and removed the surgical covers as if he were flourishing a torero's cape. The drapes whipped off dramatically. And so did the suprapubic cystostomy tube. Dr. Webster was irate. He verbally cauterized his chief resident, and demanded that the chagrined doctor obtain a blood level of his thyroid to see if he was a cretin or if he was just born stupid.

"So, scrub up, Garven," Dr. Webster said. "We have to put the tube in again. This time you do it; so it won't get pulled out. Our Dr. Nordstrom can watch and see how a real surgeon does this very difficult case."

It was a calculated insult; the intern showing the chief resident how anything was done.

Garven tried not to look at Andy. He and Dr. Webster took forty-five minutes and replaced the tube in the bladder. Garven put in an entire layer of additional securing sutures for good measure. Once again, the two surgeons relaxed.

"Take off the drapes, Garven. Careful now," Dr. Webster said with a snide glance at Andy Nordstrom.

Garven carefully removed the drapes. The tube stayed in. Garven gave out a small sigh. The OR team turned the patient on his side to remove the wet drapes beneath him. The tube fell out. Garven gave out a big sigh.

Dr. Webster had to be called back into the room. Words nearly failed him, but with an effort at control, he was able to launch into a fairly adequate verbal castigation of the imbecilic intern and the cretinous chief resident. It seemed to be cathartic for the unfortunate professor of urology.

Dr. Webster concluded with the fairly mild invective, "Now, you half-witted, fumble-thumbed cretinoid morons, I will do it myself and show you how to do the simplest operation in all of urology. The two of you retarded simpletons stand by and watch while I do this!"

It really did not take too long to repeat the procedure—about thirty-five minutes. Practice had made the steps move by efficiently. Dr. Webster made a new opening into the bladder and assiduously closed the previous one. He layered suture lines and secured the flare-tipped tube into place as securely as a molly bolt. He sarcastically pointed out each layer and its proper closure to the two silent house staff men. The chief was an excellent technician even though he was getting on in years, and he did a superb job with every facet of the simple operation.

Garven and Andy stepped back. Dr. Webster moved away from the table, de-gloved, and removed his gown. He could not resist a parting insult.

"Miss Demarco," he said to the scrub nurse, "you take off the drapes. I can't trust Lenny here—a classical reference to Faulkner's character—and Dopey—another less classical literary character—to do it without screwing up my work."

That seemed to exorcise the remaining demons of anger. He walked to the writing desk and scribbled his op note.

Miss Demarco removed the drapes and the suprapubic cystostomy catheter with consummate ease. It happened so smoothly and quietly that, at first, none of the OR team recognized what had happened. Miss Demarco turned pale. That was what Garven saw first. Then he saw the abdominal suture line devoid of a protruding latex tube. He did not feel that it was his place to report the happening, him being the lowest person on the totem pole, a mere "thing" and all—and a half-witted, fumble-thumbed, moronic, retarded, cretinoid, dopey simpleton to boot.

Andy Nordstrom looked at the cystostomy tube lying on the floor. He had a sad face. Part of the job of chief residents is to deal with bad news. He took in a big breath and walked over to Dr. Webster. Garven and the nurses could not hear Andy because he whispered. All they heard was a voluble flow of inventive expletives, obscene and scatological characterizations, and blasphemous importuning that called for lightning strikes and damnation of all present. The curses were uttered in a low-voiced monotone without shouting, but Dr. Webster's face was purple. Garven was afraid the man would have a stroke or, at best, would have to be carried out of the operating room in a straitjacket and have to go directly to the "bug ward."

The circulating nurse did her best to comfort the distraught surgeon and finally succeeded in getting him to go to his office. He was still talking to himself as he left the surgical area altogether. Andy and Garven replaced the tube without incident and with very little conversation. All in all, two hours had been expended in placing the suprapubic cystostomy tube—a half-hour procedure. When they got to the doctor's lounge to change clothes and found themselves alone, the two surgeons in training broke into peels of insane laughter and kept it up until they were too tired to stand and too drained to shed another tear.

106

CHAPTER
Thirteen

There were no Jews on the G-U service that year. That was a serious drawback because Jews usually took call on Christmas day, and the Christians, even the nominal ones, like Garven, gladly spelled their Hebrew brethren off on Rosh Hashona, Yom Kippur, and even Thanksgiving in return. Garven drew the black bean and was on call on Christmas day. John Jacob Webster, head of the urology department, scheduled the removal of a cancer of the kidney on that day. He met the protests of the nurses and anesthesiologists head-on; those of the G-U house staff went unspoken and ignored. Dr. Webster needed the help of one of the town urologists who had made himself an expert in renal vascular reconstruction. The tumor was so invasive that Dr. Webster was sure that they would have to sacrifice the main artery to the kidney, and he wanted the expert help. Hyman Safir was Jewish, and it was the only day he could come and help.

"Hyman Safir!" Ken Ashton, the unlucky anesthesiologist, fairly yelled. "He's nutty. Completely bonkers!"

"I know," Dr. Webster said, "but I need him. You can put up with him for one day. He's a bit excitable, that's all." He was trying to mollify his colleague.

"Are you kidding? A bit excitable? Sharks in a feeding frenzy are 'a bit excitable.' They are nothing in comparison to Hyman. When he's calm, he's like a chimpanzee on amphetamines! He gets crazier than the proverbial outhouse mouse!" He was getting more strident and hyperbolic by the minute. "What have I ever done to you, J.J.? You know the nurses hate him. He has the biggest fund of anti-women jokes in the country. It drives them wild."

Garven kept to himself. It was apparent that he was not expected to enter into the conversation, being a mere "thing," so he kept quiet.

Hyman Safir moved into the room like a turpentined cat. "Merry Syphilis and a Happy Gonorrhea!" he chimed as he swept about the room, disrupting nearly everything.

He rearranged the Mayo trays, altered the drapes, insisted on doing the positioning, scrubbing of the patient, and draping himself, then rushed out to scrub his hands. The chief of urology scurried to keep up. Garven was ignored.

"Hey, J.J., did you hear about the murdered woman out in The Valley—the one that all they found was her head?"

Dr. Safir appeared quite serious. He was busily dissecting in the depths of the wound as he spoke.

"No," said Dr. Webster, hoping it was not another one of Safir's sick jokes.

"Yeah, it was terrible. She'd been raped," he continued.

"How'd they know that if all the cops found was her head?" Dr. Webster asked and instantly wished that he hadn't.

"By the smile on her face," Dr. Safir guffawed.

Garven made himself as small as possible. The nurses cast dirty looks at the infamous woman hater.

As advertised, the tumor was a crab-like monster that enveloped the ureter, vein, and artery, infiltrated the lumbar muscles, and had very nearly replaced the entire kidney. The two senior surgeons sweated and grumbled, but did a beautiful job in cleaning off the ureter and were working on the artery. The atmosphere was calm and professional, belying the anesthesiologist's apprehensions. Garven was having a hard time seeing around Dr. Webster and Dr. Safir or Andy Nordstrom, the chief resident, into the wound, and his arm was getting tired from holding the idiot stick retractor at arm's length, but otherwise was picking up a tidbit here and there.

Dr. Hyman was a generally pleasant and congenial fellow, if "a bit excitable," but he had one blind spot. He roundly disliked women, and thought they had no place in medicine. If he had his way, he would have had all male nurses. The women in the operating room did not take him altogether seriously, but from time to time, he got on their nerves, and rarely they allowed themselves to get back at him. At least, that was how Garven reconstructed the scenario that transpired that afternoon.

Dr. Ashton told a few jokes as the surgeons went about their meticulous work. On a serious note, he said, "I read a scary statistic, one that we could probably verify through our ER. Somebody did some research and found that every twenty minutes in our country, a woman gets abused, beaten, or murdered. That's terrible, don't you think, Hyman?"

Garven would not have thought that the urologist, who was so engrossed in his dissection, had heard the anesthesiologist.

But the surgeon said, without looking up, "Yeah, that is terrible. You wouldn't think that there were that many women misbehaving."

His statement set the nurses' teeth on edge.

He compounded the offense by muttering, "Most women should just be regarded as passing fannies anyway."

"Really, Dr. Safir," complained the circulating nurse.

"Didn't like that one, dear?" he said sweetly. "Did you hear about the woman who was raped in all three orifices and was robbed of twenty-two bucks?" He looked around and got nothing but cold-fish stares. "No? It's a true story."

"I grant you that," said the scrub nurse. "I read it in yesterday's *Republic*. That was terrible. Now, don't you really think that, Dr. Safir? You can't be that against women. What have you got to say about that?"

"All I can say is that she sure got her money's worth." He guffawed again.

Nothing more was said. Dr. Safir announced that he had to leave for a call of nature.

"I still have to get to the back of the renal artery. Once that's clean, we will have a specimen, and we can close up. Don't touch the artery, J.J.; I'll be right back."

He left wearing his gown and gloves.

J.J. Webster did not like being condescended to in front of his house staff. He, like every other surgeon in the world, was averse to being given orders and was contrary enough to do the opposite of what he had been told. He took up the dissecting clamp and scalpel, and started to cleave tumor off the artery.

Suddenly, a geyser of blood erupted from the tumor bed.

"Put a clamp on it, Andy, before it gets away from us!"

Andy put several clamps near the furiously bleeding artery but was only partially successful. Dr. Webster was too old for this sort of thing and was becoming very excited.

Garven strove to staunch the bleeding with the use of the large pool sucker, then jammed a large sponge. The bleeding subsided, but the artery was still ready to bleed as soon as the sponge tamponade was released. Dr. Safir reentered the room, unaware of the bleeding problem.

"*Schreckligen!*" he howled when he looked in and saw the soaked sponge. "*Putz!*" he called Dr. Webster.

That was not particularly helpful.

Dr. Safir hurriedly stripped off his gown and demanded a new pair of gloves. He moved so quickly that the nurse could not do up the back of his gown. He icily moved Garven aside and inspected the wound. He calmly demanded a set of draping towels and applied them unnecessarily around the opening, fixing them in place on the skin with towel clips. Towel clips are clamps with talon-like ends that bite into the flesh and clamp shut to hold the tissue and towel in place.

The circulating nurse said, "Dr. Safir, I have to towel clip the back of your gown. Hold still please."

He ignored her and created a moving target for the woman, who was only trying to maintain sterility.

"So let's see the damage you've done, J.J.," said Dr. Safir to his colleague.

Dr. Webster nodded to Garven, who gently lifted up the compressing sponge.

The nurse applied the towel clip to the back of Dr. Safir's gown at the exact moment that Garven fully released the pressure on the large tear in the major artery. Unfortunately, Murphy's Law, or some close corollary, came into force. Coincidence then wreaked havoc. The artery erupted, the nurse caught the skin of Dr. Safir's back with the claws of the towel clip, and Dr. Webster successfully applied a clamp to the bleeding end of the artery simultaneously. The bleeding ceased immediately.

Dr. Safir screamed in genuine agony, "Take that thing off, aaa, aah!"

Knowing nothing about the towel clip in the surgeon's back, Andy Nordstrom swiftly unclamped the artery, following what he thought were the surgeon's orders. The nurse released the towel clip in Dr. Safir's back at the identical moment. The blood again geysered.

"Put that clamp back on, you idiot!" yelled Dr. Safir, beside himself with rage.

Andy reapplied the arterial clamp, knowing that the order and the descriptor were aimed at him. The nurse reapplied the towel clip to the back of the gown, resenting being called an "idiot." Fortunately, the bleeding stopped. Unfortunately, the towel clip was once again clamped into the already tender skin of the irate surgeon.

"Take it off!" he screamed.

Dr. Webster was getting confused. He could not fathom why his excitable colleague wanted him to, but he undid the clamp. The nurse undid the towel clip. Blood once again pumped out of the open artery.

"Put it back on!" Dr. Safir barked.

On went the arterial clamp. On went the towel clip. Another scream.

"Take it off!"

This time, Garven, who had been obliged to stand aside, prevented the removal of the arterial clamp by shouting, "Andy, not the clamp on the artery! Leave it be!"

The surgical dissection bed remained dry. The nurse was a trifle slower to catch on and left the towel clip in place. Dr. Safir did a pirouette with the circulating nurse circling him. Finally, he stopped long enough for the offending towel clip to be removed, and things settled down.

Dr. Safir insisted vehemently that the nurses had done this to him on purpose despite equally impassioned denials. For all of that, the operation went well in the end. Afterward, Garven ran into the nurses as they were leaving to go home. While they continued to protest their innocence, he noticed that they went into fits of undisciplined laughter when they came to certain parts of the retelling of the story. Garven felt weakened by the release he obtained from his own jocular reaction.

The story of the day's events did little to assuage Elizabeth's upset at having had to celebrate Christmas alone. She did not see Garven until the following evening, when he arrived at their suite in the Beverly Hills Hotel too exhausted even to maintain his end of a long conversation. He had a day off on the twenty-seventh.

The last thing she said to him, as he wafted off to sleep was, "I have something important to say to you tomorrow."

Although Garven had to be on the ENT ward to start his rotation at six the following morning, Elizabeth had gotten up earlier than him. She was in the bathroom with the door closed, a departure from their usual very open policy about bathroom matters. When she came out, she looked pale and ill.

"What's the matter, Elizabeth?" Garven asked.

He was afraid that she might have been vomiting and might be getting the flu. He hoped that she would not ask him to stay with her for the day.

"Oh nothing," his wife said.

Despite her wan facial aspect, she appeared to be quite cheerful. Garven felt better; it did not look as if he were in for any kind of argument about his lack of consideration for her needs, a not-infrequent complaint leveled at him of late.

"I thought you might be sick," Garven said.

He hoped that might be a safe thing to say now.

"Well, I am, kind of," Elizabeth said coyly.

Garven was not sure what that meant; so, he waited.

"Don't you want to know what's going on?" she asked.

Whatever it was, Garven hoped the conversation would not have to drag on overlong. He had a thing about being late to rounds.

He plunged right in. "I do," he said. "So what's the problem?"

"Oh, there's no problem," Elizabeth responded unhelpfully.

Garven arched an eyebrow at his wife. She started to laugh.

"Okay, Elizabeth, I give up. Out with it."

To his surprise, Elizabeth rushed to him and threw her arms around him, pinning his arms to his chest. She squeezed hard and wobbled him about.

"We're going to have a baby, dear!" she exulted.

You could have blown Garven over with a whisper. They could not be having a baby. It was impossible. It would have had to be by parthenogenesis, he thought, for as much as he was home.

"Are you sure?" he asked once he collected his thoughts.

"You bet I am!" she said excitedly.

"How long…I mean, when?" Garven queried bemusedly.

"About six weeks. During the two full days of our November honeymoon," Elizabeth said with a delighted laugh.

His face was a comical study in perplexity, an archetypal husbandly response. Whether Garven was glad about the impending blessed event or not, he would have to ponder.

But, at least, he had the good grace to break into a wide grin and say, "Great! I'm thrilled! Let's hope it's a girl and looks like her mother."

It was exactly the right thing. Elizabeth hugged him right out the door.

112

CHAPTER
Fourteen

The ENT resident was reading the *Arizona Republic* when Garven walked onto the floor. The front page carried the headline: "MINIMUM WAGE NOW $1.00." The article said that 2,000,000 people would be affected. There was a rehash editorial about the Supreme Court striking down the southern "separate but equal" laws and its effect outside the South that did not interest him, and another that was written by a committee of Hollywood writers and actors who had been blacklisted as communists. They raked up the unfortunate condemnation of Senator McCarthy by the Senate and pleaded for justice for themselves now that their arch nemesis was gone from the scene. Garven picked up the editorial page out of the surprised resident's hands.

"It's all right, I'm finished with it," the resident said, looking as if it were not altogether all right.

The article decried and condemned the Wisconsin Republican's conduct in his Senate subcommittee activities. Garven felt almost personally humiliated. His prevailing thought was that the country was absolutely going to the dogs, the communist dogs. At least, he had not ruined his own career by attaching himself to Joe McCarthy's coattails. That was the only bright side to the editorial written by the local pinko sympathizers.

Ear, nose, throat was a weak service at Osterlund Memorial, overshadowed by plastic surgery and a strong oral surgery teaching program. It was good for Garven because the workload was fairly light. The main reasons for staying up at night came in the form of calls to the ER to do the initial evaluations on facial injuries in conjunction with the arrogant plastics residents and to see nosebleeds. He was able to do more actual surgery on the ENT service than on any of the previous rotations. It was such a standard practice to do T&A's—tonsillectomies and adenoidectomies—on children at the age of two that it might as well have been California law. Garven did T&A's every regular OR schedule day. It was on ENT in a T&A that he came to grips for the first time with what it means to have real surgical responsibility.

Rebecca Joust had enormous tonsils and had had frequent bouts of tonsillitis that prevented prophylactic removal of the easily infected glands. She was almost three by the time she had a long-enough infection-free period to have them out. By any standard of the day, she needed the operation. By the time Rebecca came along, Garven was three weeks into the program and was judged by the senior residents and attending staff to be so proficient that he could do the operations without direct supervision in the operating room. He had done dozens with the same morbidity and mortality rate as the rest of the ENT service could boast—zero.

The tonsils filled the back of Rebecca's throat to capacity. It was very difficult to work around them. Garven had to get them dissected free and a suture ligature into the tonsillar bed to prevent bleeding. The first tonsil was extracted with considerable difficulty and with more bloodletting than Garven had wanted. He had to press a sponge into the site of removal of the tonsil for a full five minutes to get the area dry. He put in the figure of eight suture in the bed of the tonsil, then worked on the second one. He did not relax until the three-year-old was in the PAR.

It was his night on call. He was in the ER, tending to a posterior nosebleed, and working hard at it, when a call came for him from the peds ward. It was from the pediatric resident, and the woman was shrieking. Garven could scarcely understand her.

"Get up here, on the run. Kiddo is bleeding…choking…Hurry it up!" the resident yelled.

Then Garven heard her say to someone in the background, "What? Oh no!" and she evidently dropped the phone.

Garven imagined the worst and tore out of the ER without explanation. He ran to the elevator and ordered everyone in the conveyance to keep their hands off the numbered floor buttons. The elevator was interminably slow. They finally reached the thirteenth floor—hospitals were not superstitious— the pediatrics ward, and Garven dashed off. He did not have to ask which patient was in trouble or which room she was in. There was a crowd of nurses,

114

aides, medical students, and house staff clustered in and around 1324. He made record time in getting to the room.

Garven pushed his way in. "What happened?" he asked one of the doctors.

The resident surveyed Garven rapidly to ensure that he was not some unwelcome intruder. Pediatricians are, by nature, very protective.

"Hemorrhage from the tonsillar bed. Kiddo is asphyxiating from the blood she swallowed. She aspirated. The blood is so thick that we can't get a tube down."

He held a small tracheal intubation tube in his hand, waving it in frustration.

"You the surgeon?" the intern asked.

He and a second resident were trying to put in a subclavian line. They, too, were frustrated.

"Yeah, Garven. I'm Garven," he said.

"Glad you're here. Do a trach. None of the rest of us has a clue about how to do one."

Garven was, at least, on familiar ground with that request. He had done several tracheostomies on goats in medical school and had practiced on dead people whenever he could. On ENT, he had done several, although none on a child.

"Get the trach tray open!" Garven said to one of the nurses.

She sprang into action.

"Slosh her neck with iodine!" he said to another.

He did not bother to scrub his hands. Garven swiftly cut a vertical incision in the soft tissues of the fragile little girl's neck. One of the peds residents stepped in to hold small retractors; so, Garven could see. Garven daubed up the small amount of blood from the skin incision and dissected deeper. He moved aside the strap muscles of the neck and pushed the little thyroid down out of his way. He was moving very calmly and rapidly.

The trachea came into view. Garven swept it clean of connective tissue. He took a number 15 blade and made a transverse incision in one of the middle spaces between the harder tracheal rings. Clotted blood instead of air bulged into the opening. Garven cut through the ring above and below his transverse incision. More clotted blood pushed its way out. The intern took a sucker and removed the big clot. Bright, red blood began to be evident.

"Get Dr. Sawyer," Garven said without looking up. "He's the ENT resident on tonight. Also, call the OR. We have a stat case. We'll have to take her to the OR to stop the bleeding."

He pushed the trach tube into place in the tracheal opening. The nurse attached an ambu bag and tried to hand pump in some air. The air would not move.

"I have it in the soft tissue," Garven moaned.

He had wanted to look smooth, like a surgeon should in front of all of these kiddy-swamis. He quickly removed the tube and tried again. This time, he got it in the correct site, and the nurse was able to ventilate Rebecca. In two or three minutes, the little girl began to move about, trying to get away from the doctors.

Garven sewed the tracheostomy tube in place. He looked into the mouth and saw a considerable amount of bright, red blood.

"Let's get her to the OR! Get a T&C—three units!"

After the blood was quickly drawn, everyone rushed to help get the girl's hospital bed to the OR.

Dr. Sawyer was able to stop the bleeding. He showed Garven his own suture, located too far forward, in relation to the bleeding site.

"That bleeding is coming from the common carotid. You were lucky this time. As it is, this kiddo will have a tough time of it," the ENT resident said as he and Garven finished the case.

And Dr. Sawyer was right. Rebecca developed pneumonia and required bronchoscopy to clear out the old blood and the infection. She was on a pressure respirator for three weeks and IPPB for another two. Rebecca spent three months in the hospital being weaned from the intermittent positive pressure breathing apparatus. Garven learned a lesson from the case. He had a much clearer concept of where the critical suture was supposed to be placed, but that was not the main lesson. Garven learned some humility. Not enough that he lost his nerve for surgery, but enough to make him feel vulnerable.

February was orthopedics month for Garven Wilsonhulme. The orthopods were burly men interested in the mechanics of injuries, the position of bone fragments, and in hammers, chisels, nails, and screws. They spent two or three minutes per patient on rounds then hurried off to operate or to make or change casts. From the first day to the last, Garven was up to his elbows in plaster. Most of the patients were young, relatively healthy, with short medical histories, and none too bright.

Garven put casts on simple non-displaced fractures—the intern cases—with considerable care. With wild abandon, the young patients, usually men, walked holes in the bottoms of their fresh casts, kicked footballs, went out in the rain, and one even went swimming in his cast. Cast clinic would have been a nightmare of frustration had Garven given in to the urge to care whether or not the walking wounded obeyed his advice and acted in their own best interests.

Half the day, he put on casts, including the hundred-pound body casts with a steel frame attached to the skull for broken necks, and the other half, he bivalved casts to open them up to relieve pressure or used the Strykker cast saw to remove casts and then to replace them, only to repeat the process on the same patients in a week. The final half of every day—total, three halves— was spent in ordering, then trying to find, X-rays.

Downtown LA was full of derelicts, and the bums were the most prevalent kind of patient at Osterlund Memorial Hospital. The heroin addict bums had the worst time of it everywhere, including on orthopedics. In cast clinic, Garven had the opportunity to remove casts that smelled so bad that the other street people complained about the stench that would gag a mule. As often as not, Garven could expect to find an infected leg ulcer by the fracture site. All too often, the ulcer had burrowed an infection to the bone, and the X-ray revealed osteomyelitis, true bone infection. It was a good way for bums to get in off the street for a few months. There were risks in that reasoning on the part of the patients, many of whom would do anything to get into a decent bed and to have a run of edible food for a while.

Some of the patients developed systemic infections from their bad fractures. Some died. Many of the old men were in the hospital so long that they had neatly printed cards pinned to the back of their hospital robes, denoting their names and stating: *"If found wandering, return to 4C – Ortho."* Old ladies fell and broke their hips. Especially among the poor, the specter of falling and of sustaining a hip fracture was viewed as a death sentence. One of the most common operations done in the night was hip nailing.

It was Garven's job to put the old ladies' legs into the Thomas splints, the temporary traction device, until the old patient could be taken to the OR. He then helped to place the patient on the fracture table, a modified operating table designed to permit variable traction during surgery. Thereafter, Garven languished in boredom as the residents incised, looked at X-rays, and plated and nailed the fractures while Garven pulled on a retractor or suctioned blood. He learned a lesson from the experience. Sometimes, doctors had to accept less-than-perfect alignment in the plating. The general principle was that "perfect is the enemy of good"; the incorporation of that profound canon of medicine into his thinking was likely the most beneficial thing Garven got out of his rotation on orthopedics.

The only other thing he really remembered about the rotation was how much better neurosurgery looked to him than orthopedics. That revelation came fully home from two of Garven's experiences with orthopedic surgical procedures. The first was a tendon repair.

The patient was the victim of an aggravated assault with a knife. The assailant had slashed at the victim and had inflicted deep cuts on the volar surface of the man's arms—the classical defense injuries. The ortho resident very neatly repaired the severed tendons. The problem was that he did not know his anatomy particularly well and succeeded in sewing the victim's tendons to the ends of his severed nerves. The result was tendons that did not provide mechanical function and nerves that did not afford electrical function to the unfortunate double victim's upper extremity. Garven had a firm conviction that the neurosurgeons could have done better.

The other evidence of the superiority of neuro over ortho came in the matter of how back surgery was done. The head of the department, Dr. Mohler, was the nation's renowned expert on the treatment of scoliosis. Teenagers and a few subteens flocked into the clinics, and Dr. Mohler ran one operating room exclusively for the surgical straightening of backs. The house staff, Garven included, spent considerable time applying an assortment of back corsets, braces, and plaster casts to achieve the straightest back possible for the patient. When that proved to be inadequate in twenty-five percent of cases, the patients were scheduled for surgery.

The operations consisted of long, bloody incisions over the spine—all orthopedic incisions were bloody—and placement of long steel rods that were cranked gradually to straighten the abnormal curvature. The Harrington and Mohler rods sometimes caused constriction of the spinal cord and required revision, and sometimes they broke off and perforated out of the skin, or caused severe back pain and had to be replaced or removed. The surgery was done in a fashion that impressed Garven. It was major, painstaking, and rewarding surgery despite its difficulty and the occasional complications.

Garven was less than impressed with the propensity of the orthopedic surgeons to do a back fusion on anyone who would hold still in the charity hospital. The private practice version of the indications for the operation was that anyone who could pass the "wallet-check" test was a candidate. Everyone has had back pain some time in their life. These operations were big, bloody, crude, and inventive. Backs were fused in front, in back, along the sides, and in the disc spaces. As near as Garven could tell, the fusions produced long hospital stays—upwards of twelve weeks—and resulted in a very small percentage of people who were pain free and could return to work. In fact, the fusion surgeries produced a significant number of back cripples who were worse than they were before their operation. It was evident to Garven that fusions were only rarely indicated, since nothing about the patients' tests gave any indication of back instability preoperatively, and were a remarkable financial drain on Los Angeles County and the State of California.

It was in one of those back fusion cases that Garven had the faith and admiration he felt for neurosurgery once again vindicated. The senior orthopedic resident was doing a lumbar spine fusion with Garven as assistant. Lemuel Jefferies, the resident, was fairly experienced in doing the operation but had never been particularly enamored of treating back pain patients and had no intention of seeing them when he finished his residency. As a consequence, he had not learned to do them well.

The patient was markedly obese, and the exploration was very bloody because the man was lying on his protuberant abdomen, a position that compressed his abdominal vessels and backed blood up into the spinal veins. Garven could not see a recognizable landmark. There was so much blood and muscle trauma that he could not tell where they were. Lemuel extended the incision twice to get more exposure, and that did not help.

Finally, he admitted the obvious. "Garven, I'm lost. I don't dare take off another scrap of bone or I'm going to rooster this guy. He'll be paraplegic, and I'll be sent off to do something dreadful, like dermatology."

Dermatology was considered to be the second worst career fate that could befall a man, right down there below psychiatry and peds.

The very sound of the specialty's name evoked derision on a regular basis: "If it's wet, dry it. If it's dry, wet it. Or else, rub it with cortisone. Now you know all there is to know about dermatology."

It was that grim specter that moved Lemuel to a rash action. He called for help from senior staff. That was not the rash action, in and of itself. The ortho staff surgeons were all otherwise occupied, so Lemuel took it upon himself to call for help from the neurosurgeons. That was the rash action.

David Stark himself responded to the call. He came into Lemuel's operating room and greeted him politely, and thanked him for consulting the neuro service.

He took a quick look at the huge trench of an incision and said, "Why don't you just pack it for now, and come and show me the myelograms?"

Garven packed the wound and stayed with the patient. Lemuel and Dr. Stark walked over to the rack of X-ray view boxes, and Lemuel put up the films. Dr. Stark looked over the images of the lower spine enhanced by instilling a radioopaque iodine contrast material called Pantopaque.

"So what do you see, Dr. Jefferies?"

Lemuel used an opened paper clip as a pointer and indicated an area on the X-rays. "Indentation here is a big ruptured disc," he said.

"I agree," said Dr. Stark. "Which level?"

"L4-5," Lemuel said.

"Do you have the motion films?" Dr. Stark asked.

Lemuel showed the professor of neurosurgery the X-rays taken with the patient forward and back, and to each side. There were a set of good quality tomograms, images that intentionally blurred out everything except the center portions in order to focus on that area.

"Do you see any instability, Dr. Jefferies?" asked the senior neurosurgeon.

"Not on the films, Dr. Stark."

"So what is your diagnosis?"

"Orthopedic ruptured disc," Lemuel said.

To the orthopedic surgeons, discs were divided into huge and obvious lesions that were a clear indication for surgery and into small ruptured discs, known as "neuro" discs. The orthopedists regarded them as being too small to warrant operation and privately castigated the neuros for doing unnecessary operations on the small lesions.

"And what is your operative plan?"

"McGill fusion."

"Why?" asked Dr. Stark.

"Well, if you really want to know, it's what Dr. Mohler told me to do," Lemuel responded defensively.

"Did you plan to take out the disc?"

"No. They don't let anyone but the chief resident and the staff men open into the spinal canal. Might hurt the dura and the nerve roots."

"Well, that's certainly a good policy," Dr. Stark said with a tinge of sarcasm creeping out. "'At least do no harm,' as Ostler said. There is a little problem with the operative plan. When you are done, the guy may or not have a fusion, but he will certainly still have his disease and his pain. What do you say about you and I taking out the man's herniated disc, and get him well?"

"Okay, Sir. I have gone as far as I can go."

Lemuel had lost confidence in himself, a fatal flaw for a surgeon. Surgeons are described as being arrogant. That may be true, but self-confidence, even arrogance, is critical to be able to cut and remove, and commit during an operation.

"Mind it I have a look?" asked Dr. Stark.

"Have a look" is a euphemism for "steal the case."

Dr. Stark cleaned up the blood and evaluated the incision. The reason for the bleeding was that the orthopedic surgery resident had gotten himself out into the bloody muscles alongside the spine, and could not see any of the bony landmarks. Dr. Stark took a pair of dissecting chisels and, in two minutes, had separated the lumbar muscles for the backbone in the correct plane of dissection. He packed the dissected area with sponges, and they waited for a few minutes. He removed the sponges and placed a right-angled retractor, called a Taylor retractor, in one space, the L4-5 level. He packed off all the rest of the unnecessary incision and left exposed a neat view of the one segment that needed surgery.

Lemuel looked at the small operating space suspiciously but did not say anything. Another criticism that the orthopedic surgeons leveled at the neurosurgeons was that the latter liked to work through "keyhole" incisions, instead of in a "real" incision with adequate exposure.

Dr. Stark removed snippets of bone on the laminae, the layers of bone overlying the spinal cord and its coverings, until he had opened an area about the size of a quarter. He put in a slender retractor and had Garven very gently hold the dura and its precious contents to one side. He told Garven at least three times to be careful.

"Take a look, Dr. Jefferies," he said to the senior resident.

Lemuel looked in to where the neurosurgeon was pointing. There was a huge ruptured disc, a fragment that had broken loose from its connective tissue bindings and was jammed up against the swollen and reddened nerve root. Lemuel nodded. It was an excellent orthopedic disc specimen. He had never seen one so well exposed, he thought, and said so to Dr. Stark.

The neurosurgeon removed the disc piecemeal using fine curettes and biting instruments, disc rongeurs. In a few minutes, the entire offending disc was gone and sat, like pieces of crab meat, in a small, metal surgical bowl.

Dr. Stark looked up at Garven and said, "Wilsonhulme, isn't it?"

Garven was flabbergasted that the eminent head of neurosurgery recognized him. He blushed.

"Yes, Sir."

"Can you close up this gash?"

"Yes, Sir," Garven said.

That was something of an exaggeration. He was at the "see one" stage in the progression from "see one" to "do one" and on to "teach one." Lemuel gave him a look, but Garven already had the needle holder loaded with the deep suture in hand.

"What about the fusion? That's what we came for," protested Lemuel mildly to Dr. Stark, who was already taking off his gown and gloves.

"Let's you and I go out to the lounge while the 'thing' finishes up," said Dr. Stark. He looked back over his shoulder and gave Garven a smile and a wink.

The fat patient got up to walk on the day after surgery. It was unheard of on orthopedics and was only permitted because the professor of neurosurgery had insisted. The patient was overjoyed to be able to walk free of pain in his leg for the first time in months. The back pain from the large incision was considerable, but was destined to die down to near nil over the ensuing months.

While making hurry-arounds on the patient, Dr. Stark found Garven on the ward and asked him to have a chat with him.

"So, I understand you are interested in going into neurosurgery. You want to come over and see how back surgery should be done?" Dr. Stark asked Garven.

Garven wondered how the professor knew that he wanted to be accepted into the program of neurosurgery training. He had only told every person who would listen since he left medical school of his ambition.

"I am. I would like to apply. I still have to finish the straight surgery internship and the core year of general surgery before I can apply," he responded.

"Apply now, Dr. Wilsonhulme. I'd like to get the decision made for who is going to come on my service more than a year in advance. I think you'd like it here. Why don't you give it some thought?"

CHAPTER
Fifteen

Garven's first thought, in terms of applications, had to be for a residency position for the upcoming year. Whatever else he did, he would have to secure a "core year" general surgery residency and thereafter apply for the subspecialty of his choice—neurosurgery—at the institution of his choice—UC Osterlund Memorial. Elizabeth was good at filling out forms, and she served as Garven's secretary. They worked together to apply to more than a dozen training institutions. The time was opportune because he was rotating on anesthesiology, the easiest rotation in the entire straight surgical year.

Rounds were simple and cursory on anesthesiology. Garven and the anesthesiologist went to see the patients for whom they would give anesthesia that day and to review their charts, and in the evening, they made a tour to be sure that the patients were not having any anesthetic problems. There was scarcely any follow-up responsibility.

Once he had been on the service long enough to feel comfortable, Garven made the comment that, "I could get to like this. Every doctor I know hates to see patients, and anesthesiology seems perfect."

His mentor on anesthesiology, Dr. Howard Cartwright, responded, "That may be true, but every specialty has its problems. Surgeons think anesthesiology is boring. We say that we have a specialty of hours and hours of boredom mingled with moments of sheer terror. No Specialty—at least none that you can make a living doing—has it all good or all bad. With the exception of internal medicine, of course."

That went without saying.

123

Garven liked anesthesiology. He got there early, learned to put in sophisticated lines, like arterial monitors and central venous pressure lines that were threaded all the way into the heart. He became familiar with the anesthetic drugs and emergency cardio-pulmonary resuscitation medications. Garven was even able to continue his education in neurosurgery while on anesthesiology.

David Stark scheduled an aneurysm, a difficult anterior communicating artery lesion, for the first Monday after Garven started on the anesthesiology service. Aneurysms are thin blisters pouching out from the walls of arteries, and are prone to burst with serious, even catastrophic, bleeding. One of the most dangerous times for that devastating hemorrhage to occur is during surgery. Anesthesiology provided two of the safeguards against hemorrhage during aneurysm operations.

Garven and Dr. Cartwright planned to give the patient drugs to hold her blood pressure to the lowest level consistent with maintaining vital brain blood perfusion during the surgery. That was the easy part and could be accomplished in a matter of seconds, when Dr. Stark indicated that the time was right. The difficult measure was to induce hypothermia—to cool the patient and her metabolism down to the point that the nutritional demands of the brain were minimal. Both hypotension and hypothermia resulted in a concomitant decrease in the cerebral blood flow and reduced pressure in the aneurysm.

Mrs. Sanderson was wheeled into the operating room at four o'clock in the morning in anticipation of the start of actual surgery three hours later. Dr. Cartwright induced the patient into deep anesthesia. Garven, Dr. Cartwright, and the neurosurgery resident, Hal Chandler, then lifted Mrs. Sanderson into a plastic tub filled with iced saline and immersed her up to her neck. She started to shiver, despite the anesthetic.

"Give her fifty of Thorazine, Garven," Dr. Cartwright ordered.

The shivering decreased.

"Give her another fifty," Dr. Cartwright said after a few minutes of observation.

The shivering stopped.

The OR nurses started continuous iced saline enemas. The process of dropping the temperature was a slow one—about half a Fahrenheit degree an hour to begin with, then the fall in temperature accelerated. It was painful work. Everybody's hands were blue and freezing cold. It was hard to make them function normally and effectively. By six o'clock, the core temperature, recorded on a rectal thermometer, had dropped to ninety-four °F after two hours of the rather primitive cooling process.

"Think we'll make it by seven?" Garven asked Dr. Cartwright.

124

Their goal was ninety-two degrees.

"Right on schedule. She is where I want her to be. Take the temp recordings every fifteen minutes now. I don't want her to get too cold and have a cardiac arrest. That would be a poor way to start the case," Dr. Cartwright said.

"Like the old saying that you know it's going to be a bad day when you wake up face down on the cement," Garven quipped.

"Yeah, that's about it," Dr. Cartwright said. "I remember a sign in an airport control tower I toured one time that is even more apropos. It said, 'Remember, one midair collision can spoil your whole day.' I can identify with that."

Garven laughed.

At fifteen to seven in the morning, the circulating nurse announced, "Ninety-two degrees. What do you want to do, Dr. Cartwright?"

"That's cold enough, and we're just about exactly on time. Let's get her out and onto the OR table."

The crew hoisted the dripping patient out of the freeze bath and laid her on the table. The nurses and orderlies toweled her off. Her skin remained icy cold to the touch and a pale, bluish-gray in color.

"I hope I never have to go through anything like that," observed the scrub nurse.

"You won't," said Dr. Cartwright. "That's just for patients. We know better."

They all laughed.

The anesthesiologist continued. "Do you know what they call a person who still has his or her tonsils, appendix, uterus, leg veins, and hemorrhoids?"

His audience smilingly shook their collective heads.

"A doctor," the anesthesiologist said, delivering the punch line.

They all laughed heartily, knowing that there was more than a little truth in that bit of humor.

The neuro resident, Dr. Chandler, shaved Mrs. Sanderson's scalp. He was swift and skillful. There was not so much as a nick. He painted the shaved skin with iodine. It was 6:58.

"Temp still ninety-two degrees," reported the nurse.

At the stroke of seven, Dr. Stark and Danny Tucker, the chief resident on neurosurgery, strode purposefully into the room, hands scrubbed and dripping.

As they toweled off, Dr. Stark recognized Garven.

"Good morning, Dr. Wilsonhulme," he said. He nodded to everyone else and called them all by name, including the nurses and orderlies. "Have you done a good job getting my patient ready for her operation?"

"Yes, Sir. I did it all by myself," Garven said as he stood among the seven people who had worked all morning on Mrs. Sanderson.

The assemblage laughed.

"Spoken like a true neurosurgeon," Dr. Stark said.

"I'll give the pentobarb now, David," said the anesthesiologist. "By the time you're down to the aneurysm, her brain metabolism should be the lowest it can get."

"Good. You are a fine gas passer, Howard. Mary Ruth, hand me a draping towel and a towel clip. Let's get this show underway," said Dr. Stark.

On anesthesiology, Garven learned about human physiology and frailty, about medications and emergencies, and about the personalities and foibles, and at times, the flaws of the surgeons. There were surgeons who were slow and never shed a drop of blood, ones who were fast and bloody. There were imperturbable practitioners and volatile martinets. There were important professors who could not cut their way out of a wet paper bag, and interns who were naturally gifted despite knowing almost nothing about the surgical problem beyond the technical aspects of the operation itself. The vast majority of the surgery witnessed by Garven was competent, skillful, and altogether appropriate. There were exceptions—surgeons who joked that they were doing "acute remunerative surgery," and it was not really a joke. There were men wielding the scalpel who were unsafe, and no one stayed their hands. Garven learned the first rule of surgery: What is seen and done and heard in the OR, stays there when you leave there.

Garven finally made up his mind where he wanted to go to do his core year of general surgery in the middle of April, a couple of days before the deadline for applications to be in the hands of the program directors. He was serving his rotation at the Rosewood VA Hospital at the time. The experience was so positive that Garven put in for the VA service.

The VA hospital, located from Figueroa to Grand Street between Pico Boulevard and Cameron Lane, was huge and sprawling. There were multiple red-brick buildings on the grassy campus. Flower Street cut through the middle of it. All around the VA center lay teeming downtown slums with urban decay rife and obvious. The VA maintained its facilities in immaculate condition; the buildings and grounds formed a handsomely kept oasis in the middle of the sea of dilapidation. The pace was slower than at UCOMH, almost tranquil. The number of emergencies, the screaming down the hallway from the ER to the OR, was minimal. The number of bread-and-butter surgical cases was large, and there was an inexhaustible supply. It was an ideal place to learn surgery. The patients were in true need, and were grateful for the care. It was neat and orderly. And the residents were on only every fourth day. To Garven, it seemed like a little slice of heaven in comparison to the big city charity hospital where he was to spend eleven of his twelve months of internship.

Granted, Garven knew, he was not going to see the exotic cases. All of the very complicated surgery was transferred over to the Osterlund Medical Center by contract. There was a close affiliation between the University of California and the Veteran's Administration; but it was contractual, not direct. The VA staff strongly preferred it that way, and Garven liked the idea as well. He reasoned that he was going to be a brain surgeon, not a chest or belly cutter. He did not need to spend miserable nights taking care of the skid row train wrecks. He could learn to be an entirely adequate cutter and sewer at the VA without the hassle of Osterlund. At the VA, the central pharmacy even made up the IV solutions, and the nurses started the routine IVs.

On his rotation at the vet's center, Garven had his specific cuts: he got to do all of the appys, gall bladders, hemorrhoids, vein strippings, and vagotomy and pyloroplasty stomach ulcer procedures. He worked up all of the patients that came on the service—he and the other intern, David Caplan. He assisted on the larger bowel and stomach and chest cases, and he observed his operating skills increasing by the day.

Henry Winston, the chief of surgery at the VA, noticed Garven as well and asked him if he wanted to consider doing his year of general surgery at the VA. Garven was a good choice for Dr. Winston's program. It was a pyramidal program, unlike the straight, vertical arrangement at Osterlund. That meant that, although several first-year residents—usually six—entered the training program, only one would be able to be the chief resident at the end of four years, and he would be the only "graduate" of the program that year. At Osterlund, anyone who entered as an intern could expect to have a period as chief resident so long as he proved his competence. Garven's avowed desire to pursue neurosurgery meant that he would be a source of one painless attrition. Garven thought about the offer, and accepted.

CHAPTER
Sixteen

In May, Garven started his rotation on neurosurgery as the general surgery resident on the service. For a month, he learned what work was really about. He only thought that he had worked hard in the previous months. On no other service at Osterlund was the intern regarded and treated so wholly as a "thing." There were no "intern cuts" on neurosurgery, no rewarding little operations to break the drudgery cycle of scut work. It was little wonder that few interns ever applied for a neurosurgery. The dismal character of the problems that the neurosurgeons dealt with was enough to keep any but the very few from becoming interested. Dr. Stark described those very few as having a "thought disorder" not unlike his own.

Elizabeth could not, for the life of her, understand why Garven wanted to dedicate so many years of his life into a training as oppressive as neurosurgery, at least if the internship were any indication of what lay ahead. Garven was rarely home; and when he was, he was a zombie. Elizabeth provided food, massages and comfort, and a living. Garven provided nothing. He did not even have the time or the energy to listen to her minor gripes about her pregnancy.

The first-year neurosurgery residents worked harder than the intern rotating on and off the service, if such a condition were possible. They assisted all day in surgery, took care of the desperately sick patients all night, and, in their free time, did the "studies"—pneumoencephalograms, ventriculograms, arteriograms, lumbar punctures, and myelograms. Garven endeared himself to the two first-year residents by doing all of the scut and writing the results down; so, they could look good on rounds. He made sure that the patients were where they were supposed to be when they were supposed to be there, which was historically unheard of. That made the residents' workloads a little lighter, and they were favorably disposed to Garven.

The payoff came in a form that further endeared Garven to his nominal superiors. Garven showed an interest in doing the studies. By the end of the first year of residency, the neurosurgery residents could only regard them as drudgery. They did not take very long to learn how to do; and after that, the pneumos, ventrics, and LPs could almost be done in their sleep. They knew Garven wanted to get into the residency program and wanted to learn the techniques. They knew he wanted to shine in Dr. Stark's eyes; after all, that was exactly how they had obtained their own residencies. So they taught Garven how to perform diagnostic studies.

Garven was already good at doing LPs, so he found every one of them relegated to him within days of his coming onto the service. The basic technique of a pneumoencephalogram (PEG) was to do a spinal tap with the patient in a sitting position, so it was not particularly difficult for Garven to do the actual test. The pneumoencephalogram was done to determine if a tumor was present and its location. A small amount of spinal fluid was removed through a needle placed into the lumbar spine. Then a similar quantity of air was instilled through the same needle. The air, being lighter than the CSF, rose to the top. The patient was sitting, so the air made its way into the water chambers of the brain—the ventricles. By taking X-rays from several directions and with the patient in a number of different positions, it was possible to tell if there was a mass distorting the ventricles and to infer indirectly its location and size.

Pneumoencephalograms were miserable experiences for the patients. The air inside the brain caused a terrible headache. The neurosurgeons regularly did the procedure to evaluate chronic headaches and commented that, "If the patient thought they had headaches before, they won't ever complain again once they have the pneumo. Then, they know what a real headache is like."

If the patient was annoyingly persistent and insistent in his or her complaints, the pneumoencephalogram would be ordered and was referred to by the residents as a "punitive pneumo."

Garven learned to work the pneumo chair in which the patient sat to have the test. The chair allowed the patient to be turned upside down, on the side, frontward and backward. The positions all enhanced the headache and the punitive quality of the test. Once, Dr. Stark came into the fluoro room in radiology while Garven was doing a PEG. He was sure his patient had a tumor, but nothing was really showing up on the PEG X-rays. The patient was whining with pain and retching. It was a standard wretched experience.

"Too bad we don't have some kind of tomogram X-ray that would show the inside of the skull without all of this, without having to use a contrast material."

He sighed and left.

The second, fairly common test, the ventriculogram (VEG), was a variation on the pneumoencephalogram. When a large mass was suspected by the neurosurgeons, in contrast to the neurologists, it was deemed dangerous to do a lumbar puncture. In this case, a small drill hole was placed in the side of the skull; a blunt needle was passed through the brain and into the ventricle. Again, CSF was removed, and air was instilled. It was a harder test because sometimes, the ventricles were so distorted by a mass that they were not in their normal location or they were so small that they were missed. Because of Garven's experience with goats in Dr. Harralsen's lab, the residents soon trusted him to do that test as well as doing their PEGs.

While it was all right for selected interns to do LPs, PEGs, and VEGs, arteriograms and myelograms were reserved strictly for the residents. The service was so busy that the residents and Garven seldom saw the staff men as they went about their scut work. Garven gradually worked his way into doing the two forbidden procedures as a matter of course.

The arteriograms consisted of puncturing one and then the other carotid artery in the neck, the right brachial artery in the bend of the elbow anteriorly, and rarely, for the back part of the brain, putting the needle into the back of the neck from the side and puncturing the vertebral artery where it enters the back part of the brain. Arteriograms were harder to do for the resident, and traumatic for the patients, but not as bad as the PEGs. It was often frustrating because the resident could not get the needle into the artery or got it only partway in and no good pictures could be obtained. When the needle placement was accurate, iodine contrast material was instilled under pressure and serial X-rays were obtained at two per second for four seconds and then one per second. The normal arterial configuration was well understood, and books and manuals abounded to clarify any vessel that might be demonstrated on the studies. Abnormalities of position and stretch of vessels were evaluated to try and outline tumors. The studies also showed blood vessel abnormalities such as the aneurysms Garven saw in the OR and arteriovenous malformations. By the end of the month, Garven could get into the arteries as well as the residents.

Myelograms were lumbar punctures followed by placement of ten or twelve ccs of an oily iodine contrast material called Pantopaque. X-rays were taken from back to front and side to side. Indentations of the column of contrast material suggested masses pressing on the nerve roots and spinal cord. The only two critical things about the test were that the needle be all of the way into the spinal fluid compartment, and that the patient be moved carefully, so that the heavy, oily contrast would not get into the head of the patient and cause granuloma foreign body reactions. Garven was not supposed to do those procedures, either. But the residents taught him how, and he became quite proficient.

It was in the last week of his neuro rotation that Garven learned why the training in some centers was referred to by outsiders as "the SOB school of neurosurgery," and it was his very proficiency in doing the tests that caused the painful lesson. Garven was called into Dr. Stark's office.

"You have been a very good intern, Dr. Wilsonhulme," Dr. Stark said as soon as the two men sat down.

"Thank you, Sir. I tried my best," Garven said.

"I take it that's altogether true. You learned how to do the routine tasks on the ward with real proficiency, I understand."

"Pretty much, I guess," said Garven with a little self-deprecating smile.

"Now, don't be modest, Dr. Wilsonhulme. I will tell you something I prize highly and that's simple, direct honesty. That is something I would use in determining who will be in the residency program and who will not. I have some questions that I would like to ask you with that caveat as a preliminary."

Garven was afraid that the preamble about honesty was going to lead to something he did not want to discuss. He was not quite sure what that would be, however. He looked around the somber dark room. It was paneled with rich teak and mahoganies, and had oil paintings of English foxhunts and personally inscribed photographs of famous neurosurgeons on the walls.

"Sure," he said to the professor.

"Is it true that you do pneumos, LPs, and ventrics as well as the residents?"

"I don't think I would go that far, but I can do a credible job on all of them. I think the residents would tell you that I can work unsupervised on those kinds of things," Garven said warily.

"So I hear. And, Dr. Wilsonhulme, have you been doing myelos and angios?"

Garven knew that that question was coming. He presumed that Dr. Stark knew that he had been doing the prohibited tests. Since he knew that, he did not hesitate, and he made no effort to shave the truth. "Yes, Sir," he said.

He looked Dr. Stark right in his eyes.

"And the residents taught you how, right? I mean, you didn't just sneak down, kidnap the patients, and do those procedures on your own?"

"No, Sir."

"Did the residents stay with you all the time? The way I mean that question is, were they essentially doing the procedure and letting you have some experience to learn, or were they turning over their work to you and absenting themselves?"

This was the crux of the issue. Garven knew that, and he dreaded answering. "Well, a little of both," he replied.

Dr. Stark raised his eyebrows into question marks.

"I mean, at first I watched; then they showed me how. Then they let me do a little to see if I had the hang of it. Then they gave me more freedom; until I did some all by myself."

"Some?" asked Dr. Stark archly.

"Eventually, quite a few."

Dr. Stark studied Garven for a full minute. It was evident that he was trying to come to a decision.

Finally, he broke the awkward silence and asked, "Dr. Wilsonhulme, do you want to be my resident year after next?"

"Yes, Sir, Dr. Stark, I certainly do. That's why I came to Osterlund."

"I've put a lot of thought into this…about you. You are something of a nonconformist, I have observed. You are aggressive, maybe the most aggressive young doctor I have encountered. You knew what you were doing when you did these tests. You knew that you were breaking my rules. Maybe I can overlook that; everyone gets to make a mistake…once. I will put it to you straight, Dr. Wilsonhulme. Are you disciplined enough for this program? Here, you have to do it my way. Maybe, should you ever have a patient of your own, you can do it your way; but in this program, there is one boss. Me. Can you obey my rules and do it my way, if I give you a chance?"

"Yes, Sir. I'm sorry I violated your rules. I was overenthusiastic. I wanted to learn everything. I looked at it as a competition, and I did everything I could do to win. What I wanted to win was a place in your program. I will kick my own butt from here to kingdom come if I have screwed up my chances. I can do exactly what you want, if you'll give me the chance."

There was a momentary pause. Then Dr. Stark stood up and walked to where Garven was sitting. The professor offered Garven his hand, and Garven shook it firmly.

"Done," said Dr. Stark. "I want you to know something. That handshake is a contract. I will not back out, and I expect you to do the same. Now, I have a harsh lesson for you to learn. You have one more month in your internship, and I want you to spend it here with us as a junior resident. If you agree, I can arrange it with Dr. Lyons. You can live without a rotation on surgical path or one of the subspecialties, can't you?"

"Yes. I was assigned to surgical oncology. I can always have the rotation next year. It won't be any great loss for me or the program, I'm sure. But...I don't understand. Are you going to have three junior residents, Dr. Stark?" Garven responded.

"No, Garven," and Garven took note of the fact that Dr. Stark had called him by his given name for the first time. "That is the harsh lesson I spoke about. I know you're busy, but I want you to come with me to another meeting."

Garven followed the chief out to the ward. Neurosurgery had had a small conference room built as part of the ward. The two junior residents and the chief resident were sitting in the room, waiting for the arrival of the chief. They turned to face him as he and Garven entered.

"I'll get directly to the point, gentlemen. I have one question before I say what I came here to say," Dr. Stark announced.

Except for the background noise coming from the busy ward, it would have been possible to hear the proverbial pin drop.

"Elmo," he said to Dr. Johannsen, the chief resident, "did you know that the intern was doing resident-level studies?"

"Not really, Sir. I probably should have. The whole service is my responsibility, and maybe I even suspected it. Garven there is one aggressive guy, and he would eat your lunch if you gave him half a chance. But, I really didn't know it."

"Typical neurosurgeon," Dr. Stark commented.

The others nodded. It was not to be interpreted as a compliment necessarily; Garven could tell that.

"I'll accept what you said, Elmo. You have always been truthful with me."

"Yes, Sir," Elmo said.

He was very tense.

The two junior residents were pale and sweaty.

Dr. Stark looked hard at the two of them.

"Pretty hard work, this neurosurgery residency business, no?"

The question was rhetorical. It was clear that the professor did not want an answer from either of them.

133

"I gave you a few general absolutes to go by and some specific rules to obey at each level in your training. I did so for a reason. I gave the two of you a warning a couple of months ago about shifting your work. Maybe I was soft, and maybe I just thought you were so busy that you hadn't remembered my rules. Now I learn that the two of you have given over your responsibility to an intern. Never mind that he might be capable. You acted in violation of my rule. This is the point in the conversation when I should say, 'What have you got to say for yourselves?' But I'm not going to do that. I will make it very simple. You're fired. Both of you. And today."

The two junior residents had to hold on to their chairs to keep from falling off. Their faces were so pallid that they could have fainted. They knew Dr. Stark well enough that they knew it was useless to protest. He was the first of the first in the famous SOB school of neurosurgery.

Dr. Stark dismissed the two of them with a wave of his hand.

When they were gone, he said to Elmo Johannsen, "Don't look so put upon, Elmo. Here's your new resident." He nodded perfunctorily at Garven. "And it is not going to be as bad as all that. Those two are not cut out for this ball-breaking residency. Tell them I have put in a good word for them with Angus Bradshaw at White Memorial. He is willing to take a couple of second years in his program. They are a little shaky over there in San Bernardino, and he has a couple of unexpected vacancies. They can start next week. You handle it, though. You're the boss."

"Okay, chief. One question, though. Do you really mean to have just one junior resident?"

"Just for the month. Dr. Wilsonhulme has been doing the work of two for a month anyway. He can handle it," Dr. Stark said. "Better get him to work; we've wasted a lot of time this afternoon in administrative matters. Why don't you take a few minutes to bring Garven up to speed about his new duties? Then you and I can make rounds on my new private patients."

Elmo turned to Garven as soon as Dr. Stark stepped out onto the ward.

"Boy, Garven, you have bitten off a big mouthful. I hope you can chew it. I hate to sound like Simon LeGree, but you are going to have to be on call every night for a month. Hope you're not married or anything."

"I can handle it," Garven said.

He hoped his face did not reveal the mixture of his feelings—regret for the passing of his resident friends, grim determination to be able to survive the upcoming ordeal, gratitude to the powers that be that he did not get fired,

134

and elation that his neurosurgery training career was assured if he could but last out for a month and prove himself.

"Do I need to tell you the resident's job?"

Garven could not suppress a little sheepish grin.

"No, I guess not," Elmo said. "That's what got us up this proverbial creek without a paddle. You and I will have to become real friends. We are going to have to do it all. Hang in there, Garven. You can do it, and I will help you."

Garven was allowed to have one last night off before the month-long ordeal was to start. Elmo volunteered to stay in the house and to take call. It was unheard of for a chief resident to do that, and Garven felt like he would do anything for the guy in return. He went home and did not say word about his new job to Elizabeth, at least not until the evening he planned was over.

"Hey, Miss Elizabeth," Garven said as soon as he entered the Beverly Hills Hotel residence suite that he and his wife shared.

"Yes, dear," she said.

She was prepared for his comment about being exhausted. She knew that he was having a tough time of it, and she tried not to complain about her own loneliness and boredom.

"Give us a smile," he said.

He had practiced all the way home to be light and ebullient. He thought he was doing quite well. He hoped his basic sleepiness did not make him look cross-eyed when he worked his face into a party grin.

Elizabeth gave him a grin.

"Good. Tell you what let's do. I'm in the mood to get out and do the town. How about dinner at Chasen's?"

"Have you gone a little crazy, Garven? You need your rest. Don't you think we'd better just heat up something on the hot plate?" she said but with completely transparent hope that he would not want to stay in coming through her voice.

Garven burst into laughter. She tried so hard to look concerned and sincere about staying in the suite. She shook her head.

"So, put on your party duds, girl. We're starved, and we need good grub. I hear that Chasen's place makes pretty good ribs and fries."

He was giving his best imitation of a desert rat from Phoenix. Elizabeth had to laugh. For one thing, the day Chasen's served ribs and fries, the famous gourmet restaurant's roof would cave in.

135

Garven was actually dizzy when he finally got himself cleaned up. He put on a new black suit, new white shirt, and the red "power" tie Elizabeth had bought for him, so he would not look down at the heels if and when he ever faced her father in a family gathering again. He took a Dexedrine so he could keep awake. It did the trick, and he felt nearly normal again.

Garven had a corsage brought to their table at Chasen's. He smoked part of a Havana cigar just to complete the picture of luxury. It tasted awful, and he merely pretended to drag the smoke into his lungs. Elizabeth was aglow when they left the fine old restaurant. They got into her car.

"This is not the way home, Garven," Elizabeth said as if she were worried.

"Nope," he said. "I have a little surprise."

He would not answer her questions.

They drove to the Crystal Ballroom, and Elizabeth laughed out loud with pure delight. He was a rotten dancer and was on top of her feet as much as he was on the floor, but Elizabeth could not recall ever being that happy before. She was completely caught up with the romance of the evening.

"I am so tickled that you would bring me here, Garven," she said, "an old pregnant lady like me."

Garven patted her stomach and said, "Best lookin' young socialite in the city. I am charmed to be your escort, I'm sure."

He allowed the glow to persist until the Dexedrine wore off, and he was rapidly crashing into uncontrollable sleepiness. As they climbed into bed, he told her of the day's events and about his new job.

"A whole month, Garven? Is that even possible? I mean, dear, everybody needs some rest sometimes," she said, genuinely concerned for him over and above her pique at the grim loneliness that she foresaw for herself.

Garven was rapidly slipping away into the comfort of the fancy hotel bed. Just before he went completely out, he said, "Not the iron man of neurosurgery."

And he smiled in his sleep.

CHAPTER
Seventeen

On the first of June, Garven received a formal letter from the VA hospital:

June 1, 1957

Garven C. Wilsonhulme, MD
C/O Office of Chief of Surgery,
UC California Osterlund
Memorial Hospital
7220 Hill St.
Los Angeles, California

Dear Dr. Wilsonhulme,

It gives me great pleasure to inform you that your application for one year of general surgery training in the Rosewood Veteran's Administration Hospital in Los Angeles has been approved. The period of your contract will extend from July 1, 1957 to June 30, 1958. Please present yourself for orientation at 1000 on July 1. Your duties will commence the same day.

If there is anything this office can do to assist you in your arrangements to come to Los Angeles for the period of your contract, please do not hesitate to inquire. The payment schedule, obligations, rules, and regulations will be outlined on orientation day.

Sincerely,
Henry D. Winston, MD
Chief of the Department of Surgery
(Letter dictated but not read by Dr. Winston)

The letter was not signed, which Garven thought was odd. However, the secretary in Dr. Lyons' office, where he picked up the VA envelope, assured him that it was the common practice in busy doctors' offices to leave the mailings to secretaries, and often, communications were not signed. He was told not to worry about it.

With his upcoming year's work confirmed, Garven went back to his duties on the neurosurgery service. The service had four staff men, including Dr. Stark, the chief, and a Dr. Crendarte, who was strictly a researcher. When the full complement of house staff was present, there were two junior residents, two middle residents, two senior residents, and two chief residents. Most of the time, there were two interns as well. The service at Osterlund consisted of the chief resident, a junior resident, and an intern. Dr. Stark maintained a very active service at the VA and had a senior resident and an intern there. The other residents were sent on rotations to LA Children's Hospital, to the LA County Hospital, and to a cushy three-month stint at St. Paul's, an upscale private hospital in the Hollywood Hills District. One or two of the residents were assigned to the off-service rotations of neurology and neuroradiology, and to the medical school for three-month courses in neurophysiology, neuroanatomy, neuropathology, and neurochemistry.

Garven served as both intern and junior resident at Osterlund Memorial for his last month in the formal internship. A small but significant change occurred from the first day he started in his new capacity. No one called him "thing" anymore. Nurses followed his orders without quietly checking with a staff man or resident first. No one had to countersign his orders on the chart. He was expected to be able to answer the nurses' questions. He was regarded as a doctor.

Garven had learned very early in his short medical career to treat the nurses, the aides, and the secretaries with respect, and he even made it a point to cultivate an acquaintanceship with the people on the ward as coworkers, something approaching friendship. He had watched nursing staff and secretaries put up little impediments to progress, engage in unprovable work slowdowns, lose lab and X-ray reports, forget to do or postpone tasks on patients, and to fight back with a host of similar small passive-aggressive weapons against an intern or resident who was abusive or arrogant. The attitude was that the hospital could always get a new intern or resident, but the nursing and ancillary personnel were important and enduring. Garven found the nurses and secretaries to be genuinely pleasant and helpful as long as he treated them the same way.

During June 1957, that personal policy paid big dividends. Garven brought in a couple of dozen doughnuts once or twice a week. The secretaries set out his lab chits every morning before his rounds so he would not have to hunt for them. He asked the advice of the head nurse on procedural matters and about how the staff men liked to pre- and post-op their patients. He defended the nurses' aides against verbally abusive patients, even private patients. More than once, Garven glared down a nasty and demanding patient who cursed out an aide and told the patient that that sort of behavior would not be tolerated—ever. The nurses and nurses' aides sought out ways to make Garven's work go faster and easier, as a payback. The nurses rewrote pages of orders for Him—one of his direct duties—that was a requirement by the hospital for each patient each week. They had his procedure trays ready and in the room. They got permission slips signed on time. They started his IVs and put in his Foleys. The aides made sure the patients were in their rooms when Garven made his rounds and railed at the indigent patients who dared to complain at small inconveniences caused by the "poor, overworked doctor."

He never forgot to thank even the janitors and aides. He remembered the nursing and administrative staff's names and the names of their families. When one of the nurses or a member of their family got hurt or sick, Garven enlisted the help of his wife Elizabeth to buy a small gift and card. As a consequence, Garven's month was not much more difficult than his previous intern rotations, and he was freed up to do more interesting and educationally beneficial things. The month was not without its stresses, however.

The second Monday of the month had been a grueling one. Garven and Elmo had assisted Dr. Stark in an eighteen-hour-long brain operation—removal of a huge acoustic neurinoma from the posterior part of the brain. Garven had spent the remainder of the evening in the neurointensive care unit, working on a patient with multi-system failure who had been admitted for evacuation of a chronic subdural hematoma the previous day. The man, Clarence Bearer, was a wealthy movie producer. Dr. Stark moved in his glitzy social circle, and the family demanded Dr. Stark and Osterlund Memorial when Mr. Bearer developed serious neurological problems.

The operation on Mr. Bearer had been simple and uneventful in and of itself. Six burr holes—each about the size of a quarter—had been drilled in his skull. "Woodpecker surgery," the aides called it. And the serous fluid accumulation from an old hemorrhage on the surface of his brain had been removed and had not re-accumulated. Postoperatively, the sixty-year-old man had a series of problems. He developed thrombophlebitis in his right leg and had to be treated with bed rest with his leg elevated and hot packed, and given anticoagulants. He had emphysema from fifty pack years of smoking Camels. His lungs barely functioned post-op, and he had had to be intubated and placed on an IPPB machine. Finally, the stress of it all resulted in a small myocardial infarction. The heart attack produced an irregular heartbeat. Mr. Bearer was now known as Dr. Stark's "train wreck" in the ICU.

Garven and Elmo Johannsen, the chief resident, were both asleep in the house staff quarters building at two-thirty in the morning when the telephone rang.

Garven sleepily answered, "Hello, this is Dr. Wilsonhulme, what's up?"

He would have threatened mayhem if some nurse were calling for a routine sleeper or stool relaxer or to give a routine blood value. That was the sort of thing the nurses did to interns and residents they did not like.

"It's Dr. Stark's 'train wreck.' I think he's got a real problem with his rhythm. I think he's having runs of ventricular tach," the nurse's worried voice answered.

"How long are the runs of PVCs?" Garven asked, coming rapidly awake now.

"Some are a few seconds long, some more than a minute… Uh oh, Dr. Wilsonhulme, you'd better get over here. I think he's going to arrest."

"Give him a bolus of lidocaine. I'll be right there," Garven ordered and dropped the receiver back into its cradle.

He sprang out of bed and hurriedly forced on his shoes. He had learned to sleep in scrubs and to wear nothing but slip-on shoes. His activity woke up Elmo.

"What's going on, Garven?"

"Stark's train wreck's arresting. I'm on my way."

"Wait a second, I'll go with you. We can't afford to have famous and important Mr. Bearer croak on us. Stark would put our butts in a sling."

He was in his shoes and lab coat in fifteen seconds.

The house staff quarters were located in a separate building adjacent to the main Osterlund Memorial Hospital patient care center. There were six floors in the quarters building, and three of them connected to the main building via double doors. That was during the day. At night, only the third floor doors

140

were kept open. Everyone knew that, and the arrangement provided security and worked well. Except on this Monday night, a janitor had locked all three doors. Garven and Elmo raced to the locked door, and kicked at it and cursed it futilely. They made an about-face and ran down the three flights of stairs, and out into the courtyard between the two buildings. There were two entrances on that side of Osterlund Memorial. The two harried house staff men chose the south door first.

That entrance was locked. So was the second one. They rushed back to the quarters building, planning to run through it and down the main corridor into Osterlund's lobby. That door had locked behind them. They shrieked curses.

"What now?" demanded Elmo.

It had been a while since he had had to fight the inconveniences of the sleeping quarters arrangements, and he was rusty as well as frustrated.

"Let's run around the building until we find an open door. I'm afraid the security arrangements require that only the front door and the ER entrance are open at night. We are about up the creek without a paddle," Garven said, a little out of breath even before they started.

Both doctors were worried and upset. The clock was ticking rapidly against their patient.

Garven was right. They checked the six entry doors all around the building. Every one of them was locked. The Osterlund Memorial building was nearly a mile around, and the two men had to run all the way to the main front entrance to get in the hospital. They were sweating and gasping when they burst into the lobby. Neither man was in decent physical condition. The training program was not conducive to the health of the trainees.

The ICU was on the tenth floor. Elmo punched the UP button on the elevators. They waited and fumed. Osterlund bought its elevators at the "World's Slowest Elevator Company," and serviced them with "Unavailable Repair Company" workmen. On the best of days, the elevators were dirty, unreliable, and maddeningly slow. There in the middle of the night, no elevator came at all. Elmo punched the UP button fifty more times, venting his frustrations. Nothing happened. The UP button did not even light up.

"Not working," said Garven. He turned around and spied a sleepy security guard. "Elevators work, Sir?" he asked.

The security man took several moments to analyze the difficult question. He checked over the questioner and satisfied himself that it would be all right to answer. He pondered the information he had been given.

Garven's eyes pleaded with him.

The guard finally said, "No, suh. Ah don' reckon they do. None of 'em. Bein' repaired tomorra—that's today now. Nope, don' work."

Garven did not punch the man. He sped past Elmo.

"Up the stairs," he called as he ran through the door of the main floor.

"This better not be some joke," groaned Elmo.

He was not in shape for this.

Garven and Elmo somehow made it the entire ten floors. By the eighth, they were walking, and by the tenth, they took two steps on each stair. They walked into the ICU. The frenetic activity of cardiopulmonary resuscitation was obviously underway. There were machines, drug trays, IV stands, and a host of people working on Clarence Bearer. The people at work had the frustrated look of failure on their faces.

The cardiology resident, Peter Dalkins, looked up and saw Elmo.

"Glad you could saunter over. I know this wasn't a regular neurosurgical emergency, but the nurses thought it was important. When you didn't come for half an hour, they called me. I hope you don't mind," he said, his voice dripping with the sarcasm of an overburdened real doctor having to come to the rescue of the technicians.

"Stuff a sock in it, Peter," said Elmo. "It's a long story, but we couldn't get here. You know how this place is. Nothing worked tonight. Now, just tell me the straight skinny on Mr. Bearer."

"Okay. It's a complete bust. He's deader'n a doornail. We might as well have been doing closed-chest massage on the bed board for all the good we did. I have shocked him, gave every drug on the tray, jabbed his heart, you name it. I can't get a thing going. He's had a flat EKG for more'n half an hour."

"So, even if we got his heart back, his brain would be mush?"

"That's about it. I kept on because I knew you guys were on your way. He's your patient; you make the call, Elmo."

Elmo and Garven moved in to look at the patient and at the ongoing resuscitation.

"Stop for a second," Elmo asked the medicine intern who was pumping on the chest.

The intern backed off.

They all watched the EKG tracing revert to a flat horizontal line of light coursing across the oscilloscope screen. The tracing had been wildly erratic while the intern was pumping the chest and disturbing the mechanical connections of the electrodes to the skin. Now, all was quiet. The nurses stopped their activities and looked at Elmo expectantly. The only sound in the room came from the respirator.

Elmo watched the oscilloscope for a full minute.

"Okay, it's over. Let's pull the plug." He reached over and undid the connection of the respirator to the patient's endotracheal breathing tube. Then he evacuated the air from the balloon that held the tube inside Mr. Bearer's trachea and pulled the endotracheal tube out.

"Cut off the IVs, but leave the needles and the cannulas in. This will probably be a coroner's case," said Peter Dalkins.

The nurses were well versed and did not need instructions. They set out on the big task of cleanup. The nurses hated CPR because they always had to work overtime without pay to clean up the horrendous mess, and they could remember very few CPR efforts that had ended in any other way than the present one.

CHAPTER
Eighteen

Rounds that morning were a very solemn affair. Dr. Stark was furious with Elmo and Garven. His rational mind had to deal with the impossible situation the two residents had found themselves in during the night, but his emotional one wanted to throttle them both.

"I don't want to see either one of you today," Dr. Stark said when he had waited long enough to gain his composure before responding to the terrible news that his prominent patient had died. "Dr. Johannsen, you get to work on this ward and shape things up. Get the charts in order. See that everything our patients need is done. Dr. Wilsonhulme, you spend the day in the 'pus pit.' Don't come out until the neuro patients have been reviewed and cleaned up. They have been woefully neglected."

That statement of Dr. Stark's was grossly untrue, and he knew it. It was all he could think of as an insult and as a means of exacting a punishment. It was also hypocritical. He would not admit it, would not admit that any neurosurgery patients ever got post-op infections, but both of the neuro patients in the "infection ward"—better known as the "pus pit"—were his. He had been the surgeon on each of them. It galled him to know that, and both patients had been in there for months. Garven had been in the pus pit, taking care of them twice a day since he had been on the service. Dr. Stark, in keeping with his unwillingness to admit the existence of neurosurgical infections, had yet to darken the doors of the unpopular ward.

As Elmo and Garven left in dejection to do their K-P duties, Dr. Stark shot off a parting salvo: "I foresee a great future for the both of you in the laundry

144

room. I don't want to hear about another problem or that's exactly where you'll head!"

Garven made his way to the pus pit. The infection ward was located in an inconvenient wing of the hospital, on the top floor. There were two sets of double doors marked with skull and crossbones "HAZARD" signs, but no indication of the nature of the patient care ward otherwise. There was very little traffic in an out of the area. Members of the attending staff were conspicuous by their almost universal absence.

Garven put on new sterile scrubs, a mask, and cloth booties over his shoes, scrubbed up, and put on a gown and double gloves, the standard procedure for entering the large ward. It took fifteen minutes. The smell of pus exceeded that of the room deodorants and the antiseptics, and defeated the efforts of the room fans. As a matter of routine for such exigencies, Garven carried a small bottle of Mentholatum and rubbed a dab across his upper lip. It was a trick he had learned from the first deiner in the morgue where he made his summer money in medical school. Garven made his way around the equipment to where the first of his two patients lay in his bed.

The man was C.M. Brody. He had a moderate-sized fungating brain infection. He had had a craniotomy for a severe head injury in which he had been struck in the head with the sharp end of a pick. The wound had been grossly contaminated and, despite every effort at lavage and debridement, had become infected. Not only had the scalp become purulent, but C.M. had developed an osteomyelitic bone infection of the skull plate that had been replaced. Not only had the bone become infected, but eventually, his dura covering and even the brain itself had been involved in the very resistant abscess. Dr. Stark and Elmo Johannsen had taken C.M. back to the OR and removed the infected bone plate and a portion of the scalp, and had had to suck out the evidently infected brain. C.M. went on to form what the neurosurgeons referred to as a "brain fungus," a very rare, persistent infection in which the brain gradually swells into the skull opening and becomes progressively necrotic. Day by day and bit by bit, the involved brain was removed.

It had been Garven's distasteful job to come into the "pus ward" twice a day and cut off a little more of the infected brain as it pushed its way over the surface. Remarkably, C.M. had lost very little function of his cerebrum; his thinking was still clear.

"Hey, doctah!" he called to Garven as soon as the young man came into sight.

145

He was genuinely happy to see the resident because Garven was nice to him, and more importantly, he was the only person from the outside who ever came in to see him.

"How'ya doin', shorty?" he called irreverently.

"Doing okay, C.M., how about you?"

"Cain't complain, cain't complain," the old Negro patient said cheerfully.

Garven marveled at the old man's ability to maintain his sanity in that pest hole. It was worse than being in jail. Death row inmates had better accommodations.

"We better do a big clean up job today, C.M. Dr. Stark's orders. Okay with you?" he asked.

The materials were at the patient's bedside.

"Yep, sure. Ya is the doctah. Who's Doctah Stark?"

"He's the big boss doctor. He's the one who did your operation."

"And a fine job the man did," C.M. said.

He meant it exactly as he said it; there was not a trace of irony in his voice.

"Ah'd kinda like to meet the man, shake his hand an' all."

C.M. was born in Osterlund Memorial. He got his name from the hospital. The C.M. stood for "colored male," the indicator of race and gender that had been stamped on his birth record. His mother, like many others in Los Angeles and other large city hospitals of the era, had thought that C.M. was the name he had been assigned, and who was she to go against the big doctors and nurses? There were many C.M.s in Los Angeles in his generation. The next generation produced a plethora of B.M.s, for "black male," by the same default mechanism.

Garven took off all of the old head bandages. The brain fungus was frightening to look at, but the patient seemed to tolerate the grotesque, infectious abnormality without too much trouble. Garven trimmed off the necrotic-appearing tissue down to bleeding brain, then desisted. One good sign was that the edges were beginning to turn into pink, healthy granulation tissue.

"We'll beat this thing yet, C.M.," Garven told the pleasant old man. "Just you hang on."

"Doin' the bestis Ah kin, doc. Thass all a man kin do, Ah reckon. An' I gotta tell ya, thass more'n the othah po' infected soul you sees in heah. Looks like he done gone plumb crazy this mornin'. Bes' ya go an' see him; see if ya kin do somethin' 'bout his bein' so upset an' all. Mebbe ya needa lynch his risin' or somethin'. Boo-oy but he did carry on!"

The other patient was Lamar Willis Jones, half C.M. Brody's age. Until he developed a huge ruptured disc, Lamar Willis had been a successful, well-

146

paid iron worker and the sole support of a wife and six children. He was a pillar of his local community and served as a deacon in the AME church in Compton. He had the same obligatory drinking problem as the rest of the iron workers, but it never interfered with his work, his family, or his church activities. Judging by the clientele coming into Osterlund Memorial, alcoholism was a prerequisite for obtaining work as a stevedore, dock worker, fry cook, or iron worker. The differences between those people—the alcoholics—and the skid row bums—the drunks—was that the former drank beer and cheap whiskey, and the latter drank vile wines like Muscatel, Midnight, and Revel that sold for fifty cents a gallon. The other distinction, according to the skid row dwellers, was that the alcoholics had to attend meetings.

Like C.M., Lamar Willis had come by his name from the hospital. In his case, an obstetrics resident had been inordinately proud of his own name. Day after day, as he delivered babies for the downtown and South Central LA mothers, he corrected their notion that the baby boy should be called C.M. or B.M. as was written on the birth form. Instead, the child should be given a good name, a proud name, a name like Lamar Willis. As a consequence, there were a surprising number of Lamar Willis this-and-thats living in LA and frequenting the hospital.

Mr. Jones was quiet and calm when Garven approached his bed. He was lying on his abdomen, as he had to do constantly to allow his back infection to heal slowly. Lamar Willis was mumbling to himself, talking to people who were not there. The nurses' aide came over to Garven as he looked down on the patient.

"Went bonkers this a.m.," she said, taking care not to confuse Garven with technical psychiatric terms. "Started to yell and holler. Talkin' to hisself. Took us three hours to get the shrink up here."

That came as no surprise to Garven. The psychiatrists were notoriously reticent to leave the security of their offices.

Garven quickly went through the chart. Poor Lamar Willis had had DTs early in his hospital course—had the whole gamut of seeing snakes and tarantellas and men from Mars. He was relatively young and healthy, and had come out of the alcohol withdrawal psychosis without persistent problems. The nurses' notes recorded a progressive course of depression at being cooped up and anxiety for the complication of his lumbar disc surgery. Finally, his mind must have reached the end of its reserves and snapped. The psychiatric resident had loaded Lamar Willis up with Thorazine and gave orders for him to have a regular routine dose of the drug, and some meprobamate to keep him calm. The quiet, sedated, hallucinating man before him was the improved result of the therapy.

Garven could not get through the psychotic shield Lamar Willis had set up. Garven spoke of the weather, politics, and about how the wound was improving. Lamar Willis rambled around a wildflower meadow of conversational snatches that made sense only to himself, if anyone. Sometimes, his speech was little more than a tossed word salad. Garven gave up and worked on the wound.

Lamar Willis' back incision had become inordinately painful six weeks after his surgery. The residents had made the correct diagnosis—discitis, an infection of the disc space. The infection was far enough advanced that it was evident from the outside, and a disc biopsy had grown Staphylococcus epidermidis, ordinarily a benign skin bacteria. In the patient's case, it was a virulent pathogen, eating into bone and soft tissue. Dr. Stark had had to reoperate and to remove all of the infected tissue, and to leave the wound open to heal in by granulation—by scarring. Mr. Jones had been on the pus ward for a month when Garven arrived, and was now well on his way to being healed. The wound was clean, filling in with the healthy, pink scar tissue, and was no longer painful or tender. He was able to be up and around on the ward freely. His psychotic break came as a surprise to everyone.

Garven washed out the wound. He removed the old, moistened gauze pads from the depths of the incision. He removed the Montgomery straps, the tapes that stuck to the skin well out on his back, and allowed the nurses to remove and replace the wound dressings by simply tying an umbilical tape string—like a shoelace—over the bulky bandage instead of tearing tape off the skin every time and replaced them with new ones. Garven was just laying in the last moistened sponge when Dr. Stark walked up behind him.

Garven turned to look at the chief. Dr. Stark was watching the young man's work intently. From the scowl on Dr. Stark's face, Garven presumed that there was something wrong with what he was doing.

"Dr. Wilsonhulme," Dr. Stark began.

Garven knew that he was not going to like the rest of what he was about to hear just because the chief had stopped using his first name.

"Is that how you always pack infected wounds?"

"Yes, Sir," Garven said, a little mystified.

That was standard throughout the hospital. He was doing what he had been taught on all the services he had rotated on thus far.

148

"I don't know where you learned that inappropriate, inadequate, and improper wound-care technique. It's no wonder these wounds have not gotten better."

Garven presumed it would not do any good to tell the boss that he had been shown exactly this method by none other than the number two man on the neurosurgery staff, Dr. Chou. He gritted his teeth.

"Well, Sir, I am doing it the way I was taught, and—"

"And hereafter, we will do it my way; the right way. I will show you this one time. Try and pay attention. If you can't do this right, maybe the rotation through the laundry service is what you need," Dr. Stark interrupted.

The chief had the nurses' aide bring a bottle of strip gauze that was impregnated with iodine solution. He meted out length after length of the gauze into the open wound until it was filled to the top.

"Now that's the way I want it done. Can you grasp that, Dr. Wilsonhulme?"

"I think I can handle it, Dr. Stark. Do you want it done every day like that?"

Dr. Stark looked at his new resident as if he had just scored under 50 on his Stanford-Binet I.Q. test. The chief shook his head.

"No, young man. I want standard treatment, nothing innovative. I want it done my way."

Garven was trying very hard to figure out what "my way" was.

"You pull out one inch of gauze a day and snip it off. When the gauze is all out, the wound is healed, and our man here can go home. Is that clear?"

"Yes, Sir. Perfectly clear."

Garven figured there were some 600 inches of gauze strip in the wound. Old Lamar Willis was going to need a lot of Thorazine and meprobamate before this was over.

As an afterthought, Dr. Stark looked perturbed at Garven.

He said, "What are you taking so long for? You've been in here all morning, on two patients. There's work to be done. I need you with me on the glioblastoma from Palmdale. I'm supposed to start in fifteen minutes. Instead, I have to be up here doing your work. Get a move on!"

Garven waited until Dr. Stark had left the ward altogether before he shook his head. He shook off the insults and rushed to change into a new set of scrubs to go to the OR. He changed again; so, no one could blame him for bringing contamination from the pus ward into the brain operation. They were going to remove the most malignant of all brain tumors from a woman who lived in the high desert area of Los Angeles County. Her husband was an aerospace engineer and a very detail-oriented, nervous man. Fortunately for

149

Garven, the patient arrived late. Stuck in the elevator. That made it possible for Garven to place the patient in the proper position for the incision and to attach the drapes. The patient was completely ready when Dr. Stark entered the OR with his hands freshly scrubbed and ready to go.

Garven was pleased with himself. He started walking to the scrub room.

Behind him, he heard Dr. Stark bellow, "What idiot was responsible for this draping? Who? Who?"

"*Menschen und kinder!*" Garven groaned to himself, reverting to an expression he had learned in prep school German. "*Immer schlimmer!*" [Lit. Always worse—going from bad to worse]. "I am the idiot who did it, Dr. Stark. What's the matter?" he asked his angry boss.

"It's all wrong, all of it!" Dr. Stark said in a menacing growl. "Who told you to drape a head this way? Was it that imbecile, Paxton? I should have fired him months ago."

It was indeed "that imbecile, Paxton," one of the residents Dr. Stark had fired on Garven's first day.

Garven just nodded.

Dr. Stark shook his head, expressive of the troubles of a man who did not suffer fools with any comfort and was obliged to endure an endless stream of mental cripples. The boss proceeded to take off all of the drapes and, in the process, to contaminate the entire field and all of the instruments. That served to aggravate his already roiling temper even further. He then scrubbed the patient's head himself. He then elaborately placed each drape in the exact position he wanted it with a running patter of explanation suited to the teaching of a four-year-old.

"No towel clips on the scalp. How many times do I have to tell you?"

He put sutures in to hold the drapes in place.

"No plastic sheet over the area of the scalp flap. Holds in germs. How many times do I have to tell you?"

And on and on. When the draping was complete, it looked for all the world exactly like the job he had done, but Garven felt it prudent to omit any comment on that observation.

There was no let up during the case. Garven, the moron, and Garven, the idiot, or the panda bear or the one wearing the boxing gloves or the one with ten thumbs could do nothing remotely right. He applied the Bovie electrocautery too long and charred the bleeding site, or he did it too briefly; and Dr. Stark knew that it would bleed again. He pushed the Bovie wand too hard and bumped Dr. Stark's hand. He was not able to suck out the accumulating blood fast enough. He had a palsy when he held a fine-curved brain retractor to keep the normal brain away from the tumor for an hour. He splashed in too much wash water, squirted the saline in too slowly or too late. His knots were too loose on the deep layer of the scalp and too tight on the skin. He put the bandage on too tightly and with too little padding, and had to replace it. He forgot to put in a scalp drain. It never occurred to Garven to mention that that was regularly the surgeon's prerogative and responsibility.

Dr. Stark left the room to find out what the other moron was destroying while he had been tied up in the operating room; and Garven took a deep breath, a sigh of relief for the first time that entire day. He was pooped.

Gail Dendricks, the circulating nurse, came up to him as Garven finished helping slide the patient onto the gurney to move her into the PAR.

"Garven, I cannot for the life of me see how you guys can put up with that. I would have punched the old SOB in the nose a long time ago. He treats you like you were three years old and like you were retarded. He told you every move to make and got on your back when you did exactly what he told you to do. How long do you think you can put up with that kind of crap?"

Garven was too tired to mount much of a reply or discussion.

"As long as he doesn't tell me when, where, and how often I can screw my wife, I guess I'll just take it. Someday, I expect to make it pay off."

"Another one of the 'iron men of neurosurgery,'" Gail said with a shake of her head. "It's not too difficult to see why you are all such miserable jerks, present company excluded. Try hard not to be like him and the rest of them, okay, Garven? Think about how this feels."

CHAPTER
Nineteen

June 27. Three days to go in the internship. Garven had not been home to see Elizabeth in twenty-six days. She had come to have lunch with him several times. She, more than Garven, looked forward to the VA residency and some semblance of a civilized life. Garven heard his name paged over the hospital loudspeaker:

"Dr. Wilsonhulme. Dr. Wilsonhulme."

He hated to hear his name paged. It always meant trouble or work.

"Come to Dr. Lyons' office. Come to Dr. Lyons' office."

Since he had nothing to do but a full day's work and had not even had time to shower or brush his teeth, he dropped everything cheerfully and made the long trek to Dr. Lyons' office. The departmental secretary handed him an envelope with the UC Osterlund Memorial logo and address. Garven turned to leave.

"Please open it here and put your signature in the space where it goes. We need to have this paperwork in today," the secretary instructed him.

Garven opened the envelope and examined the enclosed letter:

June 26, 1957

G.C. Wilsonhulme, M.D.
University of California
Osterlund Memorial Hospital
Department of Surgery

Dr. Wilsonhulme:

Your first three-month assignment for the junior residency year at Osterlund Memorial Hospital will be on the surgical oncology service under the direction of Theodore Keuffel, MD. Subsequent rotations will be posted in the department of surgery office. We are pleased to announce that the pay scale for first-year residents has been raised to one hundred dollars a month, an increase of twenty-five dollars.

Signed
Lamar Witkins, MD, PhD,
Chairman of Postgraduate Education,
University of California Medical School System

Garven presumed that the letter had been misaddressed. He had a residency, and it was at the VA Hospital, not at Osterlund Memorial. Also, it would be unreasonable for a person to have to make such an important decision and commitment with only three days to go before the actual start of the new hospital year. It would be impossible to find a new job.

"This looks like a mistake to me," Garven said to the secretary. "I have a contract for a junior surgery residency year at the Rosewood VA."

The secretary was mildly annoyed to be interrupted while she was dealing with the chief of surgery's important matters.

"What was that?" she asked.

"This letter says I'm supposed to have a residency here, and I already have a job at the VA," Garven said.

"Oh, you apparently have not heard," she said.

There was always the ten percent who did not get the message. You'd think these youngsters would pay better attention. It was their careers after all.

"The university has absorbed all of the training programs associated with the VA system in California. We supply the residents and the training standards. We will provide the teachers. The old VA doctors will do their clinical work, but the university will handle everything else."

"So, all of a sudden, I am an Osterlund resident. All of a sudden, I lost my right to choose?"

Garven's voice was angry.

The secretary looked at the young man with a very sour expression.

"I am sure you can find a job elsewhere if this does not suit you. But, let me underscore something, there are dozens of applicants trying to secure this

153

residency. You might want to give that some thought before you do something adolescent and damage your career. Of course, you can always see Dr. Lyons when he comes back next week."

She returned to her work, exasperated with the ingrate.

Garven had to restrain himself from leaping across the secretary's desk and wringing her imperious neck. He left in a fog of frustrated anger. He had fleeting visions of burning the place down, of trashing Dr. Lyons' office, of putting a bomb in somebody's front parlor, but he did not even know to whom he should direct his fury. He knew what it meant to be powerless. There was nothing to do but to swallow this lump whole. He dreaded telling his wife more than anything else.

He told Elmo what had happened.

"Typical," said the chief resident.

Elmo all but had his bags packed to get out of Osterlund and to his new private practice job in Sacramento. He had been through the whole gauntlet and had become a thoroughgoing cynic like almost all of his predecessors.

"Let me tell you a little story, Garven. It illustrates the system here. Seems there were two Bedouins lost in the thirsty and trackless wasteland of Arabia. They used up all of their food and water, and were hopelessly lost. Death was soon to overtake them. Abdullah and Achmed discussed what to do the following day. If they did not find sustenance, they were finished. When they awakened, Achmed was too exhausted to do anything, so it fell to Abdullah to make the one last effort.

"Abdullah was gone for three days. During that time, he had circled the area where he had left Achmed. Finally he returned, exhausted, barely able to whisper. Achmed was at death's door. Achmed asked in a weak voice, 'I beg you, brother Abdullah, tell me, what did you find? What is the news?'

"Abdullah whispered, 'I have some bad news and some good news, my brother. Which would you like to hear first?'

"'The bad news. Might just as well get it over with,' said Achmed sadly.

"'The bad news is,' said Abdullah, 'there is nothing out there but the dung of camels.'

"Achmed pondered about what possible good news there could be after that terrible news. 'And pray, what is the good news, brother Abdullah?'

"'Well,' Abdullah said, 'I told you there was nothing but camel dung out there…I am pleased to report that Allah has provided us with all of the camel dung we could ever want in all of our lives!'"

Garven thanked the chief resident for his uplifting story.

The last three days of June were relatively easy. The division of neurosurgery did not admit anyone but emergency patients and did no elective surgery in anticipation of the dangerous transition days from the old to the new house staff. Garven had a little time to establish for certain that he had been officially ill-used and to be used to the idea. He tried to learn to accept his windfall of "all the camel dung he could ever want."

He called Dr. Wilsonhulme in Arizona to complain to him. His father reminded him of the old Slavic adage, "Don't worry; everything will turn out bad."

The wary coyote and the reluctant skeptic in Garven did not doubt it, and he seethed with ruminations of eventual revenge as he contemplated the hard core general surgery residency year he faced.

CHAPTER
Twenty

Elizabeth Wilsonhulme appreciated the transition from intern to first-year resident. At least, Garven was home some nights; his call schedule was every other day, but most of the days when he was not on call, he could come home. He was less exhausted, not a lot less, but some. Garven even started to read some nonmedical books. In the evening, Elizabeth sat by her husband and read a strange book by William Faulkner called *Fable* that told about the crucifixion of Christ as set in World War I. Garven read at *No Time for Sergeants* by Mac Hyman and *The Bird's Nest* by a woman author named Shirley Jackson. Elizabeth found it odd that Garven would want to read a medical kind of book, especially one about a psychiatric disorder. Garven told Elizabeth that it was about a girl who had four personalities. He was inclined to doubt the reality of the disorder and said, cynically, that he was sure that the therapist had planted the idea for the personalities in the young girl's mind.

Garven was on the oncology—cancer—service at Osterlund Memorial. He had two staff men over him—Ted Keuffel, the chief, and Randal Cunliffe, the number two man. Garven had two interns under him, Jeff Hodges and Marcus Whitesides. There was not enough surgery for a senior resident. That led to the two main benefits of being on the cancer service. Garven was allowed to do several large cases with supervision, and there was seldom enough work to keep him in the hospital beyond six p.m. on his night off. The disadvantages were that many of their patients had fatal problems and it was not a happy place in which to work for most people. With his naturally

156

rather cold personality, the fatalities and the dismal milieu did not particularly bother the new first-year resident cancer doctor. A thick skin seemed to him to be a prerequisite for cancer doctors and neurosurgeons.

He had come to learn not to emote, and the cancer patients provided great opportunities for doing surgery. The surgery being done was beneficial and was the best effort to attempt to get a cure or just to provide palliation that existed for them. The oncology service was the court of last resort.

Garven's first major professional mistake in medicine occurred on the oncology service and would serve as a philosophical guideline for the rest of his career. On his second night on call, he admitted a spindly sixty-eight-year-old man, John Bennion, with a temperature of 105 degrees, shortness of breath, and a productive cough. The patient was an old favorite on the cancer ward, who had been in and out many times. He originally started his course on the ward when a cancer of the tonsil was removed, along with a segment of pharynx, cheek, and lower jaw.

On this admission, the gentleman had a large hole in the side of his face that looked to be lined with frank cancer despite three surgeries and radiation therapy. The channel from the inside to the outside oozed yellow-green pus. His family told Garven that the old man had been in agonizingly severe pain until he had developed the fever and had become stuporous from the febrile illness.

Garven put the old fellow to rest, had Jeff start an IV, and got the young intern to order a stat chest X-ray. Garven asked himself if he had ever been as green, inept, and nervous as the intern of two day's service. He told himself "*no*," but was not certain. The PA and lateral chest film showed a white, consolidated lower lobe of the patient's left lung, a clear-cut lobar pneumonia.

"So what's the treatment?" Garven asked Jeff.

Jeff was eager. "IV penicillin and lots of it."

"So, get some cultures, and give him Pen and Strep. He'll be better tomorrow morning," Garven said.

He went back to the call room and read some more of *The Bird's Nest* while Jeff did the scut work and treated the old man. It felt good to have it be someone else's turn in the barrel for a change.

Garven appeared on rounds the following morning clean, shaven, and in a crisp, white lab coat. He was refreshed after his night's rest. Jeff looked haggard and unkempt. He had been up most of the night. Ted Keuffel and Randal Cunliffe were there, and they did not look happy for some reason. The other intern, Marcus Whitesides, looked clean and cherubic. He was a rotating medical intern who looked out of place among the surgeons.

157

Ted spoke first. "Garven, I need to see you privately while Randal takes the 'things' on rounds."

"Okay," Garven said obediently. "*Now what have I done?*" he asked inwardly as he always did when a professor wanted to have a private talk with him.

Ted took Garven to the call room, and the two of them sat down.

"Garven," Ted began.

He was trying to hold in his anger. Garven was at a loss.

"Do you get the hots by making people suffer?"

"No. And I haven't the vaguest idea what you're talking about," Garven replied.

He knew that he had to work some to keep from responding angrily to such an improper question.

"It almost seems like you did it for sadism. Last night, you did the most inane, stupid, and ultimately cruel thing you could ever do in medicine. The family is so mad that they would like to shoot you," Ted said with deep anger and strong feeling.

Garven was still in the dark. He raised an eyebrow to signal a question.

"I guess I will have to give you the benefit of the doubt that you were too ignorant to have good judgment. But did you stop to think that you should not have treated Mr. Bennion's pneumonia? Here's an old man suffering the pains of Job with that gruesome tonsillar tumor. We can't do a thing for him, and the tumor won't kill him. He could live for another twenty years in misery. Then the Good Lord blesses him with a pneumonia—the 'old man's friend.' He could slip away painlessly and peacefully. The family prayed, actually prayed, that something like that would happen. Then some idiot resident wanting to look like a hero comes along and cures the pneumonia. Dumb jerk."

"Jeez, Dr. Keuffel, I never thought of it that way. I'm sorry. It was a dumb thing to do. I have learned an important lesson," Garven said, chagrined.

"You'd better have. If you do anything remotely as moronic as that again, I will personally kick your sweet patatootie up around your ears; so, you have to look backward when you walk. Now get down to the OR and set up the 'second look' for today."

Garven tucked his tail between his legs and went to the OR. Sylvia Harmon had been operated on for local invasion of a cancer of the uterus the year before. A major clean out had been done and the patient had had a long, stormy course in the hospital. The extensive surgery had been done in hopes of achieving a cure. Now, on the first year's anniversary of that surgery, Mrs. Harmon was doing very well clinically. From everything the doctors could see or find out about her, she looked like a cure. She had returned for a prophylactic "second look" operation to see if she had any tumor that had escaped her extensive bowel workup and to see if it could be removed. The second look program was proving to be very worthwhile in extending patients' lives and in increasing the cure rate on chest and abdominal cancers.

Randal Cunliffe was the attending, and Jeff Hodges, the intern, was to be second assistant. Because it was unlikely to turn into a big case, Garven was the surgeon in fact. He opened the belly, taking due care to avoid contacting the bowel with the scalpel. This was a concern because of the possible adhesions caused by the previous surgery. The three surgeons carefully retracted the bowel loops aside, holding the greasy, slippery intestines with moist lap pads so they could get a good look into the depths of Mrs. Harmon's pelvis. To their mutual dismay, the pelvis was studded with small buds of tumor metastases.

"Have a feel around, Garven. Let's document the mets," Dr. Cunliffe suggested.

Garven moved his hands over the liver and found two big rocks of cancer imbedded in the soft, purple organ. He found the spleen to be dotted with small seedlings that had metastasized from the pelvis to it. The mesentery holding the bowel had hundreds of small tumors, and the lumbar plexus of lymph nodes was full of hard metastases. Garven reported his findings.

"So, Dr. Hodges, what shall we do, now?" Randal Cunliffe asked the intern.

"Well...uh...I guess we could take out as much of the pelvic tumor and maybe the big liver mets as we can. That might buy her a little more time. Might keep her from getting a bowel obstruction or something down the line," answered Jeff.

"Garven?" asked Dr. Cunliffe.

"Sew her up and get her out of here."

"I have to agree. I'm the most aggressive cancer cutter in this institution, and I have to agree that all we have here is an 'eek-a-peek-a-shriek.' Let Jeff sew her up. Give me a call in the office when you're done, okay, Garven?"

"Yes, Sir," Garven said.

The worst ordeal of the day for Garven was about to begin. Jeff was the slowest human being Garven had ever seen. He could not seem to push a needle through a tissue layer in anything under a minute and a half. He was all but paralyzed with ambivalence over how far from the edge the suture should be placed, over which suture and which size of suture to use, whether to use the big cutting needle or the tapered, curved needle. He put one stitch in the bowel, and Garven had to repair the hole. He put holes in his own glove twice and in Garven's once. It took longer to do the closure than the rest of the operation put together had taken. Garven thought he would go nuts.

159

He could do the sew-up job in fifteen minutes and was sorely tempted to steal Jeff's part of the case. But he remembered the rules, and endured in silence while the intern fumbled and bumbled his way through the procedure.

When Jeff was putting in a skin suture, he cut the previous suture with the needle and had to go back to that suture site. He tangled up the sutures, broke them when he tried to tie knots, or tied the knots so loosely that the skin edges gaped open. The intern's face was sweating so much that the circulating nurse had to mop it for him. She had a poorly suppressed look of amusement on her face. Garven felt like going over to the wall and banging his head against it because it would feel better when it quit hurting.

He said, "Hey, Jeff, do you have trouble tying your own shoes?"

Jeff looked stricken. He was hoping against hope that no one was paying attention to his ineptitude, a completely naive desire, he knew. He glanced sideways at Garven's face, and saw that his resident was laughing silently behind his mask. Jeff started to laugh as well.

"Bloody awful, right, mate?" he said in a theatrical British accent. "Right down bloody awful."

The nurses had to sit down; they were laughing so hard.

Garven acted as surgeon or assistant on major resections of lung, bowel, stomach, skin, and muscle for a month on the cancer service. He learned how to staunch serious bleeding, how to undo mistakes like tying off the ureter, thinking it was a vessel, and when not to cut—the most valuable lesson of his month. He committed his first medical malpractice while on oncology.

The case was a routine one, but on a ponderously obese woman, Geneen Crawford. She had a single ulcerating cancerous polyp in her distal large bowel. Ted Keuffel had instructed Garven to do a simple resection and primary anastomosis of the cut ends of bowel and no more if the intraoperative manual abdominal exploration failed to reveal mets. The exposure was difficult and required placement of several lap pads. When Dr. Keuffel left for his office, he complimented Garven on a nice job and left him and Marcus to close. Marcus was not the least bit interested in the technical aspects of surgery, which suited Garven fine. He made good time in approximating the several layers of the obese abdomen, and was pleased with his progress.

"Hey, Garven," asked Marcus, "do you know how to tell when surgeons are having a formal dinner?"

"Nope," Garven said and grinned.

160

Marcus had been thoroughly contaminated by the prejudices of his internal medicine mentors and had a great fund of anti-surgeon jokes. Garven loved them.

"They all have their flies zipped up," Marcus said.

Garven tied off the last fascial stitch of the linea alba, and the belly looked securely closed.

"Do you know how to save an internist from drowning?" Garven asked Marcus.

"No."

"Good," Garven said.

He began tying the big abdominal wire stay sutures in place, the insurance stitches against the wound opening up and allowing evisceration—the guts falling out.

Marcus laughed. He had developed a thick skin about the prejudices of surgeons toward internists while he had been on the surgical service.

"So, Garven, do you know what percent of surgeons have hemorrhoids?"

Garven laughed, knowing he was being set up. "I don't, Marcus. Maybe one percent?"

"Yeah, that's about right. The other ninety-nine percent are perfect assholes."

Garven laughed so hard he had to quit putting in the skin sutures.

The patient did well. She had a little post-op fever on the second day.

"Should we get a chest film and a KUB?" Marcus asked Garven, meaning kidney, ureter, bladder X-ray—a simple film of the lower abdomen.

"She probably just has a little post-op atelectasis, a few little lung collapses because she's so fat. Probably get over the fever by just getting her up and around, but do what you want, she's your patient," Garven said to the intern.

Marcus got the X-rays. The chest film confirmed the little streaks of white that indicated small areas of lung collapse. That was almost certainly the cause of the fever. The abdominal X-ray, however, showed that a large operation sponge had been left inside. The sponges had lead strings imbedded on their top surfaces so they would show up on X-ray, and this one was unmistakable.

"What are you going to do?" Marcus asked Garven.

"Move to Mexico," Garven said dejectedly. "I'm going to get sued. It's a *Res Ipsa Loquitur* ['The thing speaks for itself.'] case, like cutting off the wrong leg."

"She's perfectly fine, Garven. Even her fever went away when I got her up and made her cough, just like you said it would. She may never get into trouble, and you'll be long gone if she does. I'd hate to tell her. She probably will sue," said Marcus, trying to be sympathetic.

"So don't tell her, right?" Garven asked. It was a rhetorical question. He knew he could not do that. "That is the second best way to guarantee a suit,

161

Marcus. Right after altering the chart. Nope. C'mon. We're going to tell her and her husband."

Garven's two main dreads were not the patient and her husband. He hated to confess to Ted Keuffel that he had screwed up, and he had a niggling doubt that the university really had malpractice insurance that would cover him if he got into trouble. He and Marcus went to Mrs. Crawford's room. Mr. and Mrs. Crawford and their two grown daughters were in the room.

"Hi," Garven said. "How are you feeling?"

"Fine. Except I want something to eat," responded Mrs. Crawford.

"Clear liquids maybe tomorrow, and in a couple of more days, we'll start on full liquids, then soft diet, then lousy hospital regular food," Garven said, and the family laughed.

"So, doctor, how do you think my wife is doing?" Mr. Crawford asked seriously.

This was Garven's opening.

He said, "She is fine. The cancer is out, and there is no evidence of spread of the tumor. Mrs. Crawford will probably live to be a hundred."

He let that sink in.

The family looked relieved and happy.

"But," he added, and the family and the patient all looked at him with a flash of fear. "I made a mistake in surgery and left a sponge in her abdomen."

"What does that mean, doctor? I mean, what do we have to do?" asked Mr. Crawford.

"Is that going to hurt my mom?" asked one of the daughters.

She looked angry.

"Doctor?" Mrs. Crawford asked, looking carefully at Garven's face.

Marcus was making himself unobtrusive.

"It means that we have to go back in and take it out," Garven said. "We might get away with leaving it in. Maybe it won't do you harm; but more than likely, it will cause an infection and maybe a bowel obstruction if we do leave it in. If we take it out now, it probably won't cause you a bit of harm. I'm sorry. I know another operation is the last thing you wanted to have. It's my fault, but it really needs to be done."

"When?" asked Mrs. Crawford without hesitation.

"Tomorrow morning," Garven said.

He appeared sober and unhappy, but determined.

"Shouldn't we get another opinion?" snapped the talkative daughter.

162

"No, dear. I have confidence in Dr. Wilsonhulme. He was honest enough to tell us about this when he might have gotten away with it. I'm not thrilled about it, but we'll go ahead tomorrow," said Mrs. Crawford.

"This probably won't set you back more than a day. There won't be any blood loss, and the risk is minimal. I still think we'll have you out of the hospital in a week," said Garven.

He was right. The operation was simple. Garven only had to open enough of the original incision to admit his hand. The sponge was easily found and removed. Mrs. Crawford never turned a hair, even with the second operation. She did not file a lawsuit, although Garven sweated over that for months to come. He told the two staff men after she had been discharged.

Ted Keuffel said, "We knew about the sponge the day you found it. We were just waiting to see how you would handle it. You were right up front with me. You know how I feel about lying: Lie to me and you're toast. I think you did all right with the family, too. It's not wonderful to leave a sponge in a wound, but everybody gets to do it at least once in their career. Anyone who has never left in a sponge either has not done enough cases or is lying. Patients should beware of the surgeon who has never had a complication. You can be glad that this happened early in your career. You know how careful you have to be. It's no fun having that conversation with the family, right, Garven?"

"You're the master of understatement," Garven said.

"I liked the way you told the family. You were a stand up guy. They responded to that. I think you have learned several lessons, hard ones, like most of the lessons of surgery. Let's get back to work," Ted concluded.

CHAPTER
Twenty-One

For their first anniversary celebration—six weeks late—Garven took Elizabeth to dinner at Scotty's Castle in Death Valley. He had an entire Saturday off before starting his three-month rotation on general surgery. It was scorching hot; they sweltered. Elizabeth was in her eighth month of pregnancy, and she suffered. But the day of freedom and great food was rejuvenating to each of them, and more importantly, to their marriage. Elizabeth had been unhappy and felt roundly neglected. Garven felt frustrated, guilty, and powerless against the demands of his training program. The day together served to erase almost all of Elizabeth's growing dark moodiness. Garven spent his entire month's earnings on the splurge, insisting that this little vacation had to come from his own funds. He forgot to get her flowers or a card.

Elizabeth went into labor on August 12. It was a long, drawn-out, debilitating struggle. The only saving grace was the paracervical block administered by the overworked resident during the twentieth hour. The block served to stop all of the pain, but also shut down all progress of the delivery. Elizabeth's water had broken six hours earlier, and there was concern about her developing puerperal sepsis. When the baby's heartbeat began to slow, they took her for a C-section. It was a boy—a six-pound, eight-ounce boy. Garven missed most of the labor because he had to assist on a GSW to the abdomen. The ER had been inundated by the aftermath of a gang fight, and all of the on-call residents were called into service. He barely made it to the C-section. Garven was exhausted from his night's work but was excited and proud at the arrival of the baby. Elizabeth was still sleeping off the effects of the anesthetic,

164

and Garven did not get a chance to tell her about his joy at the birth of Peter Arthur Wilsonhulme, named, at Garven's request, after the two grandfathers.

His next assignment was on Surgery A, Peter Lyons' service. Before Garven came, the services had been designated by color, and the chief's service had been purple, referred to as "royal purple" by everyone else. Green surgery had drawn an unacceptable number of comments over the years about the observation that pus was green, and "white" surgery seemed to be so pristine and angelic a choice that the rough-talking and living surgeons always felt uncomfortable with that color. Lyons gave the staff men a choice—numbers one through four or alphabet letters, A through D. The numbers connoted ranking, and they rejected that option. That was how Garven came to be on "A" surgery. The irreverent referred to that service as "any old surgery" or just "a surgery."

The work resumed in earnest. Garven was paired up with Harry Chang, who was no less of a red-hot as a resident than he had been as an intern. They were on call every other day—thirty-six hours on and twelve hours off—in theory. Most of the time, they worked well into their twelve hours off.

Garven did less scut. He had to back up the interns and clean up when they messed up or forgot or failed. One of the interns was lazy and slow, and had an attitude problem. Garven left it to the nurses to straighten him out. They made life miserable for the arrogant peds rotator, and he was slowly beginning to come around. Garven had more responsibility now.

When something went wrong, the senior resident, the chief resident, or the staff did not go to the intern, even if it were his fault. They went straight to Garven. Garven did not think of that as being unjust. He knew it was part of the training; he had to be a leader and he had to learn responsibility. He learned to let it run down hill. The interns screwed up, and Garven landed on them with both feet. He learned why they were called "thing." They did not deserve better. He regularly treated them like "things," just like Harry and all of the other residents and staff men, and he did not have a moment of trouble with his superego over it. Garven saw it as a necessary part of the "thing's" educations.

In his position as a resident, Garven had new responsibilities on the ward and in the operating room. He had new things to learn. It was his responsibility to keep beds available for new admissions, so he had to get patients out, either by discharging or by dumping them. The beds were chronically full because of the necessity of keeping their indigent and drug addict patients overly long to treat their many side ailments and because they were so irresponsible.

"Dumping" was a time-honored, universally-practiced, and despicable method of transferring undesirable patients from one service to another, either by deception or by intimidation. Internists dumped on surgeons by sending chronic belly pains for surgery, knowing that they had alcoholic gastritis, and surgeons dumped on internists by transferring post-op patients who had lung or heart problems. In each instance, the condition of the patient would be exaggerated. All services deplored dumping, and they all did it.

Garven's major coup in dumping came when he was able to move a woman to psych. Ordinarily, it was all but impossible to get a psych resident even to come and do a consult on a surgery patient. Garven had an extraordinarily unattractive, obese, foul-mouthed woman on his service whose wound would not heal. Fat people have a worse time healing in general. She was taking up a bed, and Garven needed to admit a gall bladder for himself. He called the psych secretary and told her that he had a great consult for them.

She said, "None of the residents or staff is available. You should try again tomorrow, maybe."

He said, "But, you don't understand. I can't put this on the written consult, but this is a great case. Take one of those guys and tell him that I have an absolutely gorgeous young woman, a starlet, who is in sexual storm down here. We can't deal with her. She's all over us. We need help. She's threatening to leave AMA. I don't know if I can keep her any longer."

Leave against medical advice? Not likely. The woman, a derelict, loved being in the hospital. The wound infection was the best thing that had happened to her in fifteen years.

"Well, I'll check with our first year. He's only been on the service for a month. I don't know what he'll do. He might not like to take the responsibility," the secretary said.

"You do that. I'm sure he'll be interested," Garven said.

He held on the line.

In a few minutes, the secretary returned. "You did say 'sexual storm,' did you not, doctor? I'm sorry. I've forgotten your name."

"Lyons, Peter Lyons," Garven said. "And, yes, it was 'sexual storm,' bad case of it. We can't handle this starlet."

"Our Dr. Dupres said to send her up then. You need to send a written consult along with her," the secretary said. "Thank you for consulting us, Dr. Lyons."

166

"Oh, the thanks is mine, Ma'am," Garven said. He wrote out the consult and put it in the envelope. Every word in that consult was the truth:

Fifty-two year old woman post-op bowel resection for diverticulitis has poorly-healing wound. Patient picks at her wound, is uncooperative, profane, and combative at times. Unable to control her on our service. Thank you for your help in accepting this fine lady in transfer.
Signed (illegibly)
Garven C. Wilsonhulme, MD

Of course, there was trouble the next day. But no one could read the signature, and no one challenged Dr. Lyons, the chief of surgery, when he said that he knew nothing about the matter.

Garven had to learn to protect his turf from dumpers, and to become clever and quick on both offense and defense. In matters pertaining to the operating room, he had to learn the best devious ways of getting the good cases for himself and of dumping the bad ones on Harry Chang or even on another of the surgery services. There was serious competition when it came to surgery, unlike when dealing with psychiatrists or internists, who were gullible enough to make Garven almost regret some of his better coups.

Harry's best feature was that he was such a conscientious and hardworking doctor. His second best feature was his honesty. Garven liked that aspect of Harry's makeup best of all. He did not dump on Garven, i.e., saw to it that Garven got the bad cases. He did not steal from Garven, i.e., took the good cases out of the proper rotational sequence. That made him very vulnerable to Garven, because Garven had no qualms about dumping or stealing when it came to surgery. He considered all to be fair in war, and this was a sort of war. Harry's honesty was so deeply rooted that he tended to consider other people honest as well as himself. Garven thought Harry had a lot to learn.

While Harry patiently waited his turn for the good junior resident cuts—gall bladder and common duct stones, intermittently bleeding stomach and doudenal ulcers, simple bowel resections and colostomies, lumbar sympathectomies, uncomplicated inguinal and abdominal herniae, and splenectomies—Garven figured out the system and found ways to circumvent it. The supply of patients came to the surgical services from the emergency room and from the clinics. The elective cases were apportioned on a strictly fair basis. One patient to Surgery A, one to Surgery B, etc. On the day that Garven was on call, he got the patients that were electively admitted that day, and Harry was supposed to get the patients on the days when he was on. That was what was supposed to happen.

What did happen was that Garven went to the medicine clinic and looked up the patients they were seeing that day and which would be sent to the next surgery clinic. He expressed an interest and took over the good surgical patient then and there. The medicine interns and residents were spared the extra work of writing up the consult and arranging the clinic visit, and Garven was able to arrange for the patient to come in for admission to Surgery A on his day, and everyone was happy. Garven learned that the best way to get the patients he wanted was to visit the admissions office late at night. The poor admissions clerks were always overwhelmed with elective admits for procedures the following day and with emergencies. They paid Garven scant attention.

The patients in the admitting room were listed by diagnosis. Garven simply made some lateral shifts and erasures, and finagled the patients into being admitted to his service on his day. He haunted the ER when he could, and discovered a patient or two who needed a good surgeon. He acted official and took the ER patient off the intern's hands. They were so busy down in The Pit that they scarcely noticed. There were comments about the fact that Garven seemed to be the luckiest resident in history in terms of getting the great cases. His stock reply was something about "living a good, clean life."

Garven had to learn to excel in another area that was largely public relations, but that impinged on his ability to get to do surgical cases. The hospital's patients required enormous amounts of blood for transfusions. The trauma from the ER and the surgical blood loss accounted for the greatest need. The problem was that need almost always exceeded supply, and there was a chronic drive to get more blood into the blood bank all of the time. It was the duty of the first-year residents throughout the hospital to procure donors. The medicine residents did not much care about the problem because there were no real sanctions that could be applied to them. The surgery residents were made to care greatly because Dr. Lyons enacted a draconian law regarding blood transfusions.

His law was that if a service used more than its quota of blood, and if it did not get sufficient donors in to replace the shortfall, elective surgery by the first-year residents was canceled. That was a fate worse than death so far as Garven Wilsonhulme—first-year resident and surgeon in training—was concerned. He learned every trick in the book and went on to invent a few of his own to procure blood so he could do his cases.

The simplest and most straightforward method was to ask the family and friends of patients who were going to have elective surgery to donate. These people were not citizens in the broadest sense of the term, usually. And they did not readily take to any sense of responsibility. Garven had to suggest, just suggest, on occasion, that if there was no blood available, they would have to give the loved one monkey or pig blood. He let the families realize that the hospital had more of the latter. He took care to explain the genetics involved. If you had pig blood, or even monkey blood, in your system, what could you expect in your offspring?

The best way, Garven found, was to get a lot of blood from patient's family when the patient was going to have a procedure that would not ordinarily require a transfusion, like an upper g-i series, a simple gall bladder removal, an appy, or was being admitted for observation. You could never tell when an emergency transfusion would be needed in an observation patient.

It was always more difficult to get people to donate after the operation was over, but it was still possible to get some blood by using the right persuasion. There were a high number of GSWs to the abdomen in downtown LA. Often, a bowel was perforated by the gunshot wound and a colostomy had to be performed. A colostomy involved taking the end of the injured bowel and bringing it out through a hole in the abdomen, closing off the distal end in the abdomen. The handsome young shooters who, in this temporary instance, were the shootees, did not at all like to have to excrete into a bag on their abdomens. It was not cool in general, and it wreaked havoc on the love life. The bowel had to be exteriorized for about three weeks, and then could be returned to its normal anatomical arrangement with a simple operation.

The patients with colostomies were required to provide at least four units of blood for their bloodless operation before the takedown of the colostomy could be scheduled, at least on Garven's service they did.

The conversations usually went like this:

"Doctah, Ah wants ta have ma colostidy (or colostopher) took away."

"Well, Sam (or John or B.M. or Lamar Willis), how long's it been since you were shot by that dude?" asked Garven.

"I come inta the mercy room 'bout a mons ago. Had the colostidy."

"Well, Sam, I think we could consider replacing it. Pretty big operation. Think you are ready for such a big surgery?" Garven queried.

"Yassah, doctah. Ah is. Ah am a tellin' ya, ma nature has come back and ma juices is all dammed up. Ah just gotta git this here thang offa ma belly."

"Okay, you get the family and friends and neighbors in and have them give a bunch of blood. We'll need a bucketful. Then we can do the operation. You understand, Sam?" Garven said with a worried face.

"Yessah, Ah does. Ah'll git right hol' of ma homeboys this verah day. Yessah, thank ya, Suh!"

Often as not, Garven arranged for Sam to be admitted on Harry's day.

Another chronic problem of surgery that Garven had to learn to deal with effectively was how to get a consent for surgery signed by an incompetent or stuporous patient. Op permits were essential for legal purposes on every person who had an operation, except in the most dire emergencies, and even then, the permit had to be signed by the patient or by someone in the family post-op. The most logical thing to do was to get the family in and have them sign for the patient who had temporarily or permanently lost the use of his or her mental faculties. That would be the way to do it with citizens. However, most of the patients at Osterlund Memorial did not have families. Garven figured that most of them either hatched, spawned, or dropped out of trees and into downtown LA. There was seldom a next of kin or guardian around and never when they might be needed.

The next alternative—another legal method—was to have the patient declared officially mentally incompetent, have a guardian appointed, and to communicate with the guardian about the surgery and to debate whether or not such an operation should be done on this poor soul for this or that humanitarian reason. It would have taken three weeks to accomplish that on every patient, and Garven and his cohorts saw several such problems every day. Perhaps, if they worked forty-eight hours a day to comply with that sort of nicety, it would have been possible. Since the residents and interns could only work thirty-six hours each day, it was impractical. And besides, the majority of the patients would be dead by the time the proper paperwork was completed.

So, the problem was handled somewhat differently. There were a couple of methods employed, depending on the mental state of the patient. If, for example, the patient was stuporous and uncommunicative, the conversation, in the presence of a nurse as witness, would be:

"Mrs. Jones. You need an operation to repair your abdominal wound dehiscence because if you don't, you are liable to suffer egregious and potentially permanent effects. To wit, your internal gastrointestinal alimentary digestive tract could be exteriorized, desiccate, and become infiltrated with microbes.

170

"Unless you have an objection, we will do the aforementioned operation this very afternoon. You may now signify an objection if you wish and in the manner of your choice."

Pause.

"If you have any questions about what is entailed in the surgery or if there are any clarifications you desire concerning the long, detailed, and careful explanation I have given you, you may so signify now."

Pause.

"Finally then, Mrs. Jones, if you have any objections to surgery, you can state them now in the presence of this witness. You do not need to say anything if you agree with the proposed surgery."

Pause.

"There were no objections, Mrs. Gillhooley. We can sign the op permit for her. Thanks for coming in and being a witness."

"You're welcome, doctor."

On the other hand, if the patient were delirious or combative and generally unwilling and uncooperative, that posed another problem for the surgeon needing the op permit. Garven knew he could submit a psych consult and wait three days, go through legal services as he might have done for the stuporous patient, *or* he could get what the nurses called a "phenobarbital consent." That was the simplest method of all because it did not even require a witness. In this instance, the informed consent conversation was considerably simpler:

"Mr. Smith, you need an operation. We need to amputate your right leg above the knee because you neglected your diabetes and let your leg rot off. If you have an objection, state it. If not, we will do the operation this afternoon."

Pause—while Garven held Mr. Smith's limp hand and moved it and a ballpoint pen in a jerky, "John Smith," or sometimes just an "X," across the line captioned "SIGNATURE OF PATIENT." An IV phenobarbital, given as a preoperative sedative, worked miracles in helping the John Smiths to be reasonable and cooperative in their own behalf.

Garven had no time to watch TV and heard the news on the radio in the OR most days, when he did pick up a headline fragment or two. "GIANTS MOVED TO SAN FRANCISCO; DODGERS TO LA." "SHERMAN ADAMS, PRES. ASST. RESIGNS." Garven's perception of the former was "who cares?" and of the latter was, "big surprise, another crook in the government."

Not all of general surgery was as stimulating and rewarding as the hours spent getting phenobarbital permits or helping family members feel good about donating blood. Garven still had to attend surgery clinic and listen to complaints from patients who had typhoid-malaria, vomiken, the yaller janders, the toenail poisonin', runnin' off of the bowels, pain in the liters, the piles, complications from the "side-car" operation (Shirodkar operation), purse, or were just on the pitiful list (critical list).

He had to look at "onions" (hernias) on dirty old men. He had to look at "'roids" (hemorrhoids) in men who, when he asked them to bend over and spread their cheeks, would grasp their faces and pull at the corners of their lips. He examined dirty old women who complained of having "fireballs of the Eucharist" (fibroids of the uterus). They had "locked bowels," eatin' cancers, "walkin pneumonia," "acute interdigistitis" (acute indigestion), and the "bloody flux" (bloody diarrhea from Shigellosis, a bowel parasite). Every day, they flocked in with "bronical exodus" (bronchiectasis) and the "fleas are bitin'" (phlebitis) and "henfections in the grimes" (enlarged, infected groins). And every day in clinic was the same as every other day, except that the names and faces were changed. Garven was not even altogether sure of that, but the nurses repeatedly averred that it was so.

CHAPTER
Twenty-Two

In the three months rotation on the orthopedics service as a resident, Garven became skilled in dealing with routine fractures such as silver fork wrist deformities—fracture of the distal forearm bones, boxer's fractures—fracture of the fifth bone of the hand, and the almost undetectable early wrist navicular fractures. He came to know a number of the patients well; many of them were repeaters, either accident prone or by lifestyle, likely to find themselves in the wrong places at the wrong times.

The experience made Garven adept at putting on arm and leg casts for un-displaced fractures, thumb-spica splints for navicular fractures and "gamekeepers thumb"—injury to the ulnar collateral ligament of the thumb or for De Quervain's tenosynovitis. He could swiftly apply a "Freddie-the-Frog" splint for finger fractures and a posterior leg splint or a stirrup ankle splint for leg injuries or a volar arm splint, extending the wrist for arm injuries. As he learned and did all of those orthopedic outpatient procedures, Garven ruminated about how much value they were going to be for him when he finally got into the private practice of neurosurgery. The answer was obvious. Garven chalked it up to the concept that the ortho rotation was just one more hole he had to have punched in his surgery education card and let it go at that.

The worst problem—at least in terms of the amount of work entailed—was in dealing with fractures of the neck. The policy at UC Osterlund Memorial was for the orthopods to get all of the neck fractures that were un-displaced, and the patient was neurologically intact. The complicated and operative cases went to neurosurgery. The treatment for the orthopedic neck fractures was monotonously similar and a major undertaking. Every patient had to be placed in a halo-chest cast for four months.

The halo was a metal ring that could be fitted around the crown of the head and secured in place with skull screws. The screws were driven into the skull after applying copious amounts of local anesthetic. Uprights—four metal posts—were attached to the halo and to a crossbar over the chest and over the back. The patient was then placed on his or her back on a special body cast table and wrapped in thick bias tape and cotton batting. Then a body cast was laboriously applied from the patient's hips to the neck to hold the metal crossbars and lower ends of the posts rigidly in place and to prevent any flexion, extension, or torsion of the neck on the body. The process took two or three hours, and the final result weighed upwards of one hundred pounds.

The patient's arms protruded from arm holes and were allowed nearly complete freedom of action. For many of the patients, the freedom of the arms was all but nullified by the ponderous weight of the cast. Smaller patients were often almost bedridden due to the weight.

The most humiliating experience of Garven's training career thus far occurred while he was on the orthopedics rotation. His scrubs were regularly coated with plaster of Paris from his work with casts, and the remaining open cloth of the scrubs was speckled with blood, pus, and assorted bodily fluids that accumulated during the long workday. Garven took two and sometimes three showers a day. The practice was frowned upon by the administration because the cost of laundering all of those scrub suits was prohibitive in their meager budget. At the end of the quarter before the next infusion of county money, the laundry piled up and old and tattered scrubs were discarded but not replaced, resulting in shortages in the dressing rooms.

Garven made a mistake. He removed his soiled scrub suit and entered the shower without securing himself a new pair. He also left his locker keys in his scrub pants pocket. While he was wasting hot water in the luxury of a shower, taking care not to notice the gray color of the tile and the furry lines where the caulking had once shown white, the janitor came by and collected all of the dirty scrubs.

Garven toweled off, being wasteful by using two towels from the large stack instead of the allotted one per showeree. He went to the shelf to find a clean set of scrubs. There were none; the shelves were completely empty. He cursed. He used the phone in the dressing room to inform the laundry service that there were no fresh scrubs in the OR dressing room. They responded politely that there were plenty of them where *they* were, all dirty. It was the middle of the night after all. They assured him that there would be a new set of washed scrubs on the shelves at ten the following morning. That was no help to Garven; ten o'clock was eight hours away.

Garven sighed and went to his locker, resigned to the deduction that he would be obliged to wear his own clothes and to cover them with the nastiness of the hospital environment. Even before he got to the locker, he realized that he did not have a key. He looked frantically around the room for his scrub pants, knowing before he set out on his search that they were not going to be there. He called the laundry room again and asked if they had seen his keys. The reply was a heavy sigh, signifying a profound wonderment that such a one as the caller could have ever gotten into medical school.

"Ain't no keys here," said the patient woman on the other end of the phone. "We'll give a look in the washer when the pants is done. Might find them then. Might not."

"When will that be?" pleaded Garven.

"About ten," came the reply from the woman with the pleasant voice.

Garven was in trouble. He wrapped a towel around his midsection and resigned himself to the long wait until he could get some kind of pants. His fervent hope was that there would not be any more emergencies that night, and he would only get behind with his mountain of work and would not have to appear in public in his Mahatma Ghandi towel. He gave himself no better that 30-70 odds.

The truth was closer to 10-90 against him. His beeper went off less than fifteen minutes later. He called the ward.

"Cardiac arrest!" the nurse shouted into the phone. "Get over here right now!" and hung up.

He had no choice.

Garven secured his towel around his waist as tightly as he could. He checked to make sure that nothing dangled out below. That was all he could do to ready himself for the public. He prayed a little rusty prayer and ran to the ortho ward.

The nurses snickered a little as he came in, but they were too busy to pay real attention, and had no time to listen to an explanation. The code-blue resuscitation team was busy on another floor and could not respond to the ortho arrest. Garven was the only doctor on the scene. He dived in, heedless of the absurdity of standing there in a Tarzan outfit. He intubated the patient, pumped on the chest, ordered IV drugs, applied the shock paddles, and pumped on the chest some more. He showed the night nurse how to use

175

the Ambu bag to pump in enough air to make a difference. It was difficult because the patient was an old, four-pack-a-day chronic lunger with unbelievably stiff lungs. They had to dismantle the traction apparatus for the man's fractured hip.

The result was the same as it was in nearly every CPR effort that Garven had ever seen. The old man's heart rhythm was briefly recognizable on the EKG monitor, but it was to no avail. The old heart would not take over and pump, and finally, Garven called it quits after two hours of futile work.

"Let's pull the plug," he said.

For some reason, the assembled nurses found that terribly funny. None of them made a move. Garven looked at them with incredulity. He could not think of a thing amusing about the situation where a patient they had been working on for hours had finally died. He found it difficult even to crack a smile at the request to "pull the plug."

Then he looked down at his feet. There lay the towel, crumpled and trodden. The significance of "the plug" became more evident; and he, too, thought it inappropriate for there to be any pulling. He blushed scarlet, which caused the nurses and the aides to howl with laughter.

The charge nurse said in a voice broken with uncontrollable sniggering, "No, Jane…the rope. Jane…just the rope!"

The allusion to naked Tarzan and Jane swinging through the trees on vines was too much, and the entire exhausted group of medical personnel broke down in a highly incongruous deathbed scene.

Garven took the opportunity to back away and to find a couple of patient gowns to cover his embarrassment.

Christmas came and went. Garven was able to be off because they had a Jewish ortho resident, Meyer Silberstein, who took call. The Jewish community had a generous program of volunteering to take over hospital work on the one critical day of the year for the Christians. The men and women from the temple congregations and their rabbis took the places of the nonessential health care personnel in Osterlund Memorial, which allowed the bulk of the workers to have the day off. The Christians substituted for the few Jews on the staff for Hanakkah and Rosh Hoshana. Garven had taken Meyer's call for him both holidays.

"Have a great Hanakkah, whatever you do on that holiday," Garven had wished Meyer.

Meyer was less than devout. He had said, "We just have a nice Hanakkah bush and some bootleg chicken."

"What's a Hanakkah bush?"

"I get mine at O'Leary's tree lot."

"What's 'bootleg chicken'?" Garven had asked his co-resident.

"I'm not really sure," Meyer had responded. "Looks a lot like ham when it's sliced, though," he laughed.

Christmas was more fun than Garven could ever remember. The baby, now three and a half months old, and responsive, was a pleasure to both parents. He had stopped bawling all night about a month ago, and Garven now found Peter Arthur not only tolerable, but laugh provoking and engaging. His developmental stages were a matter of fascination for the new father, who recognized an incipient genius when he saw one. On the twenty-sixth, Garven headed back to the salt mines of UC Osterlund Memorial, and Elizabeth took Peter Arthur back to Phoenix; so, her father and mother could see him for the first time.

From January to the end of March, Garven was on thoracic surgery. He helped a lot and rarely was allowed to be the primary chest cutter. He did come out able to do a good opening and closing; that was about all. The old resident cases of lobectomies for TB or partial resections for lung abscesses were almost nonexistent in those days of effective chemotherapeutic treatment for tuberculosis and systemic antibiotics for other lung infections. Heart and major vascular cases were reserved for senior and chief residents and staff surgeons. Garven assisted at enough that he was sure that he could do a lung resection for cancer or repair an ascending aortic aneurysm, or take care of a PDA (Patent Ductus Arteriosus), but no one ever gave him a chance. He was glad to be off the service.

Garven was the "Pit Boss" for the month of April. The ER rotation was only a month long because no one could stand up to the psychic and bodily abuse more than thirty days. The schedule was forty-eight hours on and twenty-four hours off. The beauty of the schedule was the full day off—usually spent sleeping. The ugly of the schedule was the other two days. Garven was not required to do anything exactly. He simply had to see to it that every patient sent from the triage desk to the EOR was cared for properly and in as timely a fashion as possible. He had two interns, six nurses, two deputy sheriffs, and six aides to do the work with and for him. He was good at delegating but,

177

like all of his predecessors, drove himself to exhaustion and craziness by his personal requirement to review every case—an impossibility.

The first thing he demanded of the interns was that they consult frequently and get the floor residents down into The Pit often to share the joy of caring for their special patients. FBIs were divided into simple, nonmetal foreign bodies of the eye that could be dealt with by the intern in the EOR and into the category of complicated and/or metal inclusions in the eye. All OBs were to have an excuse for a consult, no exceptions. The last thing Garven was going to allow was a bad delivery with complications in the EOR without expert help and responsibility present. All abdominal slashes that looked as if the injury were a stabbing (pronounced "stobbing")—a wound that involved deep penetration by a blade and probable intraperitoneal injury—went to the surgery resident on call. If the patient stated that he had been "jouged," that is, the knife had been stabbed then twisted about, he earned a trip to the OR under the care of the resident on call. Most "hilted" knives were obvious emergencies and got automatic consults.

In Garven's mind, the function of the ER was to stabilize real emergencies until the floor resident or intern could take the injured person to the OR or to the ward. The next lower tier of injured, the superficial lacerations and un-displaced fractures, were taken care of by the interns. The lowest tier, the regulars who got lonely or bored on weekends and liked to come in and see the doctors just to have something to do or someone to talk to were nurse problems, and Garven spent about ten seconds each with them before signing them out. Some of the regulars were so persistent that the EOR people chipped in for cab fare just to get them out. There was a universal term for the ER habitués—GOMER (Get Out of My Emergency Room). Also in the lowest tier came the crazies, the beat-up drunks, the addicts looking for a fix, and derelicts with phony complaints, looking for a place to stay that was away from the mean streets for a night. The trick was to be able to tell them apart.

CHIs—the closed head injuries—usually earned a six-hour stay in the EOR, a skull X-ray, then discharge with the head injury sheet if they could give their name, address, wife's name, or other simple personal data. The questionable ones, the ones who stayed sleepy, or who deteriorated, or who developed neu-rological signs or stiff necks, got a neuro consult. "Neuro" invariably meant neurosurgery, not medical neurology. No one really trusted the neurologists for anything serious or that needed treatment. They were all right for the FLKs, the old strokers, the people who walked and talked funny, but for real neurological trouble, the EOR people wanted a neurosurgeon, even if he was only an intern. In the medicine pit, the attitude was somewhat different. They wanted a "real doctor" and went to the greatest lengths to avoid having their patients fall into the hands of the surgeons. So far as Garven was concerned, there was no accounting for such opinions; but he, like every other surgeon, knew that he would never fathom the minds of the "lice and fleas" internists.

Garven taught his interns and the rest of the medical personnel to send broken necks to neuro despite the hospital policy that had the neurologically intact going to ortho. If the nurses and interns could not find a neurological deficit on the patient, Garven would go to the bedside and search until he could find one, however minor or contrived. He knew that one neuro could take care of a neck fracture better than a carload of orthopods. The pods were all right for the crude stuff, the mechanics, but the neuros had to be involved in the fine work, the wiring problems, even the potential ones.

The interns had plenty of work. They took care of skin abscesses from the subcutaneous infections in the addicts, the superficial lacerations in prostitutes, the PID—Pelvic Inflammatory Disease, gonorrhea) in women. In a month's rotation, the interns did I&Ds on hordes of pilonidal abscesses, perianal and perirectal abscesses—all infections near the rectum—and sent them off to sitz bath—"sit-in"—clinic. The interns were the first line of defense against surgical complications—stitch and wound abscesses and dehiscences, bowel and urinary tract obstructions, the painful hernias, thrombosed hemorrhoids, and the burns. They got first crack at all IVs and cut-downs, chest tubes, LPs, paracenteses, bone marrow punctures, skin biopsies, I&Ds—Incisions and Drainages—catheterizations, doing local anesthetic blocks, and pushing "onions"—hernias—back into their canals and at dealing with the few "hurts all over" that slipped through the cracks at the triage desk.

CHAPTER
Twenty-Three

Garven, as Pit Boss, was responsible for checking off all of the routine intern cases and for all of the unusual cases. He saw a beautiful woman who refused to allow the intern to do a pelvic exam. When Garven persisted and got angry, she got angry also and lifted her skirt to reveal positive evidence that she was a man in drag. There were men with priapism, men with wedding rings forced onto their penises, retarded boys with hair balls in their stomachs. Garven screened the clotted blood vessels, the foreign bodies in the penis, nose, ears, vagina, and the rectum, the seizures after head injuries, GSWs, chest stabbings, and people in shock. He had to see every DOA—like the floaters found in the ocean or in the Los Angeles River—rape case, major bleeder, and burn case with more than thirty percent involvement by established EOR policy and the law.

For some reason, the most memorable DOA Garven saw during his EOR rotation was a man who hanged himself. DOAs were not all that uncommon, and hangings were not so rare. Garven had seen his share. There was nothing remarkable about the man per se. He had put a rope around his neck, stood on a chair, and handcuffed his wrists behind him, then kicked out the chair. In his death struggles, he defecated, urinated, and ejaculated, all frequent concomitants of death by hanging. The cop who brought the poor soul into Garven's domain marveled at the man's ingenuity.

He showed Garven his official report on the incident: *"Subject secured hands behind his back with handcuffs. While hanging, he was still able to masturbate."*

A routine day involved an amused intern bringing Garven a frightened man with a perpetual erection—priapism. They tried ice packs, Thorazine, and sedatives. And when that did not work, they sent the poor man to GU. The standard joke was that "no one ever complained of priapism." That was manifestly untrue in reality; the condition resulted from blood clotting in the convoluted veins of the penis and preventing the timely evacuation and detumescence of the organ of copulation. It was painful and dangerous; few men ever regained the ability to have full erections again. Still, the nurses and aides always seemed to find a reason to work around the novelty patient.

Never a day passed that there was not a full-blown crazy or two for whom Garven had to make the final disposition. One day, it would be a hysterical man with paralyzed legs. Garven found injections of distilled water, which stung like everything, to be effective. He never accused the patient of faking or of having a psychological problem. Instead, he assured them that the injury would clear with the shot, and they would be able to go home in a couple of hours. He was invariably right, and regularly received gratitude, adoration, and short-lived fame for performing a miracle.

He got less positive response from the illegal alien Mexican women and, worse, from the old ladies brought in faking unconsciousness for inexplicable reasons of their own. It was easy to get the Mexican women to react. He brought the male orderlies into the examining room and had them all talk loudly to establish the fact that there were men in the room. Then, Garven would suddenly grasp the hem of the woman's dress and whip the skirt up over her abdomen, baring her legs. Mexican women are modest, and invariably, and involuntarily, the woman would betray herself and grab at her skirt to cover herself.

One old lady proved easy to diagnose as a hysteric, but made Garven the butt of another lasting EOR tale. She had been brought in from her nursing home unconscious. Garven had seen her eyes fluttering and was sure she was awake, but faking. He had two nursing students and an EOR nurse in tow and was in the mood to do some teaching. He started a running patter about how to tell if a patient were faking. He demonstrated the standard measures like picking up her arm and letting it fall again and again, missing her face, tickling her eyelashes, pinching a leg, raising one leg and pushing down on the other and feeling that leg resist. She demonstrated all of the signs of malingering, and Garven made a big point of her dishonest status. As he did so, she became observably more agitated. Garven moved alongside the woman to put a hair in her ear. Suddenly, her hand shot out and made an angry grab for his

181

unguarded crotch. He made an instantaneous twist, causing her to miss the crotch contents and to end up with a handful of trouser leg.

"Not fast enough!" Garven exulted to the woman, tickled that he had forced her to demonstrate that she was indeed awake.

She had an angry and vengeful look.

"You're just not big enough, that's all," she snapped. She then gathered her things and stalked out of the front door of the EOR.

Another opportunity to excel in that general category of disease included the woman who came into the EOR hysterical, screaming that she had a rat in her vagina. Garven had seen a light bulb in a vagina, a battery-operated vibrator in a boy's rectum—that could still be heard vibrating—and a woman with a Coke bottle in her vagina that she said she put there so she would get more excitement out of sitting on her washer during spin cycle, so why would it seem so strange to have a rat in that private orifice?

She was dressed in pink slippers—a dead giveaway that she was a neurotic at best and, given the circumstances, a full-blown loony. She also had more than one ring on more than one finger on more than one hand, another prima facie evidence of bats in the belfry. The nurses had trouble holding the woman down. She was terrified, appeared to be in agonizing pain. Garven talked very soothingly to her, assured her that he believed every word she said.

"Put her up for a pelvic. I want the orderlies to go over to the rat lab and get an empty cage so we can get rid of the thing. Okay, Miss Templeton, now we're going to do an internal exam. You ever had one before?"

"No," came the quavering voice.

It won't hurt. I will be very gentle. Just try and relax."

The orderly brought in a good, solid rat cage, about half the size of a bread box. It had a hinged top that dropped down on the cage with a satisfying clang. Garven had one of the nurses show the cage to the patient.

Garven rummaged around in the woman's vagina with his gloved hands for a few moments, long enough to be convincing that an examination had been done and the rodent captured, and not long enough to give the demented woman any ideas.

"There! I have it!" Garven exulted. He kept his hands below the line of sight of the woman. He nodded to the orderly, who clanged the rat cage shut as loudly as he could. "Okay, get that thing out of here. Get it over to the medical school. They can experiment on it. It is a big one. I can hardly believe you were able to survive with that thing in you, Miss Templeton. You got here just in time!" He let her see the covered cage being whisked away.

182

Miss Templeton calmed down and went home happy and singing the praises of the UC Osterlund Memorial Hospital EOR. Another miracle.

One day, Garven saw an eighty-year-old woman who complained of severe pain "down in my privates." He had the nurses set her up for a pelvic exam. The assisting nurse told him that the old lady was senile and had never had a speculum—or anything else—in her vagina in her entire life.

"I bet this is going to be lots of fun, doc," she concluded.

Everything went well. The old lady permitted her legs to be separated. Garven leaned forward and inserted his fingers into the tight, dry, old vagina. The old lady reacted instantly and violently. She threw her legs around Garven's neck and locked her heels as firmly as the jaws of a vice. He finally had to call for help from the nurses, and he never lived it down.

A couple was brought in, locked in an amorous embrace. The woman was a young white virgin who, as it turned out, developed neurotic guilt feelings just after penetration. She developed extraordinarily painful vaginal spasms. The slightest movement caused her to have a renewal of the spasms. Disconnection proved impossible; so, the couple telephoned the ambulance and was brought to the ER. There was a crowd of helpers and well-wishers in the entryway when the ambulance pulled in. The young man was humiliated, but the woman was in so much pain that she was beyond caring about social situations. Garven cured the couple by giving both of them 150 mg of Thorazine and packing the involved area with ice. In less than an hour, separation was effected, and both of the patients were discharged from the EOR groggy and grateful.

On the heels of that couple, the ambulance brought in an elderly, blue-haired woman who had collapsed while waiting in line at her bank, i.e., a citizen. She arrested as she was being wheeled in. Garven called a "code blue," and the forces turned out to perform a model CPR. It was a rare case; the woman revived.

"I don't care what anybody else says, but we're good, aren't we?" the head nurse said and clapped Garven on the back.

"Wha... Where am I?" the lady asked, still dazed.

"Well, you know you're not in heaven, just take a look at this one's face," the gleeful nurse said to the patient.

She brought Garven's head down to where the woman could see his face plainly.

"Oh no," she moaned and turned on her side, looking away from the Resuscitation team.

Tears were welling up and running down her wrinkled old cheeks.

"What's the matter, dear?" asked the nurse, genuinely concerned and completely bemused.

The woman had just been resurrected from the dead. The outpouring of sadness seemed inappropriate even by EOR standards.

"I wanted to die," she said. "I have cancer of the anus, and I live in agony." She wept softly. "I was at the bank, winding up my affairs, so my death would not be a burden on my family. When I fainted, I was sure I was going to die. It was really quite pleasant."

In an hour, the woman was well enough to be taken back to her apartment on Wilshire.

Garven commented to the head nurse, "Great save."

Sometimes, he did not have such "great saves," and was accorded a great measure of gratitude for his work. One old man with Alzheimer's presenile dementia fell at home and was brought to the EOR unconscious from a head injury. He had a nasty forehead cut, but as soon as he crossed the threshold of the EOR from the triage desk, he arrested. The intern and one of the nurses resuscitated him before his wife could get to the hospital from her home.

Like the woman with the anal cancer, she was dismayed that her lifelong companion, who had suffered from and caused his family to suffer from Alzheimer's for nearly twenty-five years, had been rescued from a merciful death.

"Why couldn't you have just let him go, doctor?" she asked. She was neither angry nor accusative, just sad.

"I really didn't know his condition, Ma'am," Garven said. He was on her side. "Look, oftentimes, people deteriorate over a period of time after they have CPR. Let's keep him in here for a while and see how he does."

"And maybe he won't make it?" the wife queried plaintively.

"We'll just have to wait and see," Garven told her.

The old man was tucked away in the last cubicle for six hours. Garven got blood studies, skull and neck X-rays while the old man lay on his gurney, but the EOR was busy; and Garven did not bother to go over the studies.

Finally, they needed the bed, and the old man would have to be sent up to the ward. Garven gave the old wife the hard news that her husband seemed to be hanging on rather fiercely, even to be rallying.

"I need to sew up his cut, then I'm afraid he'll have to go upstairs. Please have a seat in the waiting room; I'll have the nurses fetch you when I'm done."

"There are no seats in the waiting room, young man," the wife said pleasantly. She smiled. "I'll just go out and have a stand. It'll do me good."

184

Garven cleaned up the cut on the man's forehead and put a rolled towel under his shoulders to put the cut on a level position to facilitate suturing. The scrubbing had made the cut bleed. He daubed at the bleeding, which stopped easily, then he quickly ran a row of 4-0 suture to close the opening. He became aware that the cut was not bleeding at all. In fact, there was nothing but a little dark blood under the suture line that evacuated easily. That was strange.

Garven lifted the drapes that had been covering the old gentleman's face. He was White—gray-white—and his eyes were open. He was not breathing. Garven checked his carotid artery and heart. Nothing. The man was dead.

Garven gathered up the chart, checked the lab data, which was unremarkable, and took a cursory look at the X-rays. Normal skull. But on the cervical spine films, there was an unmistakable, slightly displaced fracture of C1on C2. Garven sagged back into his chair. What he had done flashed through his mind in vivid detail in an instant. When he extended the man's neck, the fracture had slipped and severed the patient's high cervical spinal cord. Death had been as instantaneous and painless as if it had been the result of a judicial hanging. He debated about whether or not to tell the man's wife the whole story. He finally decided to do the right thing. He took in a deep breath and went out into the ER waiting rooms.

"Mrs. Farmington, your husband has had a turn for the worse." He paused. Her face was expectant.

"Yes, doctor?"

"I'm afraid that he had another cardiac arrest. We did not make any attempt to do CPR on him. We didn't think you would approve of that."

"Is he dead, doctor? Just tell me straight out."

"He is, I'm afraid."

"I loved the man for fifty-five years, made his food, cleaned his clothes, and kept him out of trouble. It was almost as if I breathed out and he'd breathe in. I could not bear to see him the way he was. Thank you, doctor. You are a kind man. You have done the right thing."

Garven guessed that she was right. He felt a small pang at her reference to him having "done the right thing." He was not entirely sure what she thought that he had done, but he let it go.

CHAPTER
Twenty-Four

In the UC Osterlund Memorial "Pit," there were two types of patients—at least in the parlance of those who worked there. There were the "customers," sometimes known by the generic sobriquet, "knife fighter"—the great majority of the patrons of the services of the ER. And there were a minority of "citizens," also known as "people," who came from Beverly Hills, Hollywood Hills, The Valley, or even Orange County. The woman with the senile husband and the lady with the anal carcinoma were examples of the latter. These patrons actually paid for their care; some had jobs and even a few had insurance. In general, they were not drunk, filthy, blasphemous, or complaining of having the "all overs" or the "miseries" that brought them to the "muncy room," in contradistinction to the "customers" who were all of those things.

Garven was the Pit Boss the night Derek Van Gildersleeve, the world-renowned pianist, the very paragon of a "citizen," was brought to the EOR by the director of the Los Angeles Philharmonic Orchestra. He was world famous, having recently won the Moscow Young Pianist Award, the most prestigious and coveted honor in the world of serious music. Garven was not a fan of any celebrity; he did not have time. But, of all the performers in the world, Van Gildersleeve was the one by whom Garven was the most awestruck. The pianist had given a virtuoso performance at the Dorothy Chandler Pavilion that night despite excruciating pain. He had a perirectal abscess that came to a point during the performance. By the time he had suffered the last of three encores, he was writhing in pain. It was unthinkable for him to sit for even a second longer with that large, pulsating boil on his bottom. He was brought to the EOR in his tie and tails because it was late at night and Osterlund was the place where he could get relief the quickest.

Garven assigned an intern to Van Gildersleeve. He was placed in a cubicle having to stand because he could hardly bend his legs now, let alone sit.

"I have a gunshot wound to check out, Mr. Van Gildersleeve," Garven told him. "Then I'll be right in. Hang on. We'll have that abscess drained in a few minutes, and you'll be fine."

"Thank you, doctor. Could I have something for pain in the meantime? I am getting nauseated," the pianist requested politely.

"Of course. Annie! Get ten of morphine IM for Mr. Van Gildersleeve in seven!" Garven called to the head nurse. "No allergies to narcotics, I hope?" he asked the miserable man standing there in his tux.

"None."

"Good, I'll be right back," Garven assured him.

Garven sent the GSW up to the OR with the "B" service resident and intern. Two ambulance loads of kids who had been attending the regular Friday Night Downtown LA Knife and Gun Club Meeting burst into the EOR at that moment. They had been in a gang fight over which group, Mexican or Negro, had the right to sit in Wesley's Eighth Street Diner. This serious question had led to an acrimonious debate punctuated with fists, knives, and clubs. Then the situation deteriorated into real unpleasantness. Eleven young gentlemen of the two sporting clubs were the recipients of gun, knife, blunt trauma, and bicycle-chain whipping injuries. Four of the injuries were serious.

"Where do we put all of these nice boys?" asked the police attendants accompanying the fire department EMTs who were treating the victims.

The police had gone through a recent sensitivity training program to teach them to avoid negative racial, religious, gender, or other characterizations that might offend the patients or the community. They seemed to be getting the hang of it, but Garven felt that the new language was not yet fully internalized.

"Move the two dopers with cuts out of the trauma rooms. Put the two worst newcomers in there. Get a couple of med students down here to sew up the dopers and get them out of here. Annie, clear out the four cubicles next to the trauma rooms. Let's move it, guys," Garven ordered crisply.

He sometimes forgot to be sensitive in his references to the lifestyles of the "customers." He was under stress.

The nurses and orderlies swiftly cleared the cubicles. Mr. Van Gildersleeve, resplendent in his tuxedo and opera shoes, stood out in dramatic contrast to the bloodied, flea-ridden, and rheumy-eyed fellow travelers in the crowded ER. An orderly who was a passionate music lover found the famous musician a reasonably safe place to stand. Mr. Van Gildersleeve was afforded an especially fine view of the goings-on in the EOR from his vantage point.

A youthful victim leaned over the edge of his gurney as it was being pushed past the illustrious pianist. The gangster vomited a projectile mixture of beer, hamburger, and blood from his fractured nose—a classical combination in the EOR—onto the opera shoes of Van Gildersleeve. Some of the pungent and chunky fluid splashed up the pianist's legs.

Another gurney swept past in its turn to find a place in a trauma room. The young gentleman writhing on the gurney was holding a wad of internal viscera that was fighting its way out of the huge laceration in his abdominal wall.

He harked up a clog and observed to the genteel citizen leaning against the wall of the EOR, "I been jouged man, I really been jouged."

Van Gildersleeve felt deep sympathy for the young gentleman, but was at a loss for words. He had never seen anything remotely like the stygian scene unfolding before him.

Garven said to the intern in charge of the pianist, "Can't you get him somewhere out of the way?"

"Which do you want me to do, boss, keep pinching off this bleeder or tend to the citizen?"

The intern had his hand deep in an open chest wound at the moment.

"Forget it," Garven said.

Neither house staff man had time to pay attention to the illustrious patron. The room was a cacophony of street talk, pidgin English, medicalese, Chinese, Spanish, Spanglish, scatology, and blasphemy.

Annie Clyde, the head nurse, moved Mr. Van Gildersleeve into a corner. There was less activity there, but the floor was covered with fresh bloody stool that had come from another of the patients in the cubicles who had been displaced by the eleven newcomers from the War Zone. The smell was horrific—old and new blood issuing from the bowel takes on a special piercing fragrance. In the confusion, a derelict with impending DDTs was wheeled up close to the musician. The derelict was visiting the EOR to have his ear sewn back on and was holding the amputated appendage in a jar of sterile saline.

Despite himself, Van Gildersleeve gave in to morbid fascination and tentatively asked the bum, "How did you happen to lose your ear, Sir?"

188

The derelict looked the tuxedoed man over carefully and gave a thoughtful answer. "Benji stoled my Revel, last ounce of it. I stuck him inna eye. Then he cut me. See!"

He showed the ear in the jar up close to Van Gildersleeve's face. The musician visibly paled. His nausea worsened dramatically.

"Hey, Jamie! Leave the man alone. He don't know about that sorta stuff!" shouted one of the orderlies.

Jamie settled back onto his chair to wait patiently for his turn.

Garven tried to get to the musician, but another severely wounded man, this time a GSW to the head, was rushed in. Garven had to trach him. Jamie's, the derelict's, eyes rolled up into the back of his head as the head wound patient rolled by. Van Gildersleeve thought the old derelict with the missing ear was sensitive to the ugly trauma that passed. He was mistaken. The display of the whites of Jamie's eyes was only the prelude to a grand mal convulsion. The bum threw his ear on the floor and vomited on Van Gildersleeve, then began to have tonic-clonic jerking movements and flung himself onto the floor with a loud, hollow crack of his head.

Garven yelled to Ofelia Sanchez, the charge nurse, "Ofelia, give him three hundred of Dilantin IM and a gram of mag sulfate. Call a neurologist or an internist. Let the lice and fleas take care of him. We'll get an ENT to do his ear once he stops seizing!"

In the scramble to tend to Jamie, Garven looked over at Mr. Van Gildersleeve, whose face was now olive drab in color. The concert pianist vomited all down his nice tuxedo, starched shirt, and black studs. Before Garven could rise to help him, the world-famous classical pianist slid noiselessly down into the blood, urine, feces, and vomitus of the EOR floor. Although he was lying facedown in the offal, his countenance appeared relaxed and finally at peace.

CHAPTER
Twenty-Five

Life in the EOR was an adventure, not every day—more like every other minute. At four o'clock in the morning, an old lunger came in gasping his last from his neglected COPD. He was scarcely moving any air because of his chronic obstructive pulmonary disease. Garven intubated him, and the old fellow did not even react to the irritating tube in his trachea at first. Garven hyperventilated him with pure O2. After a few minutes of oxygenation, the patient suddenly awakened and became agitated. He tore out his endotracheal tube despite the tape on his face and the inflated balloon below his vocal cords. He hurled the slimy tube across the room and hit the intern who had been attending him full in the face with the offensive thing.

"Guess he doesn't need the tube," the intern had time to say as his patient made a beeline for the exit door.

A child was brought into the EOR at six in the morning—mis-triaged on purpose—so she could have real emergency care. The tiny girl had been found unconscious by her parents that morning and was called a "crib death," more exactly, a "near crib death." She still had a heartbeat. The entire crew in the EOR set about to work. They could not get anything going. Garven had the nurses get the pediatricians and pediatric nurses to come over. They did their best as well. Finally, after a futile effort lasting almost two hours, the senior pediatric resident called it quits. The doctors and nurses all backed away. Garven and the peds resident headed out to break the terrible news to the family.

190

They were almost to the door into the waiting room when a breathless nurse ran up behind them.

"Come back, doctors. You have to see this."

"What is it?" asked Garven, who was weary already, and the day had only just begun.

"This you have to see."

The two doctors went back to the trauma room where the child had been treated. There was a battlefield of machines, IV bottles, and discarded medicine vials to make their way through. From the doorway, the two men could see the baby breathing. They hurried over to look at her EKG monitor. The heart rhythm was perfectly normal. The baby was beginning to stir.

The pedi-pods took the child to their intensive care unit. Less than a week later, the little girl left the hospital as normal as it was possible for a baby to be. There was no inkling of her diagnosis. Garven considered it a profoundly humbling experience, not so much because he had almost made a very serious mistake, but because he knew that he would never understand medicine, not really. The parents knew it was a miracle.

One afternoon, a farmer from Claremont was brought into the EOR after being entangled in a hay chopper. The man was missing his left arm and both legs. Tourniquets had been applied to the mangled stumps. Four bound bales of hay were delivered as well. The body parts were included in the bales, and the farmer's family presumed that the miracles of medical science would enable the parts to be reattached. Garven worked furiously to stabilize the farmer and got the general surgery resident and the orthopods in to get the man to the OR. He dispatched two orderlies to pick apart the bales of hay to find the man's body parts. There was a great deal of grumbling and protest, but in the end, the orderlies did their distasteful job. They laid out fragments of flesh and bone on sheets on the EOR floor like mixed pieces of a three-dimensional jigsaw puzzle. No body part was larger in its greatest dimension than three inches. Garven surveyed the carnage and shook his head.

When the farmer's family argued vociferously that he had to do the surgical replacements of their husband's, father's, and brother's parts, Garven could not get them to listen to reason. He was sorely tempted to take the lot of them into the EOR and let them see the pieces of the man's body and then to make their own conclusions.

Instead, he told them the truth: it was patently impossible. He was sorry, but medical science would never be able to accomplish such a feat. The man's elder brother, who served as the family spokesman, had read the medical literature—*The National Inquirer*—and had his facts straight even if the young doctor did not.

"You are a quack, young man!" he shouted into Garven's face, blowing fumes from the chaw of Copenhagen he held in the acquired pouch between his cheek and his gums. "I am a gonna get a second opinion, then I am a gonna sue your ass off! How do you like them apples?!"

Garven listened patiently. The brother was not finished.

"You will not be paid a dime, you quack!"

The farmer lacked insurance or two nickels to rub together.

"I want a new doctor, and I want him now!"

Garven was tired. He turned and left. He sent the intern to talk to the family in his stead. The intern had been a doctor for a little over two weeks.

Garven saw horrors, like the man who was bitten by his horse, resulting in exposure of the great vessels on the left side of the neck, the penis caught in the zipper—that required snipping off the end of the zipper and not unzipping—and the old miner-hermit from up near Barstow, who developed cancer in the lymph nodes in his groin, resulting in a festering sore that swarmed with maggots.

And Garven made mistakes. He killed the maggots that had been keeping the old hermit's infection at bay, and the old man died of septicemia for the spread of his bacteria after being admitted to the hospital.

He missed an impending rupture of an abdominal aortic aneurysm in a man who came to the EOR three days running because of terrible back pain. The other EOR resident left Garven a note, informing him that the man had come in on his shift in extremis from shock and died as they worked on him. His aneurysm had blown to pieces two hours after his last examination by Garven. The experience was chastening and toughening, but Garven knew he could not lose his nerve just because he had made a mistake.

He was not reprimanded by the EOR attending, but he was reminded of the valuable advice to "come up with two additional diagnoses every time you get someone in with an obvious problem."

That day ended with Chen Lum, the chief orderly, running up to Garven and shouting, "Must come berry quickly. Have GSW to the berry!"

There was something very incongruous about Chen Lum, a Han Chinese. He wore the standard hospital ID tag on his lab coat. At the advice of some unknown wag, it read, "Chen Lum, HNIC."

Garven limped into Trauma Room 2 and examined the young man with the hole in his abdomen.

Although the EOR environment was not always that tumultuous, space was always a problem—and it was Garven's responsibility, as Pit Boss, to clear out the "customers" to make way for the never-ceasing waves of newly wounded. The old excuse that the patient had been mis-triaged seldom held water. He had to come up with a better excuse to move out a patient.

The first question in any doctor-GOMER interaction was, "Are you a vet?"

If the Gomer was not a veteran, and thus ineligible for transfer to the VA, another transfer option had to be sought. Among the first things Garven had to learn to do and to accomplish with finesse and skill were how to get certain patients to check out AMA—Against Medical Advice—and how to dump patients onto the medicine service.

Most of the inhabitants of the mean streets of LA surrounding and served by UC Osterlund Memorial Hospital were unsure of their next meal or bed. A significant number of them loved being in the hospital and were very adept and convincing about why they should be in the hospital for as long as possible. They were, for the most part, irresponsible, and the medical personnel of Osterlund took that into consideration with every discharge. Often, they were kept in the ER, the clinic, or in house longer than if they had been "citizens." Getting them out was the problem; there was always a supply of new wounded to take the place of the old.

There were suggestions that worked: on the ward, it could be hinted that the only way the customer's condition could be approached was with a "spearmint." The tradition-bound and superstitious customers dreaded nothing so much as an experimental operation. Accordingly, Garven learned that it was in his best interests at times to include as "spearmints" such operations as inguinal hernia repair, uterine suspensions, and skin biopsies. For the younger set, the fear of pain was transcendent. Threats of special shots using square needles with hooks on the end and the hospital running out of local anesthetic—not always untruthful—were serviceable ploys. The drastic risk of complications from the essential surgery the resident described was pointed out in great depth and detail. Most times, there was included the most dreaded hazard of all, that of the patient losing his "nature"—the ability to achieve an erection with which he could drive nails. In a population that positively revered it's "nature" and regarded "the big nerve" as the one dangling from their pubic bones, it was often enough to discourage even the most entrenched "customer."

There were underhanded ploys that were effective but were deplored by the hospital administration. Stat emergency surgery or "elevator" cases were dispatched to the operating room with a red blanket laid over them. That ensured that they were not held up by crowds in the elevators and were not shunted off to some waiting line for X-ray or a lab. For GOMERS who would not leave the EOR, Garven occasionally cut off their wrist identi-bands, put a red blanket on them, made sure that there was no chart available and no other source of identification on the "customer," and put them on the elevator.

The elevator operators—on the automatic elevators—rushed the "customers" to the OR, where they would be asked, "Why are you here?"

The reply was always some variation of, "Dunno."

The "customer" was often simply wheeled to the exit when no disease process could be determined by the usual veterinary medical methods that had to be employed in such instances.

If the GOMER exhibited offensive behavior and incurred Garven's wrath down in The Pit, he was likely to have his identi-band removed and to have his gurney placed on the elevator with no directions given at all. In that case, the GOMER usually rode up and down on the elevator most of the day, and when the elevator operator found the individual to be obnoxious or to be taking up too much room, he would be shunted off to the X-ray line or to the lab waiting room. If he proved to be offensive there, he was dealt with in another time-honored manner. One's position in the lab and X-ray lines—which were very long any hour in a day—was determined by a number slip handed out as soon as one entered the room—a measure learned from ice-cream parlors. The "customer" had to wait his turn. Nasty and abusive GOMERS found themselves the recipients of a new number when they finally made it to the head of the line. The new number was hundreds larger and put them at the back of the line again. It could happen four times in a day in the confusion of the busy outpatient department services. For the "customer," this series of moves could prove to be hungry work.

Finally, the "law" could be invoked. The "law" set down a precise number of days allowed for a given illness, condition, or operation. The deputies would have to remove the patients if they extended beyond the legal limit, and the infraction would go on the patient's record as a misdemeanor. The doctors and nurses were sorry; their hands were tied. It was the "law." If all else failed, the medical and nursing personnel could simply contrive a means of getting the customer angry.

To get a "customer" out at the time the doctor desired, it was often necessary to get the customer to sign an AMA form, even if the pretext was fear of "spearmints," of pain, or of "the law." It was a fine point, often overlooked by the customer, that they were leaving the ER or the hospital on, not against, medical advice. Sometimes, those fine points were not discussed at length.

Dumping on the medical service was a more difficult proposition, and its practice was elevated to an art form. For all the mutual disdain with which the two services held each other, they each grudgingly granted to the other a measure of street cunning, if not actual intelligence, when it came to avoiding having unwanted patients foisted upon themselves. Garven had to find a medical disease like "sugarbetis" or "bronical exodus" in the addict leg ulcer patient that was worse than the ulcer. By definition in the EOR, any intake of drugs prior to admission to the surgery section was an "overdose." The most common "overdose" was on Pepto Bismol, and next most common was Sal Hepatica, which was taken by those who considered themselves allergic to Pepto Bismol. The worst overdose was Turpentine-in-Water that was taken when Pepto Bismol had already been used and had failed, and there was no ambulance available. Overdoses were medical problems. Sometimes, Garven could sell that idea on one of his nonsurgical surgical patients and transfer an "overdose" to the medicine people.

Or he had to find a very sleepy medical intern, who would believe a lie such as, "Yeah, we worked him up in the EOR. He's got some sort of exotic anemia, needs a real doctor like your heme team," for a "customer" with only an acute blood loss anemia from a scalp laceration that his interns had sutured. This situation usually represented a triple lie; the anemia was misdiagnosed—the diagnosis was made without a single test being done to rule out elements of the differential diagnosis because it was known and obvious, and the anemia was a surgical one according to the rules, and the surgical service was obligated to use its blood for the needed transfusion, and the derelict was about to go into the DDTs, a historical item that was omitted. The lie, if accepted, would amount to a triple coup. The medical service would have one more and the surgical service one less patient; Garven's service could avoid using up its precious blood transfusion allotment for a nonsurgical case, and his interns would not have to waste their nights taking care of a ranting, deathly sick man in the delirium tremens.

For all the lies and subterfuge, there had to be a certain honor among thieves for the system to grind along with any measure of smoothness. Sometimes, there was a genuine communication between brother residents. Garven's ward would be filled to overcapacity. To lighten the load, he might have to convince a wary medical resident to take his hot gall bladder for medical treatment until she was able to be operated upon. That cost Garven's intern the pain of hearing from the medical intern that it was a "shame that they didn't teach the 'technicians' how to give medical treatment to patients with acute cholecystitis." An understanding had to be achieved with the resident on two fronts: first of all, that the patient would come back to Garven for her surgery; Garven could not afford to lose a real surgery. And that Garven could not refuse to accept a miserable transfer from medicine some time in the future. The patient would usually be a "train wreck" with five major medical problems and a bedsore that needed debridement, a surgical condition that the medical interns were perfectly capable of handling themselves. It was a complicated system with only temporary winners and losers, and for all its machinations, an ultimately just, if not altogether friendly, one.

CHAPTER
Twenty-Six

By the time Garven was through with his EOR tour of duty and was then three-quarters of the way done with his core year of general surgery, he had learned to speak the language of Central and South Central LA. It was a language with many similarities to English but one that had its own syntax, vocabulary, and cultural background.

In general, there was only one tense, the present.

"Then these two dudes jist walks up an' shoots me fo' no reason, doctah, no reason at all!"

Garven and the other residents worried that if ever the cops got hold of those "two dudes," the hospital would have to shut down for lack of "customers."

The language had a peculiar admixture of English and Spanish:

"Hey, *medico*, my hooter esta leekiendo."

That bit of Spanglish assumed that there is a Castilian infinitive "*leekiar*," meaning "to leak," which there is not. It also assumed that one knew that a "hooter" was the masculine organ of copulation, or, as the GU residents defined the organ, "that which surrounds a Foley catheter."

These were people who requested that their friends would "*pusha la puerta*" (push the door), or "*Damé un raité* (Give me a ride), or rode to work in their "trocke"—their "peek-oop trocke." They drank "siete-oop" when they could not find Corona.

The language of the streets had a distinctive vocabulary, of which "hooter" was but one example. Garven had to immerse himself in a culture that used terms with understandings such as the following:

197

MEDICAL TERM	LA STREET UNDERSTANDING
Anemia	Enema
Barium	What doctors do when patients die
Cataracts	Cadillacs
Cauterize	Made eye contact
Clots	Clarks or clogs
Colic	Sheep dog
Culture	a) the result of being reared in a suitable environment (uncommon usage) b) a medium for growing germs c) what the lab won't plate out after midnight [intern definition]
D&C	Where Washington is at
Enema	Opposite of friend, one of the famous "two dudes"
Epileptic convulsions	Athletic conversions
Fester	Quicker
Glucose	Bluecoat
Gonorrhea	Strain; also clap (not in the sense of applause)
Grandmother	Mother dear
Huh?	"Say whaa?"
Impotent	Distinguished, well known, as in the "toughest mother on the street"
Impotence	"Loss of mah nature" (a truly grave condition)
IV	a) vine growing on the walls of Eastern liberal schools (uncommon usage) b) essential UC Osterlund equipment, painful for the "customer," "work" for the intern (not resident)
Node	Was aware of
Outpatient	Anyone who just fainted
Rectum	Directum or Volectum; also, "Near killed him"
Rectal exam	What the patient gets if he makes the doctor angry
Ruptured uterine	Busted my brains membranes
Seizure	Maybe a Roman emperor?
Sharp implement [any]	Butcher knife (wielded by a woman)
Strep throat	Strip phroat

198

Subscription	Suxcription or suscription
Syphilis	The "bad blood" or "haircut"
Liter	Tendon (any elongated structure with the exception of the hooter)
Tumor	More than two
Vaginal hemorrhage	Floodin'
Varicose	Nearby
Wound (verb)	a) Scratch – any cut less than an inch deep
	b) Cut – any laceration that does not enter a body cavity
	c) Stob – to stab, a deep penetration by the sharp object, usually into a bodily cavity
	d) Hilt – very deep stob
	e) Jouge – hilt then twist

Garven knew that he had come of full age in the institution and that he spoke its language when he was called upon to render translation for an admissions clerk on one of his last days in the EOR. The young woman was from New York City, a debutante who had taken the job as an admissions officer for Osterlund Memorial for the adventure of it and to assuage her liberal sense of having so much while the "customers" had so little. She was waiting for the right proposal of marriage by one from the social register.

Garven overheard the futile conversation between the young woman and Jonas N.—for Nitrogen—Canary, a twenty-three-year-old knife fighter who was being admitted for surgery for a stobbing of his abdomen. He was in pain and was not altogether communicative or cooperative, being in no mood for such nonsense.

The admissions clerk, smartly dressed in a business suit, asked, "Mr. Canary, could you spell out your middle name, or is it an initial?"

"Whaa ya'll sayin', girl?"

"We need your full name."

"Jonas."

"And the middle name?"

"N."

"What does 'N' stand for, please?"

"My middle name, girl, whatchu talkin'? Cain' y'all unnerstan' plain English?"

"Last name, please."

"Canary."

"Canary?"

"Ass right."

"Like the bird?"

"Yup. Y'all makin' funna my name?"

Jonas was very serious now. He did not take to being put down, disrespected. That was what had caused him to have to come to the EOR in the first place. But you should have seen the other dude.

"Oh no, Sir. Perhaps we should go on to another question."

The last thing in the world the young admissions clerk would want to do was to appear to be treating one of the downtrodden "customers" with deprecation.

"Could you please tell me the place of your residence?"

"Say whaa?"

"Pardon me. I need to have your full current address."

"Whaa say?" He was looking perplexed and beginning to get angry. Anger came fairly easily to Jonas.

The admissions lady felt defeated. She felt as if she had dropped into a foreign country and did not speak the native language. She was afraid that she was going to cry.

At this juncture, Garven stepped in and asked, "Can I help?"

"Oh, doctor. You're too busy for his sort of thing. I was just trying to get the admissions information from Mr. Canary. I feel that we will be successful if we just keep persisting," she said.

Mr. Canary looked on, convinced that he been dumped into a foreign land and was hearing the local, incomprehensible language. His personal English vocabulary was about 700 words. Without swear words and an assortment of curses, his breadth of language useful for interchange with people outside his neighborhood was nearer 500 words.

"It'll just take a minute," Garven told the distraught girl. "Why don't you just hand me the form?"

The admissions secretary passed Garven the clip board.

"What does they calls you?" Garven asked Jonas.

"Hey, man, I'm still Jonas. Have been all night."

"'Jonas', what?"

"Canary."

Garven filled in the proper spaces. "You gots a 'N' in there, too, don't you?"

"I does. Mean's 'Nitrogen.' I can spells it, too."

It was a proud family name, and Garven had no doubt that he could.

Chapter Twenty-Six

"That's okay, Jonas. Now tell me and the nice lady where you stays at."

"Is that what she wuzza axin'?"

"Yeah."

"Whyn't she jist say it? Cripes. I stays with Effie."

"Where's Effie stay at?"

"On Fish Trap Road. By the Sem-Elem," said Jonas.

Under "place of residence," Garven wrote, *"Warehouse Street, in the vicinity of Clock Street."* The old and still popular name for Warehouse Street was Fish Trap Road. He turned to the admissions clerk, who looked fairly mystified.

"That's enough," he said. "You can get the rest of the information from his old chart. Jonas is a card-carrying member of the Knife and Gun Club. He has a big chart. Have a good night."

"Thank you, doctor. I'm afraid I'll never get the hang of it. You must have been here a long time."

She looked at him with something akin to adoration.

Tom Carney, one of the interns, was in the next cubicle, patiently replacing a large rectal prolapse. Garven and the other intern, Chester Van Dorning, were sewing up a series of nasty cuts on a "customer" at midnight on Garven's last night. The smell of Thunderbird wine permeated the air. It was what passed for a contemplative time in the UC Osterlund Memorial EOR.

"Pretty bad cuts, huh, Garven?"

"Yeah, but old Tucker is tough," Garven said. "He'll be back out there after the 'two dudes' before the night is out. You can count on more customers tonight, at least one anyway."

"You know who the toughest guy in the world is, Garven?" asked Chester.

"Not offhand."

"The average UC Osterlund intern," Chester said.

Garven smiled his agreement. He knew from his own experience that the surgery interns—and maybe even the rotating and medicine interns—were the most undernourished, abused, undersexed, overworked, under-slept, greatest IV starting, dressing changing, fever worker upper, retractor holding, pig skinning (from the burn service), toughest men alive.

"And do you know then who's the second toughest man alive?" Garven asked.

"I'm not sure," Chester said as he put in another suture and daubed blood off the remainder of the laceration on which he was working.

"Hubert Smythe," said Garven.

"Who's he?" asked Chester.

He cut the knot on his suture.

"He's a guy who has been through the EOR and has been operated on twice for being stabbed in the heart and is still out there, attending K&GC meetings regularly."

Chester laughed.

"Give old Tucker here 1.2 million units of Bicillin IM," Garven instructed his intern.

"How come? I mean, wounds are all clean."

"Because someone will bug you about it. It's easier than having to explain to a 'customer' about the viruses-don't-need-antibiotics theory, too. It's a good shortcut to learn early in your career, Chester. Save you precious minutes, and it's satisfyingly punitive."

"Thanks, boss," Chester said and smiled at the little pearl of wisdom, another insiders' joke.

As they finished, Tucker looked up at Chester Van Dorning in his blood-spattered, dirty lab coat and asked, "Is you a intern or a real doctah?"

Chester looked at Garven and shrugged in benevolent resignation.

"You're welcome, I'm sure," the intern said to his patient.

Shortly before the end of March and his EOR rotation, Garven came to the realization that Elizabeth and Peter Arthur had been gone a long time. He vaguely recalled that she had said that she would be gone for two weeks. He was sure it must have been near a month now. Something like that long anyway.

CHAPTER
Twenty-Seven

Garven called the Fletchers—Elizabeth's parents—in Phoenix.
"Fletcher residence," answered the maid.

"This is Dr. Wilsonhulme. May I speak to Mrs. Wilsonhulme?"

"Miss Elizabeth?" the maid asked sweetly.

"No, Mrs. Wilsonhulme. She's married now," Garven said not-so-sweetly.

"Yes, Sir. I will see if she is at home and receiving callers."

That response was formal and a bit acerbic.

Garven waited for what seemed like a long time. He was glad that he had called collect.

The maid returned.

"Miss Elizabeth is indisposed at the moment. She asks that you call later."

"I will be indisposed in a few minutes. If we don't get to talk now, it will be quite a bit later," Garven said, his voice tinged with anger.

"Miss Elizabeth had me tell you that it would be all right if you could not complete your communication right away. She told me to thank you for calling."

"Tell her thanks ever so much, too," Garven snapped.

He hung up the receiver with more force that he would have liked to.

There was no time to wait until "Miss Elizabeth" was redisposed. Garven had to start his rotation at the VA Hospital, and he would be late for his first day if he procrastinated any longer.

There were forty-two patients on the Rosewood VA surgery ward when Garven arrived to start his belated contractual residency—the contract that

203

had been so abruptly abrogated by the university. He was scheduled to stay on the service for three months. The physical setup of the ward consisted of six private rooms, six double rooms, and four large rooms with six beds each. Garven had to get used to the idea that he could not see every patient all of the time. He arrived on time for rounds—nine o'clock—three hours later than the latest rounds on any service at UC Osterlund Memorial. The bulk of his fellow doctors did not arrive for another half an hour. Garven had to work to adjust. In the meantime, he perused the charts. There were patients who had been in the hospital for six weeks, a couple for two months despite having no very serious problems that Garven could detect. The first four weeks of every patient's stay had been for his pre-op workup. He could only shake his head. He would have had to answer to an irate resident if he had taken more than a full day for any of his workups back at Osterlund during his internship.

The VA worked on a different premise than that prevailing at charity hospitals or private centers. Funding from the US government was predicated on the number of beds filled for the quarter. It was critical to keep patients in house as long as possible; the worst sin for a physician was to allow his census to fall. In his stay at the VA, Garven found men who had taken up semipermanent residence. They had return address stickers made for their outgoing mail that listed the VA as their address. When one of them eventually left walking or, at least, apparently alive, the nurses often gave him a farewell party and loaded the stuff he had accumulated during his VA stay into a rented truck.

The abuse of taxpayer money briefly rankled Garven. Then he remembered that this was the very reason that he had applied for the VA residency and had been so angry when he was screwed out of it. The pace in Veteran's Administration Hospitals was consistently much slower than in the nongovernment facilities. The pace was not just slower; it was like swimming upstream through molasses. There was a rule, or a policy, or an impediment to swift progress at every opportunity, and the gung-ho house staff people simply had to adjust or go crazy.

Every technician, nurse, administrator, aide, and functionary at the VA knew that they had been there before the energetic house staff man came, and that they would be there after the house staff man left. They also knew that they were hired under a standard US government civil service mandate that made it impossible for them to be fired barring the actual commission of murder in full view of the nonmedical staff. They knew themselves to be absolutely impervious to criticism as a result. Garven made an effort to adjust during his half hour of waiting for his fellow doctors to arrive on the ward.

Garven met the two staff attendings, the senior resident, the other junior resident, the two interns, and the four medical students assigned to the general surgery service when they collected at around nine-thirty. Rounds took three hours, with the medical students giving the histories and physical exam data, and going through the hospital courses of each of the patients, then the attendings waxed eloquent about such fascinating subjects as bedsores, hemorrhoids, the burning controversies about which was the proper way to do an inguinal hernia, and why small incisions for gall bladder removals would never catch on.

The attendings and the senior resident left shortly after noon to go to the OR for their two cases of the day. Monday was long-rounds day after the events of the weekend; so, it was not possible to start the surgery schedule until noon, which meant one o'clock. The OR staff shift quit at five o'clock, not five-oh-one. It was referred to as VAST—VA Standard Time.

Garven and Tiny Francisco, the other junior resident, scoured the charts and went over the patients for an hour to find scut work for the interns to do.

"Where are the students?" Garven asked Tiny.

"Gone to class," Tiny said and shrugged.

No further explanation was necessary. "Class" was where the med students went whenever there was any scut to be done, like blood to be drawn. In fact, the very term "student" was defined by the interns as "those who do not exist anymore."

Garven and Tiny flipped a coin to see who would go to the OR and be the fifth wheel in the simple operations and who would take the nap. In fairness, the loser, i.e., the one who had to take the nap, also had to supervise the scut work. Garven won the toss and headed for the OR. He could hear Tiny organizing the interns as he left.

"Okay," he was saying, "Jeff, you give old man Smothers the ride on the steel stallion (proctoscope), and Danny, you sew up Petersen's wound again. He's made of PPPPPT—Piss-Poor-Protoplasm-Poorly-Put-Together—but we have to give it another try. He 'vomicked' on me; so, use 'O' silk (huge, thick suture that went in painfully and caused a more prominent scar)."

Garven spent a boring afternoon learning how to tie knots again, so he would feel that he had been educated. As third assistant, he could scarcely see the actual surgery. He was not forgotten, however. The patient was in extraordinarily poor condition, an old lunger with cor pulmonale—heart failure due to the terrible work of having to pump against the severe, venous pressure caused by the tobacco-induced lung disease. The underlying reason for the operation was that the intern had never done a large, abdominal incisional hernia. The attending knew before they entered the room that the patient was likely not to make it through the operation. Garven was unfamiliar with the patient or with the attending's motives. When the old vet had a cardiac arrest, the crew was unable to resuscitate him with external measures.

"Crack his chest, Garven!" the attending shouted.

It was more excitement than the VA had seen in years. Garven obediently did a lateral thoracotomy. It seemed to him remarkably convenient that the thoracotomy tray was already out and ready.

He put in the rib retractors and reached in to massage the flaccid heart. The organ felt like a bag of miniature marshmallows. He gingerly squeezed and released, squeezed and released. There was no response.

"More vigorously," instructed the attending.

Garven squeezed more vigorously. The atria were the consistency and thickness of wet cardboard. His thumb pressed through the wall and into the heart chamber itself.

The attending was watching.

"You've killed him!" he exclaimed.

Garven asked for suture, but the nurse seemed reluctant. For some reason, the attending did not look very upset. He seemed mildly amused. Garven chalked it up to the general strangeness of the VA.

"Okay, that's enough," said the attending.

It was more than four in the afternoon. Garven gave the attending a very questioning look.

"I'm sorry, Garven, this old vet is just too far gone. There's no use keeping on."

Garven was certain ever afterward that he had been set up, but he could never get anyone to admit it.

They finished at 4:45, and even then, the head nurse was tapping her fingers at the senior resident to let him know that the bewitching hour was rapidly approaching. Garven had a headache from trying to stay awake during the period before the cardiac arrest. The only saving grace was that tomorrow was intern and junior resident day, and they would have their share of bread-and-butter operations to do. No one really complained about the system, at least not about the amount of surgery they got to do.

He forgot to call Elizabeth that night and was on call the following night, so it was three full days before he made the call to his wife in Phoenix.

206

"Hello, will you accept a collect call from Dr. Wilsonhulme?" the operator inquired of the maid who answered at the Fletcher residence.

There was a pause.

"No, I'm sorry, I'm not authorized to do that," came the reply.

Garven knew he was being jacked around. Apparently, he was being made to pay some penance for an imagined wrong. For the life of him, he could not figure out what that wrong could be. He had hardly been around Elizabeth enough to do anything wrong in the past three months.

"So, operator, go ahead and bill my number and let me talk to them," Garven said peevishly.

It took a several-minute muted discussion at the Fletcher end before Elizabeth finally made it to the phone. Garven was steaming.

"Hello, dear," she said. "How are you?"

"Hello, Elizabeth, finally," he said. "I'm fine. How are you and our son?"

"You mean 'what's his name'?" she asked archly.

"Oh, gimmee a break, Elizabeth. I want to know how Petey is."

"Peter Arthur is fine. I am fine. We are all fine. Thank you."

Her voice came through like jellied acid.

"I give up, Elizabeth, what is it that I am supposed to have done this time?"

"Nothing."

"Nothing?! Then why the cold-shoulder treatment? What was so bad that you decided to desert your husband? Didn't like the humble accommodations?"

"That kind of sarcasm will get you no place, Garven. You know perfectly well what's the matter."

Her voice was beginning to quaver. He was at a loss to understand what was so bad that she was going to cry. It would be much simpler just to come out with it and tell him her gripe. He did not understand the female mind at all.

"Look, this is costing a fortune. Let's skip the counts in the accusation then, if you don't want to tell me, and get right to the solution. I want you to come home with my son. I want you to do it tomorrow."

His voice had an unwanted hectoring tone; even he could hear it. But his temper was rising rapidly and he was becoming disinclined to play whatever game was going on here.

"I have a fortune, Garven. I don't care if it takes all night. We are going to have an understanding," Elizabeth said.

She was crying now and trying not to let it come through in her voice. She was failing.

207

"So tell me, Elizabeth. Maybe I can somehow make amends for the terrible things I have done. Would it be enough for me to chop off my left hand, or would jumping off the city building roof be necessary for this crime?"

The anger in his voice came through clearly.

Elizabeth was crying. She had stopped talking, and he could hear her soft weeping at the other end. A full minute went by.

"Why can't you just be nice to me? That's all I want, Garven. I need that much. You…you don't seem to have that in you."

There was more weeping. Garven was genuinely confused. He thought of himself as the abused party: exhausted and brutalized by the insensitive medical system. He needed the comforting. What was her problem anyhow? He considered hanging up.

A man's voice came on the line. It was stern and angry.

"Arthur Fletcher here. I take it you can tell what you've done to my daughter, young man. I predicted this, as you recall. I'll not have it, do you hear?"

Garven was furious.

"Look, Mr. Fletcher. This is none of your business. You are a buttinsky by nature, and this is between Elizabeth and me. So butt out."

No one had ever talked to Arthur Fletcher like that before. Garven could hear the older man's teeth grind even over the long-distance line. Mr. Fletcher took a deep breath. Evidently, he was counting to ten.

Garven went on.

"Now, I have a message for you. For the whole lot of you. I am not going to defend myself to Elizabeth every time she gets into a snit, and I am never going to defend myself to you. This one time, I am going to tell you what is going on. I work twenty hours a day, and I am tired when I come home at night. I do the best I can, but my job requires that I spend time at the hospital, lots of time. Elizabeth has led a spoiled child's life, and it is time she learned to put up with a few things. You tell her for me that I will expect to see her back at our apartment in two days from now. Then we will talk. I have had enough of this long-distance crap!"

"Now, you listen here to me, young man!" shouted Mr. Fletcher.

Garven held the receiver away from his ear and replied with icy calm, "And I am not your 'young man.' Give Elizabeth my message. Good-bye."

He put down the receiver.

No one ever hung up on Arthur Fletcher. He was livid. It was his prerogative as an important CEO to hang up on other people. He stalked out of the room without giving Elizabeth the message.

Garven was in a foul mood. Even the chance to do three good cases the following day did little to dispel his dark mood. The day after that, he allowed his personal ill-disposition to drive him to a small, ill-considered negative crusade. He was in clinic, seeing the streams of down-and-outs that came through. He chose to think of the VA Hospital mission as one of treating veterans of combat, persons injured in wars. He never saw any of those. The average patient was late middle-aged, alcoholic, irresponsible, and had a malady that had nothing to do with military service. Garven held the patients in the lowest of esteem; they had no business taking the taxpayers' money in his opinion. It was a patient who entered the clinic with such a "service-connected" disability that finally set the young resident off.

For some unusual reason, presumably from not having enough to occupy his mind, Garven read the administrative sections of the patient's chart, something he almost never did. The patient was only in the clinic for his once-a-year visit, as required by the VA rules. He was doing well, all smiles, had a good job, no symptoms, and drove a big car. He had an eighty percent disability for stomach ulcers, for which he was paid $818 a month by the federal government. The stomach ulcers had occurred during boot camp seventeen years ago, and the patient had been discharged as disabled less than a month after induction.

Garven asked about the man's history. How was it that he felt so well for a man having a serious stomach ulcer?

"Oh, I don't have it anymore. Had surgery. You guys did a great job. I don't mean you young fellas here today, understand. But the VA surgeons. I haven't had a lick of trouble since surgery. Don't even have to take medicine anymore. How about that?!" said the grateful patient with a broad grin.

"Well, good. I guess we won't see you again until next year, same time, same place," said Garven.

"Nosiree. Just sign on the line there, and I get my pension; and everybody's happy," said the man with his used car salesman grin.

He gave Garven a little conspiratorial wink.

It should not have, but the encounter bothered Garven. He let it fester through the day. By the following morning, he had a head of steam up enough to pursue the matter of the unneeded and undeserved pension. He went to the administration and explained his discovery, expecting to be met with praise for his endeavor to save Uncle Sam some money. Instead, he was met with the standard gray people response, the government functionary solution. With a look of profound disinterest and diffidence, the secretary gave Garven a stack of forms to fill out and told him where to send them. There was no need for the forms to come back to her office.

Much as Garven detested paperwork, he went ahead and took up his valuable nap time to fill out the extensive form in triplicate. He mailed the envelope off. It was seven weeks before he received a reply. The matter had been evaluated, and no reason had been determined to change the administrative decision regarding the patient's disability status. Garven was thanked for bringing the matter to the attention of the Veteran's Administration. It was the last time he ever bothered.

Garven met Dr. Winston, chief of surgery, in the lavatory and observed that he washed his hands before urinating. One of the internists took care to wash his hands after urinating.

The internist smiled indulgently at the chief of surgery and said in jest, "When I was in my medicine residency, they taught me to wash my hands after I urinated."

Dr. Winston smiled back, equally indulgently, and said, "In surgery residency, they taught me not to pee on my hands."

Garven laughed and told his boss about his frustrating experience of trying to get the freeloader off the VA rolls and out of the taxpayers' pockets.

"You'll never win, forget it," Dr. Winston said. "I got on my high horse one time. We had an assistant administrator, Jeffery Morgan, in charge of surgery at that time, who was a moron, completely incompetent. I protested to the director. He told me that there was no way that we could get rid of the loser and that I should just work around him. In the course of my protest, I asked the director how the guy ever got the job in the first place.

"'Oh, that's easy,' he told me. 'I know exactly how the conversation went. Morgan is the nephew of one of Ike's campaign execs. The VA job was a reward. When Jeffery came in for his interview, the administrator—my predecessor—asked Jeffery what he could do. Jeffery said, 'Nothing.' My predecessor said, 'Good. That makes it simple. We won't have to break you in.' And Jeffery had the job. Welcome to the VA, Garven."

CHAPTER
Twenty-Eight

It was a week before Garven found Elizabeth and the baby at home. He walked in at six o'clock to smell a fetching aroma of lasagna and garlic bread. Petey was burbling and crawling around on the floor. Elizabeth was all smiles.

"Welcome home, Daddy," she said.

The evening was pleasant and tranquil. It was obvious that Elizabeth had put in a great deal of thought about what she felt and what she wanted to say. She waited until Garven was full and sleepy, then gradually let him know how difficult it was for her to be left alone. She understood that he was busy, but no one could be that busy; and she felt neglected. She wanted Garven to see things from her point of view. Maybe it would be better if he went into "medicine," diagnostics and rich old ladies—that "medicine." It was not a matter of money. Diagnosticians were important, too, she opined. Her only mistake was in letting Garven know that Daddy—the real daddy—could set him up with one of the larger and more successful internal medicine practice groups in Phoenix. Then, maybe it would not be so hard. She just wanted them to be together.

Garven made a very strong effort to listen, and not to talk, to be understanding. Someone had told him that what was wrong with men was that they had a solution for everything when all the woman wanted was to ventilate her feelings. He had dispensed with the observation as being illogical, but nonetheless, he listened for a couple of hours, hours that seemed eminently satisfying to his wife. He felt very deprived and was especially nice because he did not want anything to interfere with the real reunion he had planned when they went to bed a little later. The only thing he did wrong was to bristle at the suggestion that her father could set him up with a bunch of internists.

His negative reaction to that one small segment of Elizabeth's monologue evidently set her teeth on edge. When Garven suggested that they make love, she let him know that they couldn't; it was her monthly time to "come sick," as her mother had taught her to say. Garven turned on his side and observed sullenly to himself that Elizabeth seemed to menstruate much more often as the time in their marriage increased. Originally, she had wanted to make love all of the time, and he could not remember her ever having a headache or having her period. Now, it seemed like she had two-week-long periods three times a month. He felt aggressive and angry when he went to sleep, and the feelings were not dissipated by rest.

He sent her flowers and a nice card, and made a severe effort to be polite and pleasant in his conversations with her. It was an unnatural state of communication for him, and he wondered if she was aware of the falsity of his niceness. He found himself spending a little longer at the VA each day than he really needed to; and when he came home, he made an elaborate to-do over playing with the baby. She finally got over her headaches and her period, and graciously invited his attentions in bed. Perhaps that, after more than the week and a half of denial, rankled him more than anything. He wanted her to want him, and she appeared to be making sure that he knew that her love-making was a valuable gift to be presented at her discretion for merit on his part. He missed the spontaneity of their early marriage months, and found that the anger and disappointment he felt with their relationship did not abate even in the mornings after she had given him her unique gift.

Garven learned the routine at the VA, including how to get things done so he could get patients to the OR. He learned to deal with specific individuals; the exact person who did whatever it was he wanted to have done. He found that requests through proper channels to designated offices were a waste of time. It was very worthwhile to cultivate a particular secretary or assistant administrator or lab tech to get his work done. In a short time, Garven realized that he had discovered the secret of how governments work. In the process of such cultivation, he met the linchpin of the Neuro-ENT-Plastic subspecialty services, a thirty-year-old spinster secretary who appeared outwardly austere to the point of severity, but was inwardly starved for attention and warmed to special blandishments.

Martha Storm gave Garven an education on how the VA works, who to see, who not to antagonize. He gave her smiles and jokes, a little flattery, a lot of praise. During his last month on the VA service, Garven saw Martha begin to add a little makeup, to put some color into her clothing. Sometimes, if they had a definite appointment to accomplish some secretarial task or other, she wore some jewelry. She changed her hairstyle from a bun to a wavy flourish or two. She was intelligent and easy to talk to, and the two of them began to find it convenient to have lunch in the staff cafeteria together. She gave Garven a sense of belonging in the VA world, and helped him to stop nursing a smoldering hostility at the ponderous way things worked and to accept them. He gave her sexy looks and made her blush. She had never had a date before and had never been a hand at flirting. By the time Garven had finished his final tour of duty in his general surgery junior residency, the two months on the VA, she had advanced to the point of daring to say that he had "bedroom eyes."

Martha seemed genuinely sad when he came to tell her that it was his last day to see her. He had clinic and surgery for the next two days then the academic year would be over, and he would be back to Osterlund Memorial on the neurosurgery service. He would miss her, he said with his gentlest voice and his bedroom eyes. Afterward, he found himself thinking about her, wondering what she would look like under her business suit. He had fleeting fantasies about how rambunctious she would be after thirty years of repression. He secretly bet that she would not have two-week-long periods three times a month.

It bothered him to think about the other woman; so, Garven made a conscious effort to do more with Elizabeth, to woo her, and to let her think that he was understanding the stuff she said about men having feelings, too, and how complex were her own sensitivities. Martha gradually shifted to the back of Garven's mind, but he could not quite erase her completely.

One thing that helped him not to think about Martha Storm was that he developed a genuine love for still another woman. Marlene Sewell was a veteran, a real one, a Negro woman of forty, who had been in the air force during the Korean conflict. She came to the VA general outpatient clinic on a day that Garven was filling in for a resident friend who was on a fishing trip. Marlene did not feel well and had lost weight. She was unsure of the reason. Garven found it easily; Marlene had a large breast mass and several axillary nodes.

He gave Marlene his opinion about her condition, and she put her head on his chest and cried. He put his arms around her and held her for a long time.

213

Garven did her surgery—a radical mastectomy and ovarian resection two days later. He supervised her post-op care and her chemotherapy and radiation therapy. She came to see him in the clinic almost weekly over the course of the two months of Garven's VA tour. It was evident that she was losing ground steadily; the cancer was too far advanced for any treatment.

Someone told him that Marlene's husband was cheating on her, but that she did not know it. Although Garven was a religious non-meddler, he made an exception in Marlene's case and approached the husband. Surprisingly, Mr. Sewell frankly acknowledged his involvement with another woman and promised to desist while Marlene still lived. He kept his promise. Garven helped two of Marlene's sons with their algebra and trig. He made sure that her four-year-old daughter had a birthday party while Marlene could still enjoy one even though it was months before the little girl's actual birth date.

Garven went to Marlene's house when she could no longer make it to the hospital. He gave her pain shots and started an IV line so she could be nourished when she became too weak to eat. On the last night of her life, he listened to her as she told about her life, in a somewhat rambling narrative. Then she sang:

> "Lord above, can't you see me cryin'
> Tears are in my eyes.
> Send down a chariot from up above,
> Take me to paradise.
>
> And like that lucky old sun,
> I'll have nothing to do,
> But to roll around heaven all day."

He held her hand as she died. Garven developed an attitude that many would consider odd, rather inverted, from his caring for the strong-hearted Negro woman. He considered it a privilege, even a pleasure, to serve her. He cared more for her problems than for his own. He came to love her and to feel gratitude for her. Garven Wilsonhulme became a true doctor by his involvement in the diagnosis and treatment of Marlene Sewell, and he recognized what the woman had done for him.

It also helped him to forget his infatuation with Martha Storm when he got the flu near the end of his VA rotation. The malaise, nausea, and diarrhea came on very rapidly, almost suddenly. He felt awful when he went in to work, but forced himself to push on because it was his next to the last day, and the chief was going to give him a going-away present of the opportunity to do a hiatal hernia repair, his biggest case yet. He felt progressively sicker as he scrubbed. He felt like he could not get enough air behind his sterile mask. He swore at himself, knowing that he was too sick to do the case. He pushed onward until he was fully gowned and gloved. He was pale and sweaty, and his hands and legs were trembling. Waves of nausea swept over him. He resisted. Finally, he knew he was going to vomit. They were putting on the dressing drapes. Garven had to rush out of the OR.

He struggled with his rubber fingers to unknot his mask. The emesis was coming. He was too late. He had misjudged and vomited into his mask, up his nose, and all over his cheeks. He all but fainted. The nurses saw what was going on and told the chief. He started the case. Garven went home. The good thing about having the flu was that Elizabeth tended Garven for two days as if he were about to slough his mortal coil. At first, he was too sick to think about Martha Storm, then Elizabeth's ministrations were so extensive and thorough that he did not want to think of the other woman. The flu had been the best thing that had happened to Garven and Elizabeth's marriage in many months.

Garven was only able to go back to the VA on the late afternoon of June 30, the last day of the academic year. He paid his respects to the other residents and to the staff. Dr. Winston told him that he had enjoyed and appreciated Garven's work, and offered to write him a letter of recommendation, if he ever needed one. Garven shook hands. He liked Dr. Winston and did not at all hold it against the man that he had not been able to have a true VA residency for that year. He sort of felt that the VA chief had been screwed also when the university took over. Maybe it was for the best. If nothing else, Garven had toughened up and did not have the naive expectations he used to have, and he had learned a considerable amount about being a surgeon in the last year.

The next morning, when he woke up, Garven Wilsonhulme would officially be a neurosurgeon and all that it portended. It was a deeply exhilarating thought. Since he was not on call for once, he took Elizabeth and Peter Arthur out to dinner to celebrate. Maybe, just maybe, he would be in the midst of a stable and loving family as well. He held out more hope for his success in neurosurgery.

-The End-

Synopsis of Book Five: *Law of the Jungle*

Garven accepted a referral from the medical department's division of endocrinology. He did not know that Don White had originally been consulted, but had been too busy to get to the consult the same day it was delivered. Garven never hesitated to go after a surgical case, and arranged for the patient, a woman with a very large tumor, to be safely ensconced on the neurosurgery ward and on the operating schedule by noon. She was on for surgery the following morning. Don White only learned all of that by seeing the patient's name on the operating schedule.

Garven had the woman in position and was directing the placement of the cocaine soaked cottonoids into the nose for purposes of reducing the size of the nasal arteries and mucosa and for local anesthesia when Don stormed into Garven's OR. He did not have a mask on and made no effort to preserve the sterile set-up.

He laid his ungloved hands on one of the Mayo trays and bellowed at Garven, "You rotten patient stealer! You know perfectly well this is my patient! This is my operation! I will not have you putting this woman to terrible risk by doing this experimental operation on her! Either you take her out of this room, or I am going to Dr. Stark, Dr. Lyons, and the hospital administration. This is malpractice! This is against every medical ethic!"

He went on to curse Garven roundly.

Garven was at first shocked, then annoyed, then deeply angry. He fought himself for control of the temper he had worked on for years.

He let Don finish his rantings; then, he turned his icy eyes on the junior staff man and said with quiet and measured tones, but with clearly implicit malice, "Get out of this operating room, or I will call security. We are about to start a major operation here, and you have contaminated it. Go ahead and tell the powers that be; tell the President and J. Edgar Hoover if you want. But get out of here now!"

216

The Long Climb author, Carl Douglass, a former neurosurgeon turned author who writes with gripping realism, has the luxury now in retirement to write about the turbulent era in which he lived and practiced the demanding profession of neurosurgery. His training was one of great rigor; his practice was one of heartbreaks and triumphs; and his social life bordered on nil. His good wife of fifty years and the author now enjoy their time of reflection, travel, and family relationships—all largely the product of his wife's steadfast support during the lean years, the years of success, and now the autumn of their lives.

HONORS, AWARDS, AND MEMBERSHIPS
Phi Kappa Phi University Honor Society
Alpha Omega Alpha Medical Honor Society
BS (Medical Biology) degree—magna cum laude
MD—magna cum laude
CDR/MC/USN

American Medical Association
American Association of Neurosurgeons
Congress of Neurological Surgeons
Fellow of the American College of Surgeons
The Association of Military Surgeons of the United States
Life Member of the Medical Society of Vienna
Diplomate of the American Board of Neurological Surgery

Past President, Our Community Foundation, Wasatch County, Utah
Past Medical Liaison Officer, Deseret International Foundation
Past Chief of Surgery,
Antelope Valley Regional Medical Center, Lancaster, California
Past Member-at-Large, Central Medical Committee,
Utah Valley Regional Medical Center, Provo, Utah
Past Member, Utah State Foster Care Review Committee